A NATHAN MASON THRILLER

Cabin in the Clouds

Jackson Beck

Also, by Jackson Beck.

The Sanctuary Cipher

Acknowledgements

My thanks go to Tim and Carol Harrison, Albertland Heritage Museum, Minniesdale Chapel, Ivan Butler, Emma Wilde and Janet.

Seek and ye shall find

Matthew 7:7

1

Warkworth, New Zealand 1969

FRED WALL was just about to finish his shift at the Warkworth Sawmills on the North Island of New Zealand. He was a special person, some of his work colleagues used to say. At thirty years old, of average height and with collar-length hair, he was of unkempt appearance. He wet-shaved about once every two months and his mother cut his hair every six months, give or take a week or so. Not the strongest of men physically but very wiry and agile, he looked as if he could run a marathon for fun.

A quiet man, Fred had very few friends. He wasn't the best communicator and had always struggled at school. In fact, he was a loner. He loved his mother and sister, and they lived together in a small house on the Kaipara Flats Road just outside Warkworth. His father had died from lung cancer when Fred was young.

Fred had been fortunate to get a job at the sawmills when he was fourteen and that's where he was hoping to stay for his working life. He was good with his hands, particularly when working with wood. If he needed to do any repairs to the family home or garden fences he was in his element. He was the breadwinner, while his sister Marlene worked part-time in a tobacconist shop in Warkworth but his mother Catherine was unable to work due to a physical disability that originated in her late twenties and made walking difficult.

As for mixing with other people, Fred had a one and only friend in Kaipara, who had a small house near the coast and a piece of land up in a remote part of the West Dome Forest hills. Fred would ride there on his moped that he had bought from his savings when he was eighteen. He also used his moped for transport to and from work.

The Wall family was relatively poor but happy and thankful for their little lot. They attended the Wellsford Ecumenical Church as often as they could but they relied upon a fellow parishioner who lived in Warkworth to collect them and return them in his Morris Oxford.

It was in church that Fred had first met Tawera, a local Maori who was responsible for getting him interested in geology. They used to go up into the forests and around the bays and coves looking for what they called 'gemstones', but basically anything that was different and identifiable. They were guided by their alternative bible, *The Observers Book of Geology*. They felt great pleasure whenever they identified a particular gemstone, which was usually worthless, but something that they could add to their collection.

Tawera said that there were many unusual gemstones that had come to light after an earthquake in the Dome Forest many years ago. Allegedly, the earth's crust had cracked open and multicoloured stones were cast on to the landscape. Fred was suspicious about this event as he had never heard of such an earthquake this far north, nor any multicoloured stones. He thought it could be some sort of Maori folklore story.

Fred had suggested that he and Tawera should build a log cabin and use it as a kind of operational headquarters for their hobby – a mancave if you like. Tawera had agreed and indicated that he knew just the place. So, the following weekend they had trekked up into the hills and eventually reached an area of interest. When Fred asked who the land belonged to, Tawera replied, 'It's mine, it's Maori land.' Once again, Fred was suspicious, this time about the legal ownership of the land.

They had come across a heavily overgrown old log cabin, which Tawera said was theirs to use, so Fred suggested that they may be able to carry out repairs and do something with it. The next few visits had been constructive as they began to replace some of the rotten timbers and bring the old cabin back to life.

Soon after, Tawera informed Fred that he was moving away with his family to Wellington. Fred was devastated that he was losing his one and only friend, and what about the work on the cabin? Tawera said that Fred could use the cabin and continue developing it. He could use it for as long as he wanted.

Tawera had reminded him that it was on Maori land, but what did that mean? Fred never really understood how people could own or even claim to own land on the top of a hill and in the middle of a dense forest. Where was the boundary? Could you own a whole mountain, a forest or a beach? Fred couldn't comprehend the notion.

Before they had finally parted, Tawera had given Fred his small square biscuit tin. Fred had noticed that Tawera seemed to carry it everywhere with him in his backpack. When he got home, Fred opened the tin, the contents of which just looked like a few pieces of paper and an old map, but underneath the papers there was a small quantity of beautiful stones. Fred recognised them immediately as pounamu stones, which some people called New Zealand jade or greenstone. They were incredibly beautiful and it looked as if Tawera had been polishing three of the stones, while the remaining ones were coarse and rough-hewn. Fred immediately decided to give one piece to Marlene and one to his mother. The remainder he would take back to the cabin to form part of his collection.

On previous visits to the cabin, Fred had always called for Tawera first. This meant that they had approached it from the Kaipara direction in the west. Now the route to the cabin from Fred's home was a totally different direction, from the south. On his first attempt he had become lost after walking around for hours, so he had decided to return home. He had made a second attempt the day after, then remembered that he may have previously seen some sort of route map in Tawera's biscuit tin.

That evening at home he opened the tin and found the map. It wasn't an official map but it looked as if it could have been traced from such a map. It wasn't clear, was drawn in pencil and was smudged and faded in parts, particularly where it had been folded over and perhaps thrust into a trouser, shirt or coat pocket.

Fred could make out the coastline along Kaipara harbour and could see the Dome Forest and Kaipara Flats Road. In the middle of the forest he could make out what looked like a small pinprick in the centre of the map. He wondered whether it had been on a wall and had a pin stuck into it — a sort of X marks the spot. The little hole could be the cabin. It looked to be where the cabin should be, but he wasn't sure. If it was, he could see a route up there from the Kaipara Flats Road.

Looking through the other bits of paper, Fred came across a note that looked like a list of instructions handwritten on a tracing-type paper.

ON ENTERING THE FOREST AT TAUHOA FOLLOW THE EYE TREES.

DO NOT VARY FROM THE ROUTE.

MAKE SURE TO BE OUT OF THE FOREST BEFORE DARKNESS FALLS.

WALK BACK USING THE SAME ROUTE AND DO NOT VARY FROM IT.

Fred wasn't sure whether Tawera had written this or not but he suspected he had. Fred decided to try to find this shorter route and plotted a path. He was correct, the pinprick *was* the cabin.

Fred continued with his improvements on the cabin and spent every Saturday and Sunday afternoon in the West Dome Forest hills. This was very tiring work; it took a couple of hours to walk to the cabin, sometimes carrying tools and equipment and a flask of tea, then at the end of the day carrying equipment back home that he may need during the week.

~~~

One day, when Marlene was at work in the tobacconist's, standing in the doorway, she spoke to the local librarian, who was passing and asked her about her family. She mentioned Fred's new interest in geology and gemstones. The librarian pointed out that precious gems such as diamonds, emeralds and sapphires were virtually non-existent in New Zealand, but it was still an interesting hobby. She said that there were many precious stones that could be made into jewellery, such as garnet, quartz and pounamu, the latter being extremely popular. The librarian said that there were several information sheets on certain gemstones that she would gladly pass on to Marlene for Fred.

That afternoon, the librarian was true to her word. She called at the tobacconist's and handed Marlene a roll of what appeared to her to be wall posters, held together by an exceptionally large elastic band. Later, Marlene rode home on her bicycle with the rolled-up posters under one arm. It wasn't easy and she nearly fell off numerous times, but she knew that Fred would be delighted when he saw them.

When Marlene handed the posters to Fred, he kissed her on the cheek, which was unusual because he rarely showed any emotion, mainly because he didn't know how to. He was very thankful and knew exactly what he was going to do with them.

Fred had continued with the improvements on the cabin. He had even built a stone fireplace with a chimney breast that led to an opening in the log roof. He had also handmade an extremely basic wooden chair and table and proudly positioned them in the middle of the cabin.

The time had come and the cabin was finished. Now it was the topping-off ceremony, the bottle of champagne against the bow of the ship moment as Fred proudly nailed to the wall of the cabin the posters he had been given by Marlene, entitled Obsidian, Kyanite, Goodletite, Garnet, Jasper, Flint, Chert, Quartz and Pounamu. To Fred it felt like he was wallpapering the cabin. Each poster had a colour photograph example of its header.

Fred felt immensely proud as he sat in his wooden chair and admired the walls. Very soon he would be going out to begin the search for all the items displayed on the posters and he was looking forward to crossing each one off his list. He had made a start already as he pulled Tawera's remaining pounamu stones from his pocket and placed them in a small wooden box on the table.

A couple of days later the moped was resting on its stand on the gravel track overlooking a beach. Fred was sitting on the sand in a small cove near Tauhoa. This was one of

Tawera's favourite spots. He used to say, 'Check this beach every day if you can. There are always different stones and shells being washed up here. It's like a magnet.'

It was a beautiful, peaceful location. The tree-covered hills were behind him, the beach and the sea to his front and the sun was beaming down. Fred felt he was in a special place. His memories of being with Tawera at this beach were all good and happy and he wished he were with him today.

It was a cloudless sky and Fred looked down at his tanned legs. He moved one of his socks down slightly to reveal pale white ankles, then he lifted the sleeve of his T-shirt to reveal a pale white bicep. He liked to wear the same clothes as often as he could. His T-shirts, shorts, socks and walking boots were his uniform, even at work. Occasionally he would vary to a pair of denim jeans in the winter months but not for long.

Fred opened his backpack and pulled out a thermos flask that was filled with cool water. He took a gulp from the neck of the flask instead of using the cup, then something caught his eye further down the beach. Squinting in the strong sunshine, he walked over to take a look. As he got closer, he could see that it was one of those large conch-type shells that every child used to put to their ear and hear the rushing sea. He did exactly the same and it still worked for him.

His eye was then drawn to the sand beneath where the conch had been. He rubbed the area with the toe of his boot to reveal a piece of wood. It was probably just a piece of old jetsam or debris that had been thrown off a boat or ship. It looked quite old though, and Fred was suddenly interested.

He put the conch down, got down on his knees and started to scrape the sand away from the wood.

He had already noticed that the tide had turned and was slowly on its way in, but he carried on regardless. He revealed more of the wood, which looked like three pieces of timber about twelve inches in length and nearly as wide. They appeared to butt up to each other. As he felt around the edges, he realised that the thing had sides and could well be a box.

A small wave broke, sending sea water up the beach, which lapped against Fred's arms and legs, just covering the box. As the water withdrew across the timber, Fred started to scratch away frantically along each side of the box. Another small wave broke and the sea water travelled up the beach faster this time. Fred continued to gouge away at the sand, then he was hit by a slap of water on his arms, side and legs. It splashed into his face and stung his eyes. The water level receded a little but the box remained submerged. With all his might and remaining energy, Fred placed his fingers around the bottom of the box and pulled. This was his last chance to get the box out or it may never see the light of day again.

The veins in Fred's arms and neck swelled in an effort to get more blood to the overburdened muscles. Suddenly there was a suction noise as the sand relinquished its grip on the box. Fred's knees were now sinking in the sand as he managed to haul the box out of its hole and on to the beach. As he did so he was hit by a larger wave that knocked him over and totally submerged him.

Fred stumbled to his feet, coughing and spluttering as the sea lapped around his thighs. Suddenly he was panicking because he couldn't see the box. He hoped it hadn't been carried out to sea, but he knew that because of its weight it wouldn't be far away. It wasn't. Once Fred returned to where he had been before being bowled over, the box was sitting there on the beach, fully submerged but easily accessible. He grabbed the box, straightened his legs and, staggering with his feet sinking in the soft sand, lifted the incredibly heavy box and headed for dry land. He took another slap on the back from a wave but managed to stay upright.

Fred stumbled off the beach to the safety of the gravel path. He dropped the box on to the path with a loud crunch. He noticed that one side of the box was branded with a capital 'T'. He wondered whether that referred to the contents or the owner. He thought that the box may be filled with lead because of its extreme weight, but there was only one way to find out.

He lifted the box again and this time dropped it right on one of its corners. A small gap appeared in one corner, which he presumed was the lid. The force of the drop had also left an old rusty nail protruding from it. He put one damp boot on the box then grabbed the loose piece of timber and used his bodyweight as a lever. He fell back on to the gravel path with the lid of the box in his hands. All the nails had more or less corroded away, offering little resistance.

Fred got to his feet quickly and looked into the box. It contained what looked like a leather bladder with a string around its neck. He pulled at the string, but it just crumbled to dust. He put his hand inside and the leather just fell away like damp tissue paper. Fred was aghast at what he saw. A beautiful gleaming gold bar. He picked it up and kissed it – he didn't know why. He held it in his hands and rolled it over. He could see the mould marks but there was no writing or numbers.

Fred was overjoyed and excited, then suddenly he was overcome with a feeling of apprehension and anxiety. He could see that the box contained another four gold bars and he was now worried about his safety. His head turned quickly, his eyes darting along the path into the woods and along the beach. He couldn't see anyone, but that didn't mean someone couldn't see him.

He grabbed the heavy box and headed towards the treeline for some cover but had to stop numerous times because of its extreme weight. He now had a predicament; how was he going to get the gold home? He couldn't take it on his moped. What if he was stopped by some villains or the police? Anyway, his moped couldn't take any more weight, as it barely got over the hills as it was. The cabin was closer, but it wasn't an easy option. It would take at least four hours to get there and back and he would have to do two trips and still come back for his moped. But it was going to have to be the cabin. As long as he could get the gold up there and return for his moped before dark, it should be okay.

The decision made, Fred loaded three gold bars into his backpack then lifted it to check the weight. It didn't feel too bad now, but after hiking for a couple of hours, he knew it was going to be difficult.

He started to dig out a small hole using the heel of his boot. Fortunately, the ground beneath the trees had years of rotting leaves, pine straw and other vegetation so it was pretty easy to make a hole big enough for two gold bars. Before he buried them, he took a quick look to see whether there was anyone around. He dropped the bars into the hole and covered them with his boot. He then stuck a small branch in the hole as a marker, put the backpack on and walked over to his moped. He pushed the moped into the trees and left it near the marker, then started the long walk into the forest and up to the cabin, turning around one last time to see the branch sticking out of the ground just a few metres from his moped. The gold was well hidden and he didn't think it likely that anyone would walk in his footsteps. There was no indication that anyone had seen him.

Fred saw the first marker tree directly ahead and he remembered what Tawera had said: 'Always follow the eye.' He could see the eye-shaped symbol carved into the tree trunk. As he walked into the forest there was no breeze and the sun was shining through a bright green canopy. It was stifling and humid.

As he crossed a slow-running stream and stepped into a thick fern, Fred soon became aware that he had stepped on a mosquito nest. Mosquitos flew into the air. He could hardly see them but he could feel the impact of their minute stings on his arms and legs. He walked as fast as he could away from the stream, making a mental note to move faster when he came across wet areas like this.

Next, he came across a small plantation of giant tree ferns, with their smooth velvety bark and huge fan-type leaves. For all intents and purposes, he was walking into a sub-tropical forest. There was even an abundance of yellow-crowned parakeets, endemic to New Zealand. The beautiful green parrot has a yellow crown with a crimson band about its head and a red spot on each side of the rump. Known for their loud shriek, you would be forgiven for thinking the forest was full of them.

Fred continued on. There were other markers en route that he had to look out for to confirm he was going in the right direction. Tawera had told him and shown him over the years to use certain tree stumps as indicators. Tree stumps were to be passed on the left; trees marked with eyes on the right. Think of the eye as a clock face and on the face will be a line that's the direction of travel to follow. This was a simple, vague system, but the uninitiated would fail and be walking around in circles for ever.

The bag on Fred's back grew heavier and the straps were digging into his shoulders. As he got higher into the forest it suddenly became darker, with little light spreading through the canopy. There were huge top-heavy trees with extraordinarily little lower down and a huge dark green canopy. Cedar, cypress and Douglas fir, spruce, eucalyptus and radiata pine. Growing in between these monsters, elongated cordyline stretching to the sky and absorbing just enough light with the odd flash of sunshine to keep them sustained.

Fred had just passed another marker and reckoned he was within an hour of the cabin, maybe less. The air was growing cooler by the second, so he knew he was ascending at a good rate. He stopped for a break and took the weight off his shoulders, removing his shirt briefly just to take a quick look to see whether there were any cuts. Yes, his shoulders were red, but the skin hadn't been broken. His brown forearms, however, weren't a pretty sight. He couldn't recall ever having been bitten by so many insects at once. He put his shirt back on then looked at his legs. They were the same; in fact, they looked quite swollen, particularly around the calf, but he knew there was no time to start feeling sorry for himself as he had an important task to complete. The end result would be financial security for his mother, his sister and himself.

He picked up the heavy backpack and winced as the weight of the straps bit into his shoulders. His legs now felt like jelly. He had been walking for hours and it was taking much longer because of the heavy load on his back, which was becoming agonising.

About forty-five-minutes later, Fred finally arrived at the cabin. He opened the door, took off his backpack and placed it on the table, then he collapsed into the chair. He released the pack's cord, tipped it upside down and the three gold bars dropped out on to the table with a heavy clunk. Once again, he was transfixed by the sight before him. He sat there for a good five minutes just staring at them. They looked like something from another world, these ultra-shiny, warm, glowing objects in contrast with the surrounding rustic timber beams and planks.

Fred was comfortable sitting in his chair, fatigued after the long walk. He just wanted to sleep. He closed his eyes and his head instantly lolled to the side, then he snapped his head upright to the realisation that he must under no circumstances fall asleep.

He stood up, knowing that he had to find a hiding place for the gold. He looked around the plain windowless cabin. The only place he could think of was in the fireplace or stone chimney breast. Although the chimney breast looked like a professional job on the outside, internally it was a different matter. There were several ledges created because the stone was of all different sizes. These shelves would be the perfect hiding place. One by one, he lifted the bars up into the chimney breast and felt around for a suitable place to hide them away from view.

Once he was happy that the gold was nicely hidden, Fred put on his backpack and left the cabin to start his descent. On the way back he had plenty of time to think. He realised that by the time he reached the remaining gold and returned to the cabin, he would be unable to get back down safely because darkness would have fallen. So, he decided he was going to take the remaining two bars home. There just wasn't enough time to do two journeys to the cabin.

Fred was happy with his decision. He was now extremely tired, his legs were very sore from the mosquito bites and he just wanted to get home with the remainder of his valuable find. It was a gamble, he knew. There were risks involved but they were risks he was prepared to take.

The return journey seemed harder than the ascent, as he kept slipping and falling, and on one occasion took some skin off the knuckles of his right hand as he attempted to break his fall against a fir tree. He was desperately tired and he couldn't understand why his body seemed to be giving up on him. It was much warmer now and very humid, the sweat literally dripping from his saturated shirt. Fred knew he was approaching the mosquito stream again. He could see the line of ferns ahead and knew that if he stepped into them, he would be covered again by the horrible biting pests. So, he decided to go a bit further downstream and attempt to cross in a clearer section.

He had to go a little further than anticipated, and the stream wound to the left and then the right. He noticed the light was poor, which could be because of the thick canopy in this area of the forest, but he stopped to take a look around him. There were no shafts of sunlight feeding through from above, and those lovely light-green colours from the sun illuminating the giant fern leaves had gone. Darkness wasn't far away.

In a panic, Fred leaped across the stream, slipping on the opposite bank. He realised he had varied from his route and needed to find his way back. He traced the stream back towards the area of the mosquito ferns. Without upsetting the pests, he was fortunate to find a tree marker and headed back down the trail. He reached the edge of the forest still in a panic; it was almost dark.

He ran along the edge of the forest looking for his moped. His legs were now cut to ribbons and streaming blood, as he had run through rough bush. With his arms out in front, feeling his way around, he walked into something hard and fell awkwardly. Getting to his feet, he realised it was his moped. Now all he had to do was feel about for the large stick that he had left protruding.

Finding it pretty quickly, Fred scratched away at the earth and was extremely relieved to find the two gold bars. He removed his backpack, put the bars inside and returned it to his back. The pain was like a hot knife through both shoulders, but he got to his feet and managed to lift his moped, pushing it through the bush into the open grassland. He walked towards the gravel path. Fortunately, now he was out in the open, the moon lit his way and he could see the path that he had walked earlier through the trodden grass.

The sound of the cicada was overwhelming. They must be occupying the trees and bushes around him. Their loud noise was similar to that of a cricket, which always stopped as soon as you got too close then restarted as you walked away. There was an owl making a haunting hooting noise nearby, then another further away making a similar call as if in response.

Fred reached the gravel track, hoping that the petrol hadn't leaked out of the moped as it had been left on its side. Fortunately, there was no smell of leaking fuel. He tried to kickstart the moped and the small headlight briefly flickered, but the engine spluttered and didn't start. He tried again, kicking more forcefully this time, and the same thing happened – a brief glimmer from the headlamp, a splutter, then nothing.

Fred moved the choke, a small lever on the carburettor, a quarter turn to allow more petrol through. This would either work or flood the system. He tried the kickstart again and this time the moped stuttered and puffed out a cloud of smoke that reflected like a blue fog in the moonlight. He quickly turned the choke lever back to its off position and twisted the throttle. The trusty moped, which sounded like a petrol lawnmower, hadn't let him down yet.

Fred felt relieved as he slowly drove down the gravel track, with the small headlamp lighting the way. Before long, he reached the limestone gravel road that would lead his way home. Huge moths and other flying insects were magnified and attracted by the moped's front light, while behind, the bike's thin tyres created a cloud of dust. The dial of his speedometer, which was barely backlit, indicated a speed of thirty miles per hour, which he knew was pushing the machine to its limits.

The moped's speed gradually dropped as the incline of the next hill increased. Now down to ten miles per hour, Fred started to pedal to give the engine an extra push. He made it to the top and was able to coast down the hill on the other side. He knew exactly where he was, and he knew there was a steeper hill yet to climb. He was on the Tauhoa Road and would be passing through a small village called Hoteo.

Here, in early evening, some of the local Maori men would occasionally sit outside their homes cooking on barbeques and enjoying a drink or two. Once or twice Fred had stopped and enjoyed a beer and burger. They were very friendly people as a rule and passers-by were welcomed, especially if you accepted their hospitality, but once the alcohol kicked in, some of them could turn nasty, even against each other, so he had heard.

Fred opened the throttle and this time his speedometer touched thirty-two miles per hour, then as he rounded the valley bottom, it quickly reduced on the incline. He was almost at a standstill when he decided to pedal, but the extra weight on his back brought the moped to a stalling standstill. He now had to push it uphill, which was extremely difficult. With the extra weight on his back he again began to sweat profusely. His already sweat-stained shirt was in for another dousing. Flies and moths were strangely attracted to his sweating skin.

He had to stop several times before he reached the top of the hill. It was very dark without his moped headlamp but that was how he wanted it to be for now. Struggling for breath and with every sinew stretched, he made it to the top. He looked down into the valley below and could see the small cluster of houses that was Hoteo. He could hear voices and, as he suspected, families were out barbecuing and drinking on this balmy summer's evening. If he coasted down the hill into the village, there was another hill just as high on the other side, so he wouldn't get far before stopping again. But if he stopped in the village, the men would want to know what was in his backpack. He was hesitant and didn't know what to do for the best.

Deciding to try to approach with stealth, Fred stayed on the moped but used the front brake to control his speed downhill. With the engine off, the main noise came from the gravel beneath the tyres. He was really close now to the first group of men. They were shouting loudly and waving beer bottles around in the air. Someone had set fire to what looked like a firepit and the men were standing around with large sticks as if they were cooking something. The flames briefly illuminated the dense bush that was behind the houses.

The men were becoming more raucous and two became involved in a type of play fight. All of a sudden, emanating from the windows of the house, was the sound of 'Penny Lane' by the Beatles. The men all started to dance in a drunken fashion, then the women came out and they all danced together.

This was the ideal opportunity for Fred. He coasted down into the valley but just as he approached one of the small houses a door opened and a small boy walked out. Fred swallowed hard and hoped the boy wasn't going to be followed by a big brother or father, but it was just the boy. He closed the door and Fred gave him a wave, which he returned. It looked as if he was heading for the garden at the side of the house to join in with the festivities. All the same, Fred now had to move quickly in case the boy mentioned to an adult about a man creeping around the road in the dark outside his house.

Moving back uphill, Fred was running now and blowing hard. The moped got heavier and heavier until the hill became too steep and he had to walk. The music changed; they were now on to 'Strawberry Fields', one of Fred's favourite songs. The hill seemed to take an age but eventually he reached the top and looked back into the valley. He was too far away now to hear any music and there was no sign that anyone was following him.

Fred kickstarted his moped and continued his journey home. The weight on his shoulders was causing unbearable pain and he stopped a couple more times just to take the backpack off to relieve the pressure. He knew exactly where he was with regard to the distance from home and reckoned that he should be home within fifteen minutes.

As he looked ahead, he thought he could see light coming from the road, deflecting through the trees into a large dome of light. He waited for a moment, then it disappeared. Then it was back again. It was a vehicle on the road and it had just come through the valley up ahead and was heading straight for him. Not knowing what was at the side of the road, Fred diverted his moped and pushed it into a ditch. He slid down beside it and, as he did, one of the straps broke on his backpack.

Fred lay there still, in deathly silence as the vehicle approached. It must have stopped very close by, but he didn't care to look. He just lay still and waited and hoped that he wasn't spotted. He could hear their voices now, close by, so he decided to act fast. He threw the backpack further into the ditch and coughed and groaned. He stood up so the men could see him. A large light was pointed in his direction and he was blinded.

'Can you guys help me?' said Fred. 'I came off my moped just a few minutes ago and went into the ditch.' He looked backwards into the ditch to see whether the backpack was on show. Fortunately, it wasn't. He now looked towards the light, which was mounted on the front of the truck. He could see two men just standing there with open shotguns folded over their arms. A female jumped out of the truck and Fred recognised her as a local woman. She walked over to him.

'Are you alright? Have you had an accident?' the woman asked.

'I just fell off my moped. Could you give me a hand to get it out of the ditch?'

'For sure,' she replied.

The two men just stood there, now with a lit cigarette each. It was difficult to recognise them because they were still in the glare of the light, and Fred got the feeling they were doing this deliberately. Fred and the woman dragged the moped out of the ditch, and once into the truck lights, the woman could see the state of Fred's legs and arms. She stepped back a little when she got the strong whiff of body odour.

'You look like you've been in a war,' she said.

'I got lost in the forest by the beach and it went dark.' Wanting to divert the conversation, Fred asked, 'Aren't you Walter Jones's daughter?'

The woman looked embarrassed and the men behind her suddenly looked ill at ease.

'What's it to you Fella?' one of the men said in an unfriendly manner.

'Nothing. I just thought I recognised her. Anyway, thanks for your help and, if you don't mind, I'll be on my way.'

The girl had already jumped back into the truck. The men stood there while Fred got back on his moped, kickstarted the engine and rode away. He had come across similar folk before and suspected they were poachers or at least hunters. They used the big light on the front of the truck to light up the fields so they could see their prey and were probably on the lookout for wild boar amongst other things.

Having a rough idea of his location, Fred thought he should be able to find his way back to the exact spot. It seemed to take an eternity before the truck pulled away and moved on. Fred made sure his headlamp was turned off and did a U-turn, riding back to the location where he had stashed the backpack.

He climbed into the ditch but couldn't find the pack. It was difficult, as he was looking for a bag in a ditch under speckled moonlight from the overhead trees. He searched for quite a while, sure that he was in the right place. Still nothing. His heart sank as he realised that the poachers must have found his bag and made off. He wondered why they had stayed so long before driving away.

Fred felt sheer disappointment after all his work, only to fail to get the find back home. To make matters worse he thought he could hear the poachers coming back and he could see the familiar dome of light from the headlamps, probably about five minutes away. Once again, he pushed the moped into the ditch and pulled down some nearby fern leaves to offer some sort of camouflage. As the truck got closer, he stayed low. He could hear the two men shouting joyfully as they passed by. He knew why they were so joyful; they had his gold.

Tired and dejected, Fred tried to scramble out of the ditch, kicking up dirt and snapping fern branches on the way. He was now right at the edge of the ditch, holding on to the moped's handlebars. With one almighty pull, he nearly made it out but lost his footing and ended up even further down. He lay back and began to cry. They say grown men shouldn't cry; that's what he was always told, but at this moment he didn't care – the floodgates opened.

He eventually convinced himself that it wasn't the end of the world because he still had three gold bars stashed away in his cabin. It was time to move on. He stretched out his left arm to push himself up and in so doing felt something unexpected but familiar underneath a couple of broken fern leaves. Absolutely ecstatic now, he brushed away the debris and grabbed the bag. It was empty. He looked inside, although he didn't need to, and noticed that the drawstring around the neck of the bag had also snapped like the shoulder strap. Maybe the gold bars had fallen out into the ditch and hadn't been taken after all.

Fred slid further down and, at the bottom of the ditch, partly covered by leaves and soil, were the two gold bars. Once again, his emotions had been reversed and he was so happy to have the gold back in his possession. He then managed to make some sort of use of the broken bag. He lifted it out of the ditch, contents in place, and laid it by the roadside. Now refreshed with vim, vigour, vitality and gold, Fred managed to get the moped out of the ditch. He picked up the backpack, strapped it over one shoulder and he was off.

In a cloud of unseen dust, Fred made it home. The sheer joy on the faces of his mother and sister when they saw the gold was worth absolutely everything to him. He told them that he had more stashed away and that he would be bringing it back in the coming days. He knew that the church was looking for funds to erect a new modern building and he told his mother and sister that he wanted one gold bar for this purpose. The others were for them to do with as they pleased.

That night, Fred was pampered by the two women. After he had bathed, they dealt with the injuries to his arms and legs. After a good meal and swathed in Germolene, Fred went to bed an incredibly happy man. He fell asleep almost immediately.

He never woke up. The doctor wrote on the death certificate the following day that the reason for his demise was 'Heart Failure'.

2

London, England 2014

NATHAN MASON, a Detective Sergeant in the Metropolitan Police, managed a team of ten plain-clothed constables and a Detective Constable on the Crime Squad at Southwark Police Station in south London.

He was single, Caucasian and stood six feet two inches in bare feet and weighed in at 224 pounds. With his blond hair and blue eyes he could easily have passed as a male model, but when up close you could see several scars that passed through his eyebrow line. You also couldn't help noticing the slight angle of his nose, indicating that it may have been broken in the past. His ears had a thickening too, not like cauliflowers, but you could tell that they had been on the receiving end of some repeated rough treatment.

Nathan was in love with not only his job but also rugby union. He had played in the second row of the scrum and thrived on the rough and tumble, the foul play, the gouging and scratching, and even the punching, as long as he wasn't on the receiving end, although he occasionally was. He had played for the Metropolitan Police until recently, when during a game the scrum collapsed and his head took the majority of the force. He had been left unconscious and was taken to hospital. That evening he had a stroke due to a clot on the brain. His head bore the marks of a couple of rugby boot studs; whether someone had intentionally stood on his head, only his opponents knew. Nathan had been transferred to Kingston Hospital for specialist treatment.

He had suffered an ischaemic stroke, which occurs when the flow of blood to the brain is disrupted. He had been unable to speak without slurring, and one of his legs and an arm had been affected. He had a slant to his mouth, couldn't answer simple questions and had been very unwell. Fortunately, the hospital had the right drugs and the right professionals. Within an hour, they had administered a thrombolysis clot-dissolving drug by intravenous injection.

After having been first moved to a ward, Nathan ended up in a private room, with its own toilet, washing facilities and a shower. His surroundings and treatment were conducive to his condition and he had begun to improve quite quickly.

Over the next few days, Nathan had been visited by a plethora of people, all experts in their field: a psychologist, a speech and language therapist, a physiotherapist, a consultant and, of course, the medical staff who kept a constant watch on his condition and improvement. He had resumed normal use of his arm and leg pretty quickly and the slant to his mouth had disappeared.

The Stroke Association representative had visited and left Nathan a bundle of information on subjects such as 'What Is a Stroke?' 'The Road to Recovery', 'Life After a Stroke', 'Sex After a Stroke', 'Driving After a Stroke', 'Alcohol After a Stroke' and many other topics. These were all to take home in the hope that soon he would be able to read and understand them.

Nathan had also received visits from his colleagues in the CID office, the Crime Squad and a couple of his teammates. All this overwhelmed him, partly because he couldn't remember most of their names. He was aware that they were police officers and that he was too, but he couldn't remember his role or where he worked. His memory had been severely affected and because of this he didn't like to ask too many questions for fear of coming across as totally inept.

His workmates, though, seemed to make the extra effort. They knew he was on his own and that all he had was a sister and her husband in New Zealand. It was only five years ago that his mother and father had been involved in a terrible road traffic accident near Cheltenham. They had both been killed outright when a driver, presumed under the influence of drugs, had mounted the kerb on a path of destruction.

The car front footwells were full of drug paraphernalia, which suggested that the driver had been using at the time of the accident. The car had pinned Nathan's parents against a stone wall. The driver had made good his escape. A vehicle check and the wallet found in the car had identified the driver, but he had never been seen again. He never went to his flat, never turned up for work, never used his bank account or his mobile phone; for all intents and purposes the man no longer existed.

Nathan had been notified of the news of the accident by his Inspector in CID only a few hours after it had occurred. The Inspector had received a call from one of the senior police officers at Cheltenham. Nathan had gone straight to the scene to find out what he could, arriving within a couple of hours once he had negotiated the London traffic.

This had been devastating news for Nathan. Certain quarters even suspected that he may have been responsible for the disappearance of the offender; that maybe he had caught up with him and had issued summary justice. This was totally unsubstantiated and Nathan was never interviewed or officially suspected, and after all, there was no body, just the bodies of his parents.

Nathan had fallen into a deep depression. In his world everything had turned grey and the walls had come tumbling down. His GP had prescribed anti-depressants and Nathan had been absent from work for two weeks on sick leave. But he wasn't just strong of body, he was strong of mind, recognising the symptoms of depression. He had taken guidance from various sources from outside the police on how to handle it.

It wasn't until a month after the funeral of his parents that the mist had begun to lift. Nathan had been advised that the best antidote for depression was exercise and he had jogged for at least an hour each day. Gradually, the feelings of sadness and loneliness had begun to relinquish their icy grip.

He had returned to work and been offered the position of running the Crime Squad at Southwark. He had accepted the role and the change in the type of work had helped him considerably. His mind had been occupied all the time, if not on the case in hand, then on managing his officers into their natural best-fit roles. Nathan had thrived and so had the team.

~~~

Nathan had been in hospital for a week since the stroke and was making good progress. He could now identify all the zoo animals on a series of sheets that had been given to him the day after his arrival. He could now say the words rhinoceros and hippopotamus, which had previously caused him great anxiety. He was now speaking without slurring or spraying with saliva whoever he was conversing with. He was also reading and had regular walks around the hospital.

Nathan was delighted to hear that his sister Millie and her husband Chris were on their way from New Zealand, although he couldn't understand how they had found out about his stroke. He hadn't seen them since his last visit to New Zealand.

Things were starting to look up and Nathan was looking forward to returning home, if only he could remember where it was and what it was like. The good thing was that once he had remembered something such as a word or a thought, it generally stuck with him. Unfortunately, he had been left with swathes of time and memories that seemed to have been erased and, unless prompted, may never return.

On the eighth day, the speech therapist turned up to test Nathan yet again. She had been encouraging him to use word association if he couldn't find the right words to say. When she asked him what he had for breakfast, he replied, 'Tea with brown bread, butter and ...' but he couldn't find the word he was looking for. So, he said, 'You find it in doughnuts.' The therapist waited for a few seconds before saying, 'Raspberry jam.' Nathan nodded, smiled, then gave her the thumbs up. He wouldn't forget raspberry jam again.

Little did Nathan know that he would be using word association for the rest of his life. He used it in his head when he was struggling to find a word. Sometimes though, being lost for words proved embarrassing and sometimes convenient. Some people wrongly underestimated him. On occasion he was found wanting for the best word to deal with a situation. When he couldn't find it, the sheer exasperation made him walk away in anger, or with feelings of sorrow, and the more tired he became, so the symptoms were exacerbated.

3

IT WAS now day nine and late that afternoon Millie and Chris arrived from New Zealand. They were heavily jet-lagged but had hired a car at the airport and were on their way to the hospital.

Chris had worked on the London Stock Exchange, was a wealthy man and had that stock exchange type of person look – always well presented, clean-shaven and his hair always immaculately side-parted, but stylishly so. He was five feet eleven inches tall and very lean. He had quite a strict regime of swimming in his outdoor pool every morning for thirty minutes and of walking for an hour every evening. Not an unattractive man, he even had his own light aircraft, which he used to fly and maintain as a hobby in his spare time. It could be said that he was a good catch for any woman, or man for that matter.

Chris had met Millie ten years ago at a charity dinner-dance in Windsor. She had been a businesswoman on the rise, already owner of two local high-end ladies fashion shops and part-owner of one in her hometown of Cheltenham. It could therefore also be said that she was a good catch for any man or woman. She was extremely attractive, with long, wavy, chestnut brown hair and dark brown eyes. As you would expect, being in the clothing industry, she was immaculately turned out. Chris had been unable to resist her beauty and humour and they had fallen for each other hook, line and sinker. They were an attractive and powerful young couple.

Chris had inherited some land in New Zealand and they more or less immediately started to think about a new life. Millie had already been offered a substantial sum for her two shops, one in Windsor and one in Eton. Chris had become tired of his role in the City and was wanting to work in the world stock markets from home. This he could do from anywhere in the world.

The decision had been made – they were going to emigrate to New Zealand. Nathan and his parents had been devastated, but everyone realised that you couldn't hold these two back.

~~~

Nathan was feeling a lot better today. He could think clearly, the lack of confidence that he had been suffering since the stroke seemed to have left him. He was actively walking around the ward adjacent to his room, speaking with patients and to the medical staff. This didn't go unnoticed, and when the consultant came to speak to him, Nathan confidently asked to go home.

His request coincided perfectly with Chris and Millie's arrival. They offered to take him home and look after him in the short term. He had by now remembered his home address and also the fact that his car must still be in the rugby club car park. It was agreed that he could return home. When the consultant left the room, Nathan and Millie embraced like a brother and sister who hadn't seen each other for eighteen months, although they talked regularly on the telephone.

'We've been so worried. The flight seemed to take an age,' said Millie.

'I'm so thankful to you both for coming all this way, and you're timing was perfect,' Nathan replied.

'How are you feeling today?' asked Millie.

'Every day when I wake up, I feel better. I'm beginning to remember more. I still sometimes struggle finding the words I want to say, but compared to how I was, this is a massive improvement.'

Chris came over and shook Nathan's hand firmly. 'Great to see you mate, you look much better than I expected,' he said. It was noticeable that a slight New Zealand accent was creeping in.

'I've been lucky Chris. I was treated very quickly with a clot-dissolving drug, which cleared the obstruction on the side of my brain.'

'What exactly happened to cause it?' asked Chris.

'I was playing rugby for the police when the scrum collapsed. I went down on my head, then I think someone stood on me. Apparently there are stud marks on the side of my head.'

'Is there no video footage of the incident?' Chris asked.

'I play for the Met Police not the All Blacks,' Nathan replied.

Chris and Millie laughed. 'I'm glad you haven't lost your sense of humour baby brother,' Millie said.

Nathan smiled. 'You won't believe how pleased I am to see you two.' A tear ran down the side of Millie's cheek.

4

NATHAN WAS with Chris and Millie in their hire car and was able to direct them straight to his flat at Putney Heath in south-west London.

'This is a lovely area Nathan,' Chris commented.

'Thanks Chris. It's quite a way to work in Southwark but I do like it over here. I feel as if I'm away from it if you know what I mean.'

'Yes, I can understand that in your job. You don't want to be walking down the high street and bumping into people that you've previously arrested.'

'No, that wouldn't be erm … erm … erm … good.'

They pulled up in a designated parking space to the rear of Nathan's flat and made their way to the rear entrance door. The door had a digital lock on it, the type that needs a four-digit code.

'Damn it!' said Nathan.

'Can't you remember the code?' asked Chris.

'It's okay, it's in my iPhone.' Nathan withdrew the mobile from his coat pocket and looked at the screen. 'I can't believe this. I can't remember my pin number to open the mobile. I'm sure I used it earlier.'

'Don't stress,' said Millie. 'It's early days. It may take a while to get all your memory functions back. Oh, look, there's someone coming down the stairs. They'll let us in.'

The door opened and a young man, very tall, in his mid-twenties, opened the door and greeted them. 'Nathan, how are you doing? It's great to see you back.'

Nathan couldn't remember his name but could remember that he lived in the flat next door and they got on quite well. 'I'm glad to be back. Can we catch up later?' he replied.

'Sure, no problem.'

Millie touched the young man's arm. 'Hi, I'm Millie, his sister from New Zealand, and this is my husband Chris.'

'Hi,' the man said, shaking their hands rigorously. 'I'm Daniel. Call me Dan. I work at the same police station as Nathan.'

'That's fantastic,' Millie replied. 'So, you two can look out for each other.'

'Oh yes, and we do. Not that he needs much looking after, mind.' Dan and Nathan smiled at each other.

'Well, he does at the moment and that's why we're here,' Millie said. 'Do you mind giving us the code for the front door in case we get locked out again?'

'Of course, 8257. I'll try to catch up with you guys later. Just going down to the gym.'

'Okay, bye,' they all replied in unison.

The three of them walked up the stairs and came to Nathan's flat door. He opened the mortice lock first then inserted the key into the latch, turned the key and the door opened. They stepped over quite a large amount of mail, which Chris picked up, and they walked into the lounge.

The flat was smart, modern and well presented. It consisted of a small corridor that gave access to the kitchen, lounge, bathroom, two bedrooms and a couple of storage cupboards. It was also very compact, ideal for a couple but any more people and it would become overbearing. It was, though, the type of property that was in high demand. A good example of a city dwelling in an up-and-coming location.

That evening, after Millie had visited the supermarket for much-needed supplies, the three of them enjoyed a good meal. The spare bedroom was already made up so that Chris and Millie could settle in straight away. They all had an early night.

The following morning after a good sleep, Chris went to visit an old friend in the City after they had been to the rugby club to collect Nathan's car. While Chris was out, brother and sister had ample opportunity to talk and catch up – and talk they did, for hours.

Millie was trying to ascertain what Nathan's plans were. He told her that he intended to return to the Crime Squad to continue his duties. Millie expressed her concerns as to whether that was a wise decision, or even one that would be permitted. Nathan became annoyed with his sister then; his emotions flooded out in tears. For the first time, someone had expressed the opinion that he may not be able to continue in his job. This had been eating away at him as he lay in hospital, but he couldn't accept it and was determined to continue all the treatments that had been offered. One thing he had accepted was that he would never be able to play rugby again.

Over the next couple of weeks, Nathan attended the psychologist, the physio, the speech therapist and his own doctor. What he wasn't expecting was a call from the Chief Medical Office (CMO) at the Metropolitan Police, asking him to go in for a review.

By now, Nathan thought it was time for Millie and Chris to return to New Zealand. In his opinion he was progressing well and was now attending the gym on a daily basis. However, he was still not allowed to drive, so Millie and Chris had to take him everywhere in their hire car, and he felt he was putting on them too much. He was incredibly grateful for everything they had done for him but felt as if it was time things got back to as near normal as possible. They had already been with him for nearly three weeks.

Millie reluctantly agreed on the condition that Nathan allowed her to accompany him on the upcoming visit to the CMO, as a second pair of ears. She wasn't moving on this one, so he had no choice. This was potentially embarrassing for Nathan – his hand being held by his big sister.

When the day of the review arrived, Nathan was in good form. He felt physically incredibly good for someone who had suffered a stroke not that long ago, but he knew he still had issues. He was determined to try to hide them as much as possible, but the fact remained that a lot of his memory had still not returned and at the moment this would make him incapable of doing his job. When they arrived for the meeting, Millie was asked to wait in reception. She wasn't happy but that was the way it had to be.

The officer at the review seemed to have the knack of asking questions that involved Nathan reliving part of his police past, such as important arrests and some of his acts of bravery during the course of his duties. These events were all recorded on his file, which the review officer had open on his laptop to refer to. Nathan had only his memory and it let him down badly.

Unperturbed, Nathan stubbornly made it clear that as he was allowed to drive in another couple of weeks, it was his intention to return to work shortly after that. He was then told in no uncertain terms that he couldn't return until his GP and the CMO agreed that it was safe for him to do so. He was then given a further review date in six weeks' time. Nathan wasn't happy but there was nothing he could do about it.

Two days later it was time for Millie and Chris to return to New Zealand, but not before the three of them had a good heart-to-heart conversation, during which Nathan confirmed his determination to get back to work.

'You have to accept Nathan, and I'm sorry to have to say this, but there's a possibility that they may never allow you back to work. I want you to consider moving to New Zealand. You could live with us before looking for your own place,' suggested Millie.

'Now why would I want to do that? I have everything here: my flat, my job, my friends. I just need to keep on improving. I can get through that next review, I know I can.

Besides, the last time I looked, you needed a profession or a job on the required skills list to emigrate to New Zealand.'

'You're not wrong,' agreed Chris, 'but it's also about what else you can bring to the country.'

'Such as?' asked Nathan.

'Wealth. If you can prove you're bringing your financial wealth to the country ... I'll find out how much the threshold is and—'

'Please stop,' interrupted Nathan. 'It's too much too soon and I'm not going anywhere. I really appreciate what you've done for me and what you're offering to do for me, but my place is here fighting for my job, my life ... no ... erm ... erm ... erm ...livelihood.'

'I think that what Chris is saying is that with all the money that we inherited from our parents' estate, and our financial situation, entry shouldn't be a problem for you,' added Millie.

'I'm a Detective Sergeant in the Met. I'm hoping to be promoted to Inspector within the next eighteen months, so why would I want to walk away from that?'

'For your mental health and sanity,' said Millie.

Nathan's face changed. He looked angry; about to blow his top, but Millie took the wind out of his sails. 'Right, we'll say no more about it. Time for us to be on our way, so give me a hug baby brother.' Millie stretched to put her arms around Nathan's neck, then kissed him on the cheek. They hugged, then Millie spoke into Nathan's ear: 'We need to keep in touch and speak to each other more often. Let's make a point of speaking to each other on Skype at least three times a week.' Calming down now, Nathan agreed to the suggestion.

Chris and Nathan shook hands and the visitors left for the airport. Nathan noticed that Millie had a tear in her eye as she waved goodbye from the car window. He wondered how long it would be before he saw them in person again.

Nathan was determined to try to get things back to normal as best he could. His fitness regime continued, but now he was doing more walking than running, and when he left the house he was sometimes gone for the day. His iPhone had an app that allowed free access to audio books, and he would go walking with his wireless headphones but soon realised that the battery wouldn't last for the duration of his walk, so he reverted back to his standard wired earplugs. He visited libraries, museums and many of London's attractions, quite often stopping at a local pub for his breakfast or lunch, whichever took his fancy.

A couple of his colleagues from the Crime Squad started to visit him twice weekly in the evenings to keep him up to speed on how things were progressing at work. It was during one of these get-togethers over a pint in the quiet backroom of their local pub that Nathan became aware of his shortcomings and his new lack of understanding. He was still unable to refer back to previous cases, previous names, places, arresting officers, reasons for arrest – the list was endless.

Somehow, Nathan managed to bluff his way through, or he thought he had, until the Detective Chief Inspector in overall control of the CID and Crime Squad visited him at home one day. The DCI was very friendly and very polite, but Nathan knew he was visiting him on a mission to report back to the CMO and he seemed to ask a lot of questions relating to past cases. He even briefly touched on current legislation in relation to arrestable offences. Nathan knew it was a trap but he walked right into it. They both knew that he wasn't fit to return to his job. He had forgotten too much. Again, the nagging doubt crept into Nathan's mind, niggling away at him: the fact that he may never be able or permitted to return to work.

Nathan found himself seeking solace in any library that he came across during his walks. He loved history, in particular historical crime such as the Kray twins, the Great Train Robbery and Jack the Ripper. He also loved fiction and characters such as Poirot, Sherlock Holmes and Inspector Morse. They all had one theme in common: detectives. This was what he enjoyed. He was, after all, a highly respected, fair, and unrelenting detective himself, just not as famous.

Then the doubts reappeared again. Was he going to remain a detective for much longer? He had suffered a stroke, so he could be consigned to reading about murder, robberies, rapes and burglaries for the rest of his life. He would no longer be at the sharp end, fighting crime; he would be useless, just a mere bystander as the wheels of the fight against crime kept turning.

One thing Nathan wouldn't be was a burden on society. He didn't need the welfare state, he was a wealthy man from a wealthy family. He could probably retire now, at thirty-two. He had enough money to live off for the rest of his life, but to go from a background of a rugby-playing detective in the Met to a retired unemployed man was unthinkable.

Nathan continued to keep fit and well read. A couple of days before his second review with the CMO he had an appointment at the hospital. His consultant was pleased with his progress. When Nathan asked for a possible return-to-work date he was absolutely bowled over when he was told that he shouldn't be returning to operational duties. Nathan queried the reason for this decision and was told in no uncertain terms that he would now be susceptible to further strokes. It was a fact of life. If you have a stroke, your chances of a secondary are increased considerably.

This was just another blow on this slippery road that seemed to be spiralling downhill at speed. There was nothing Nathan could do about it; the circumstances were conspiring against him – his DCI, his consultant, his GP and the CMO – and he didn't know how to slow them down, never mind stop them.

When the day of the follow-up review with the CMO arrived, Nathan was as prepared as he could have been. He had been absent from work for over three months. He was tired of being on the receiving end of bad news and negative vibes and was ready to defend his corner and go on the attack if need be.

He arrived early for his 11am appointment but was seen more or less immediately. He walked into a large office with an oval-shaped boardroom table. The office had large windows in two walls, giving a spectacular vista over central London. He was offered a seat opposite two sharply dressed men and a woman, all of whom were displaying a look of intensity that could have been construed as intimidating. On the table were two bottles of water, several glasses on a silver tray and a couple of writing pads with pencils.

With the introductions over, the chief suit informed Nathan that the Police Federation representative was on his way and due any minute. Nathan had queried why a rep was required, to which he was informed that it was standard practice for a review at this stage. Suddenly, Nathan had a bad feeling about the whole situation.

The Federation rep finally arrived and sat next to Nathan, then whispered in his ear, 'Don't feel intimidated by all this. I'm just here to make sure that you get a fair deal, and don't worry, we don't have to say yes or no to anything today; we just have to see what they offer.'

'What I want is to return to work,' whispered Nathan in reply. The rep gave him a sideways glance and a narrow smile, but Nathan couldn't read his expression.

The rep made an opening statement in which he reminded the suits that his colleague had been injured while representing the Metropolitan Police 1st XV rugby team in an authorised and approved match. As such, the injuries he had received should be construed as having been received on behalf of, if not while on duty. The meeting rolled on and on, with exchanges between the rep and the suits, which all seemed to be based around responsibility for the injury.

At one point, Nathan interrupted and attempted to turn the conversation towards the possibility of him returning to work. It was suggested to him that there could be the possibility of a light-duty, non-operational role, but that it was unlikely such a role existed with a pay grade that came anywhere near that of a Detective Sergeant. The rep was displeased with this comment and suggested a suspension of the meeting pending the employment of a lawyer to oversee proceedings to ensure that employment law was adhered to. The chief suit suddenly mentioned a medical discharge package.

Nathan momentarily lost his cool. 'I don't need a package. I want to go back to my old job. It's my livelihood; its everything to me. You can't just take erm … erm … take it away.'

The chief suit then read a statement from an official document that he had taken from the file on his desk. He made clear that the statement indicated that the CMO had confirmed, on medical grounds, that Nathan couldn't return to his operational duties. The rep reiterated that any offer to his colleague had better be a good one, otherwise the Metropolitan Police would be on thin ice. He confirmed again that Nathan had been representing the Met when the accident happened.

The meeting closed shortly after this exchange. Nathan was informed that he would be contacted in the next few days with a suitable discharge package based upon medical grounds. This was the final blow for Nathan. Mentally he was preparing for the possibility of being medically signed off, but it hurt, and unofficially his future in the Metropolitan Police was over.

For some reason, the whole process brought back all the memories from his police career – the good and the bad. He recalled vividly the trips in his spare time, travelling to Cheltenham and back, trying to locate the man who had been responsible for the death of his parents. Being a local, Nathan knew the fugitive. He knew his haunts and he knew who he associated with. But the man had simply disappeared, never to be seen again.

Nathan remembered a time when he was in uniform, persuading a mother, babe in arms and threatening to jump, to step down off a parapet of a block of flats. He remembered some of the drug busts and murder squad investigations that he had been involved in, some of which were successful, with the odd total disaster thrown in. He decided that once he received official notification about his future, he would call in at Southwark to see his colleagues, particularly those on the Crime Squad.

Two days later, Nathan received a letter in the post from the CMO. It listed how much his pension contributions were worth and made a point that they were index-linked and would be there for him to take at the age of fifty-five. They were also offering him a medical discharge payment based upon his number of years' service, his current pay scale and any mitigating circumstances. The offer was £250,000.

Upon receipt of this notification, Nathan called his Federation rep as he had been asked to do. The rep wanted to go for more, but Nathan didn't want a protracted, drawn-out affair, so they agreed to accept the package offered.

Over the next couple of weeks, Nathan continued his fitness regime. He was aware that niggling away in the back of his head, the depression symptoms were trying to find a way in, to make him feel sorry for himself, to feel desperation like he had when his parents had died. He knew that without medication, his exercise was the remedy, so he continued, walking for miles and miles each day, visiting museums and libraries, just like before.

Eventually, Nathan paid his final visit to Southwark Police Station to see his colleagues and collect his belongings. He felt quite emotional on the day, although he didn't show it. The Crime Squad had laid on a buffet in their office and all of CID were in attendance. The DCI performed a humorous rousing speech, the subject being the police life of Nathan Mason; but in all honesty, there was no other life, policing was his life.

Nathan was commended for the quality and quantity of his detective work, which for many would have catapulted them into the limelight on a regular basis, but he had liked to keep things low key, never boasting about his latest arrests, just like he had never talked about his rugby achievements, which at a small club were significant. He was a modest man, but he didn't lack confidence. It's how he was. He had lots of friends, but he was beginning to realise that they were all associated with work. He actually had no friends outside of the police.

Nathan arrived home that afternoon with an inscribed silver tankard, a Met Police ornamental wooden shield, a certificate of exemplary service, a large leaving card signed by lots of his colleagues and a large bag containing the contents of his locker. He had walked out of the front door at Southwark Police Station for the last time. The Met was losing a big asset and Nathan was losing his lifelong passion and his livelihood.

That same evening, Nathan decided to go to his local pub with his friend and neighbour, Dan. They sat in the small room at the rear of the pub and talked and talked about anything.

'What are your plans Nathan?' Dan eventually asked.

'I'm not sure. There doesn't seem to be anything for me here. I can't spend the rest of my life visiting museums and libraries and walking around the streets. For the first time, Dan, I'm actually thinking about New Zealand.'

'New Zealand! My god, it's at the other end of the world man. I take it this is to do with your sister?'

'Yes, it is. They've offered to put me up over there.'

'That's a big step.'

'I know, but it could be the opportunity I need to start again. I have no family here in the UK … well only distant relatives, so I'm seriously thinking about going Dan.'

'Only you know best Nathan.'

'I know, but if only it was that simple.'

'What do you mean? What is it that's bothering you?'

'Well, Millie wants me to move lock, stock and barrel to her place and it all seems so final, to cut off all my ties here. I mean, what if I'm not happy over there? I'll need somewhere to come back to.'

'Then don't sell your flat. Keep it. I'll look after it for you. Besides, its somewhere for my parties to overflow,' Dan said with a smile. 'And if some people want to stay over, they have somewhere to crash.'

'You're not doing a particularly good job of selling this idea to me you know,' joked Nathan.

'I know. It's because I want you to stay.'

'Why?' asked Nathan.

'Well, it's better the devil you know than the devil you don't.' They both laughed.

Over the next couple of weeks, Nathan continued exercising and reading and he was feeling very well, as well as he had for many years, but he had New Zealand on his mind. His sister had planted the seed of thought and it seemed to be growing. He found himself in the non-fiction areas of libraries looking at the history of the country: the Maori, European colonisation and the Treaty of Waitangi, when the early settlers first reached agreement with the indigenous people. He had been to New Zealand before on a couple of occasions and had always enjoyed the visits, but he was always glad to get back home. If he went again it may be different this time because he had no job and no family to come back to. He had made a point of informing Millie that he was thinking about going to New Zealand to give it a try. She was so delighted that she had cried tears of joy over the telephone.

It was now mid-November, coming into the winter in the UK, which meant it was going into the summer in New Zealand. Millie and Chris lived on the North Island, just north of Warkworth. The area was blessed with a temperate climate, nice and warm in the summer and not too cold in the winter.

Nathan had made his decision and he was going to give it a try. He decided to keep his flat in Putney as a bolthole to return to if needed, but he didn't want to let it out. He would recompense Dan for looking after it and collecting any mail and such like. Nathan enjoyed Christmas, although it was different from the norm, as he was flying out to New Zealand on 5 January. He thought he was going for a period of recuperation but nothing could have been further from the truth.

5

THE FLIGHT from Heathrow to Dubai went smoothly enough, and with a relatively quick transfer in the United Arab Emirates, Nathan was on the flight bound for Auckland.

The flight from Dubai was a torturous one. Whether Nathan read, slept, talked, ate or watched TV, there were several points during the flight when he had wished that someone had invented a teleportal device to put him out of his misery and get him there now. Hence the relief amongst the passengers was palpable as the aeroplane finally touched down in Auckland.

As he made his way through immigration, passport control and the luggage carousel, Nathan passed some of the amazing displays of Maori wood carvings, which featured serpents with large fearsome heads, sharp fangs and long tongues. The spectacular face mask carvings with their swirling and fishhook-type patterns were also on display. When he eventually passed through into the arrivals hall, he was met by a fifteen-foot dwarf statue, reminding all visitors that they were now in Hobbit country, the gateway to Middle Earth.

Nathan was tired after the long journey. His legs, shoulders and back ached, but all the ailments seemed to dissipate as he saw Millie and Chris approaching. Millie flung her arms around Nathan's neck and pulled him close. She kissed him on the side of his face and said, 'Welcome to New Zealand. I'm so glad you came.'

This time it was Nathan's turn to have a tear in his eye when he said, 'Thank you for having me.'

Chris patted him on the back and Nathan turned to shake his hand. 'Great to see you again, Nathan. Let me take that heavy-looking suitcase. We haven't got far to go.'

'Cheers Chris. I brought as much as I could within my weight limit, so it's quite heavy; just a fraction below thirty kilos in fact.' Chris pretended to buckle under the weight as he placed the case on a trolley. 'Very funny,' added Nathan as he removed his backpack and placed it in the top section of the trolley.

Chris walked ahead, pushing the trolley through the sliding doors to the car parking area. Nathan walked alongside Millie. 'Was your flight okay?' she asked.

'An absolute breeze,' replied Nathan, smiling. Millie turned to him and looked at him with narrow eyes, knowing he wasn't being honest.

'And how do you feel in yourself?' she enquired.

'Absolutely erm ... erm ... electric erm ... shock ... erm ... shocking. Sorry, I still struggle for words sometimes, especially when I'm this tired.' Millie gave him an understanding look.

As they stepped outside the arrivals lounge the heat was considerable. 'Wow. I wasn't expecting it to be this warm,' Nathan exclaimed.

'Yes, we're in a warm spell at the moment. Highs of about thirty to thirty-two degrees,' said Millie. 'It's been quite difficult sleeping, so we've been sitting out late at night, sometimes until early morning depending on how the wine stocks are.'

'Well that sounds great to me. I'll make sure the stock levels are kept more than adequate.'

Chris turned around. 'I heard that, and I'll keep you to it.'

'I'm sure you will,' replied Nathan laughingly.

They made their way to the car park. Nathan inhaled the warm air tinged with the scent of kerosene, petrol and diesel fumes, the by-products of travel. He could feel a bead of sweat forming on his forehead and the clamminess as his shirt stuck to his back. He noticed the humidity level was remarkably high.

The rear hatch of a silver Mercedes SUV opened as they approached. Chris loaded the suitcase as Nathan jumped into the rear seat with his backpack. Millie jumped into the driver's seat.

'Is this your car Millie?' asked Nathan.

'It is, do you like it?'

'Yes, it's a beauty. What do you drive Chris?'

'I have a BMW X6. We like our four-wheel drives. It means we can go off-road to some of the remote beaches and up in the hills too. I'm going to take you to some stunning places that we've only recently found ourselves.'

'I'm up for that,' replied Nathan.

As Nathan made himself comfortable in the back seat, the air conditioning washed over him. It felt so luxurious, and as his body cooled and relaxed, he soon fell asleep.

The SUV headed north, straddling the city of Auckland and crossing the iconic Harbour Bridge on State Highway 1, known as SH1. The sleeping Nathan missed the spectacular views, including, looking back to the city, banks of yachts and other boats parked in their moorings and many more coming in and out of the harbour, all glistening in the bright sunshine.

It was early afternoon and Nathan was still sleeping in the rear seat as the digital display in the SUV read thirty-three degrees centigrade. Although this was the middle of the holiday season for New Zealand, the Auckland traffic wasn't too bad. They made good progress through Albany, Silverdale, Puhoi and Warkworth. As they passed through the Dome Valley, the countryside offered views of the valley sides covered in ferns of different colour and variety as cordyline, mountain cedar, cypress, tea tree and mountain flax ascended steeply to the left and right of SH1. It was rich in vegetation and bird life and the air was clean and fresh, if a tad humid.

The car turned left and began its ascent of a hill along a narrow path. The giant ferns and cordyline seemed to bow overhead and form the shape of a long green tunnel.

'This will probably wake him up,' said Millie, looking across at Chris. The car approached a cattle grid with signs displayed saying 'No Entrance, Private Road'. Although Millie had slowed the car, the rumbles as it crept over the large iron bars were significant enough for Nathan to jerk his head upright.

'Oops, sorry,' said Millie. 'I tried to go over as smoothly as possible. Anyway, we're here now.'

Nathan looked out of his tired eyes. He now felt worse than he had before he fell asleep. 'Sorry. I guess I'm not good company at the moment. How long have I been asleep?'

'About an hour,' said Chris.

Nathan looked out of the car window and recognised the house on the hill to his left. Chris and Millie's house was called Fern Heights. Set in untold acres of land, the house had been built on a cleared hill within the Dome Forest. The car pulled left through a pair of stone pillars and ascended on a smooth tarmac, winding, tree-lined driveway, passing manicured lawns with the occasional outcrop of herbaceous planting. It was an impressive sight.

As they approached the substantial, six-bedroomed, L-shaped house, the driveway opened out to a large parking area at the side, which also gave access to three large garages that helped form the L-shaped aspect of the house. Above the garages there was a granny flat, which was used on occasions when relatives stayed. The swimming pool was outside, but on the other side of the house so that you couldn't see it from the front or as you approached the house.

Nathan knew he would be staying in the bedroom on the front corner of the house because Millie called it his bedroom. It was a pleasant room and one to which he had become attached on his previous visits. He liked the fact that he had his own room in the house, so to speak, even though it wasn't actually his. It was Millie's way of letting him know he was always welcome.

As he stepped out of the car, Nathan was immediately reminded of his first foreign holiday when he went with his then girlfriend. They had arrived in Corfu in the middle of the night. It was still very warm outside and the heat had rushed into the aeroplane as the steward opened the exit door. As they walked down the steps of the plane, they had been overwhelmed by the aroma of the nearby cedars and cypresses that covered the mountains. Here in New Zealand it felt even hotter, but it was the middle of the afternoon. The rich aroma emanating from the surrounding forested hills wafted across Nathan's face on the finest of breezes. He took a large intake of breath and closed his eyes. 'It's great to be back,' he said.

'Come on,' said Millie, 'let's take your stuff up to your bedroom.'

Chris had already opened the rear hatch and was wheeling Nathan's large suitcase towards the front door. Nathan carried his backpack as Millie went ahead, opened the door and stepped inside.

'It's lovely and cool in here, Nathan. We left the air conditioning on for you,' Millie said.

'You really didn't need to do that,' Nathan replied. 'I'll soon get used to the heat.'

'It's okay,' said Millie. 'It's needed at the moment. Anyway, go and get your things unpacked then come down when you're ready.'

'Okay, will do.'

Meanwhile, Chris had taken the case upstairs and he wheeled it across the landing to Nathan's room at the front of the house. 'Thanks Chris. And thanks for everything.'

'Not a problem.' They shook hands and Chris went back downstairs.

The bedroom was just how Nathan remembered it – quite large with a beige carpet and huge bed, built-in double wardrobes that you could walk into and a nice en-suite shower room. But by far his favourite feature of this room was its view. With one window to the front and one to the side, the views were spectacular. The front aspect gave an outlook across the manicured lawns, down the driveway into the valley and then up the wooded slopes of the hills opposite. The side window was more of the same. It was an incredibly beautiful location. Nathan just wanted to stand and admire it but instead he lifted the large suitcase on to the bed, unlocked the combination and began to unpack.

He hated unpacking. It seemed to be taking an age and he was getting hot. In the corner of the room there was a fan on a stand, which was plugged in at the wall, so he walked over and switched it on. He turned it to maximum then stripped off to his boxers and stood in front of it with his arms outstretched.

When the unpacking was complete, Nathan had a quick shower and, determined not to lie on the bed for fear of falling asleep, he quickly slipped on some shorts, a T-shirt and his holiday flip-flops before going downstairs.

He walked into the kitchen, which was like a lounge-dining kitchen where Chris and Millie spent most of their time. There was a large-screen TV on the wall above an open fireplace, which contained wooden logs. However, this was very rarely used, except on particularly cold days in the winter months, of which there were few. Immediately opposite was a large wooden dining table with eight wooden chairs. This was positioned in front of two large sliding doors.

Nathan could see that Millie and Chris were sitting outside on a couple of padded reclining chairs, so he went to join them. They were sitting by a table and were offered protection from the sun by a large rectangular parasol that had an upright stanchion to one side and a cantilever arrangement overhead. Chris had a bottle of New Zealand Chardonnay and a half-full glass. Millie was drinking her usual sparkling San Pellegrino mineral water from a tumbler.

'Look at this guy. In the holiday mood already,' said Chris.

'Yes, but no sun cream on so I'll be staying under this parasol,' replied Nathan.

'Pull up a chair,' said Millie.

'Do you fancy a glass of this lovely wine or can I get you a beer?' Chris asked.

'Well, it's a bit early for me,' Nathan said, looking at his watch then realising he hadn't altered it from UK time. He tended to use his iPhone more when he travelled because it adjusted itself to the time zones. 'Okay, I'll have a glass of that wine that you're recommending Chris.'

'No problem. I'll just go and get you a glass.'

Nathan looked at Millie. 'You're still not drinking then?'

'No, it's been over three years now. I originally stopped because I was putting weight on and it seemed to do the trick, so now I don't miss it. Also, I like a clear head in a morning.'

'Good for you.'

'Have you unpacked everything?'

'Believe it or not, yes, everything.'

'And how are you feeling now?'

'A little better. That shower is amazing. There's so much water that comes out of that shower head.'

'I know, it's good isn't it. There was a particular name for it when we had it fitted, something like storm shower.' Millie rested her hand on Nathan's. 'It's great to have you here with us again.'

'It's great to be here. I had forgotten how beautiful this country is, and this location's to die for.'

'I know, we're incredibly lucky, but Chris works hard, sometimes into the night depending on which stock market he's working on.'

'Still making money then?'

'Yes, I must admit he's rather good at it. It's all he's done for the last eighteen years or so.'

'So, what about you Millie? What are your plans? Or are you happy being an erm … home … erm … woman?'

'You mean a stay-at-home wife.'

'Yes,' replied Nathan with a smile.

'Well, I've got a few ideas—'

'What's this about ideas?' interrupted Chris, re-joining the table with a clean glass, a large plate full of crisps and a selection of nutty nibbles.

'Nathan was just asking me what my plans are workwise, but with you working from home most of the time, I'm quite happy being here with you.'

'Oh, you're such a sweetheart,' said Chris as he filled Nathan's glass with Chardonnay.

'I know,' Millie replied, rolling her eyes and smiling.

The conversation continued, and as afternoon turned to early evening, Chris cooked some large, skewered local prawns on the gas barbecue and Millie put together a salad with dressings and chunks of crusty bread.

The cicadas, resembling large grasshoppers, and which lived in a couple of nearby trees, filled the air with their unique cricket-type noises and once again it reminded Nathan of his first foreign holiday to Corfu.

As the darkness slowly shrouded them, Chris decided to lower the parasol using the aluminium winding handle attached to the stanchion. After several revolutions it closed like an umbrella. The three of them just sat and admired the amazing array of stars. There was virtually no light pollution and it really was a sight to behold. The sky was literally covered in stars. Some shone brightly, some not so, but all with crystal clarity.

Whether it was lying back looking at the stars, too much wine, jet lag or a combination of these, Nathan decided to retire to his room in anticipation of a long and restful sleep.

6

IT WAS 10.30am by the time Nathan awoke the following morning, having slept for twelve hours. He got up, turned the fan on and just lay on the bed enjoying the breeze across his body. He lay there for another thirty minutes then went into the storm shower. It still amazed him how so much water could be despatched from that shower head, but it did, and it was so effective that he didn't want to get out.

When he eventually went down for breakfast, Millie greeted him in the kitchen. 'Good morning. Did you have a good sleep?'

'The best,' replied Nathan. 'That bed is so comfortable, and it was so quiet. You don't realise when you live in the city just how much noise you get used to, so when you come into an environment that's so remote and peaceful it feels like a total switch-off of all your senses, and your body is able to totally relax. This morning I really feel better than I have for years.'

'That's fantastic. I was hoping it would have a positive effect on you.'

'Millie, you sound like my therapist.'

'Sorry, but I'm only telling the truth. I thought it was time for you to move on, and once the police washed their hands of you, that was it.'

'It wasn't quite like that Millie. I was medically discharged.'

'I know and I'm sorry, but I just thought they could have shown more loyalty to you. They're always asking for loyalty from their officers.'

It was then that Nathan realised that he hadn't spent hours thinking about his discharge and how his beloved job had been removed from his grip. He realised that he was over it. He had accepted his situation and where he stood. He didn't like being unemployed, but that's the way it was going to be for a while. But he was determined to enjoy this break as part of his recuperation.

'Millie, please let's just leave it there. I've come away to escape what's occurred in the past and now I just want some downtime in this beautiful country. Where's Chris by the way?'

'His mother's ill, so he had to go early this morning. He said he would see you when he gets back. She's been ill for a while with breast cancer and the fact that she lives in Melbourne doesn't help. Mind you, it could have been worse; she could still be living in the UK.'

'That's a shame. It's a pity he couldn't have flown there himself. I presume he's flying out of Auckland.'

'Yes, with New Zealand Air. His own light aircraft doesn't have that sort of range.'

'I'm sorry to hear that his mother's been unwell.'

'I know, it's a terrible shame. He's tried to get her to move here, into the granny flat, but she loves her home in Melbourne. I wouldn't mind, but her house must be nearly as big as this, so she must be rattling around in there.'

'And how do you feel about her coming here?'

'If she would come, I would welcome her with open arms. She's a lovely woman and a fantastic person, but she just loves being in Melbourne.'

'I can't blame her for that,' Nathan replied. 'You can kind of get used to your own company and your home comforts.'

'It's not good when you become insular though,' Millie said, looking Nathan in the eye.

Nathan was about to reply but Millie got in first. 'Okay, I'm sorry if that sounded as if it was meant for you, but it wasn't. Let's have some breakfast. What do you fancy?'

'It's okay, I'll make it,' said Nathan.

'No, what do you want?'

'Just tea and toast please.'

Millie got up, walked over to the worktop. 'You can make it tomorrow,' she said, and smiled.

'Okay.'

7

NATHAN HAD settled in well, relaxing and spending a lot of time with Millie. He knew that he still wasn't a hundred per cent back to his normal health and it was debatable whether he ever would be, but he had to admit he had felt a lot better since his arrival in New Zealand, even with jet lag taken into consideration.

Millie had told him that he could use the old Toyota RAV 4 that was in the garage. She had added him to the insurance before he arrived. This was a big plus for Nathan as he didn't fancy asking his sister if he could borrow her car every time he wanted to go out. This would give him the independence he needed.

That afternoon, Nathan moved the RAV 4 out of the garage to take a look. It was black and quite a little beast with its 2.1 litre diesel engine and its gnarly off-road tyres; it was, in effect, a small SUV. The spare tyre was bolted on to the rear door, which instead of being a hatch, swung open from two heavy-duty hinges fixed to the frame. Nathan jumped back in the car and gunned it down the tree-lined drive. He was just about to join SH1 when his mobile rang, so he pulled over to answer it.

'Nathan, its Millie. I've just received a call from our churchwarden, who's parked in the car park outside church. The alarm's going off and she seems a bit too scared to go in on her own.'

'Okay, I'll come back and get you so we can go together.'

The church was in Wellsford, a small working town of approximately three thousand inhabitants, halfway between Auckland and the Northland city of Whangerei. It's central location made it a major hub, with shops, bars, restaurants and more churches than you could shake a stick at. So, after collecting Millie, Nathan pulled into the Ecumenical Church of Wellsford car park just fifteen minutes later.

Millie had become attached to the church many years ago. Built in the late 1960s to a modern design, the roof rose to a glass pinnacle with a metallic cross standing firmly for all to see. She liked the idea of an ecumenical church, one that welcomes all Christian religions. Unfortunately, as the town had grown and the number of churches increased, the congregation at the Ecumenical Church had reduced considerably to approximately twenty-five regular takers of Communion, and that was on a good day.

Two of those regulars were now in the car park. Margaret Mills, the churchwarden, jumped out of her car as Nathan pulled up next to her. The church alarm was still sounding. Margaret, in her sixties, was a stalwart of the church, having been the warden for the last ten years. She was a stocky but gentle woman with silver-grey hair and was wearing a white blouse with blue slacks and sensible shoes.

'I'm sorry to bother you Millie, but I didn't know who to call. The vicar's in Wellington on a conference.'

'It's okay, not a problem,' Millie assured her. 'This is my brother Nathan by the way.' Nathan shook Margaret's hand and they exchanged pleasantries.

'We'll go in through the main entrance,' said Margaret. 'The alarm panel's in the hall on the right-hand side.' As soon as she had spoken, she was off, striding towards the door with her new-found confidence and with Nathan and Millie in tow.

The entrance area had that sixties look, with part-pine panelling and plastered, magnolia-coloured walls. Margaret was swift on her feet and had turned the alarm system off in double-quick time. 'It's displaying on the alarm panel that it's the vestry door alarm. Follow me,' she said.

They approached the vicar's vestry, a closed door at the far end of a small corridor. 'Margaret wait,' Nathan said. 'I'll go in first just in case.' He gave Margaret no chance to reply. He tried the door, but it only opened an inch. 'I think someone's leaned something against the door on the inside.'

'Be careful,' warned Millie.

Nathan stepped back a couple of paces then shouldered the door. It opened another inch. Then he stepped back further and ran at it with his shoulder. It was enough to move the wardrobe that had been strategically positioned on the other side of the door. A further shove and the wardrobe toppled over. Nathan rushed in but, as he expected, the intruder had long gone, so he called for Margaret and Millie to enter.

The one opening window looked as if it had been forced open from the outside with some sort of lever, which had splintered the wooden frame. The vestry was a mess. It appeared that all the books and binders from the shelves had been thrown to the floor in a big pile. Some of the older books were open on the desk, as they had been left. Margaret bent over as if to start clearing up the mess.

'Wait a second Margaret. I think it would be wise for us to leave the vestry exactly as it is until the scenes of crime officers have had a look,' Nathan suggested.

'Yes, you're probably right,' Margaret agreed.

Nathan had a quick look around the vestry. Some of the white albs and cassocks had fallen out of the wardrobe as he had pushed it over and there were some plastic coat hangers lying on the floor.

'Just before we leave, Margaret, what are those books that are open on the desk?' Nathan asked.

Margaret looked over. 'Oh, they're just the minute books for the Church Council meetings.'

'Why do you think anyone would be interested in those?' Nathan enquired.

'I haven't a clue. It's all pretty mundane stuff about the condition of the church, fundraising ideas, upcoming events, church finances and the like.' With that, the three of them left the room.

'I take it you've already called the police?' asked Millie.

'Yes, I called as soon as I got here because I saw some broken glass by the window. I was too scared to look properly. They said they would send someone over but they were dealing with a nasty road accident on SH1, so I suppose that's more important.'

Millie and Nathan nodded in agreement, then they all walked back to the car park. 'Sorry for calling you out to this Millie. I was just too scared to go in on my own,' said Margaret apologetically.

'Don't worry about it. I would have felt the same myself,' replied Millie.

'It was nice to meet you Nathan. I'm sorry it wasn't under better circumstances.'

'Not to worry, and take care,' said Nathan.

'I'm going to wait in the car for the police to arrive,' Margaret informed them. 'So I'll see you in church tomorrow Millie. How about you Nathan?'

'At the moment, Margaret, it's a possible, not a probable,' Nathan replied, smiling.

Margaret waved and jumped into her car. Nathan turned to Millie and asked, 'How do you fancy a visit to the rugby club? There could be a game on this afternoon.'

'That's okay by me. I like the atmosphere in there on matchdays.'

8

NATHAN AND Millie pulled into the rugby club car park. 'Plenty of cars here. There must be a game on then,' observed Nathan. They parked up and walked into the clubhouse. Millie followed Nathan into the bar area. It was quite a big function room with large windows that overlooked the rugby field. There was just one barmaid, who was cleaning the glasses.

'Look what the cat dragged in,' the barmaid shouted at Nathan, then quickly apologised to Millie.

'Hi Hayley, how are you doing?' Nathan walked over and gave her a hug across the bar. 'This is my sister Millie.'

'I know love, I see her quite often in town or in here, unlike some people, who I only see every blue moon.'

'That could be something to do with the fact that I live in another country halfway around the world from here.'

'That's no excuse,' Hayley replied.

'Where is everyone?' asked Nathan.

'They've just gone out. The game starts in five minutes.'

'Oh, okay. Do you know if Rico's here?' Nathan enquired.

'Rico's always here. He never misses a game,' Hayley said.

Nathan looked at Millie. 'I'm just going to go and find Rico. You can come if you like.'

'No, it's okay, I'll stay here and catch up on all the gossip.'

Nathan left the clubhouse and walked around the corner to the rugby field. It was basically just an open field with a ridiculously small stand on one side, which looked a bit like a large shed, but held about eighty people. The spectators were using it for shade on such a hot day like today. Nathan spotted Rico sitting in the front row. A creature of habit, he always sat in the same seat. It was only the unfamiliar who dared to sit mistakenly in Rico's place.

Rico Manu was a local man. Although he now worked and lived in Auckland, one hour to the south, he was born in Wellsford and his parents still lived in the town. He was a Detective Inspector in the Criminal Investigation Branch in Auckland and Nathan had met him a few years ago at the rugby club and they got on like a house on fire. Rico was thirty-six years old, about the same height as Nathan at six foot two, but he was about a foot broader. A proud Maori and ex-rugby player, he was very smart in appearance, with closely cropped hair and a beard.

Rico spotted Nathan approaching, jumped to his feet and left the stand. They greeted each other with a huge hug.

'How are you doing man?' said Rico.

'Pretty good, considering.'

'I know what's been going on with you man. I was deeply sorry to hear about your stroke and losing your job.'

'I didn't know that you knew.'

'I have a spy in your Crime Squad. He's been keeping me informed.'

'So that's no doubt how my sister Millie came to find out.'

'Yes, I told her about your stroke. I hope you don't mind.'

'No, it was a godsend as it happens. They helped me so much. It would have been difficult without them.'

'Let's go into the clubhouse and have a chat and a beer,' suggested Rico.

'I'm in agreement with that,' Nathan replied, as Rico gave him a hearty slap on the back.

~~~

Later that afternoon, Millie, Nathan and Rico went back to Fern Heights and collected Nathan's overnight bag. He was going to be staying that evening at Rico's house in Auckland. That usually meant lots of booze and food, which they were both up for. What Rico hadn't mentioned was that evening they were going out for a meal with his girlfriend Marika and her friend Loretta.

When Rico eventually told him, Nathan thought he was being set up with some kind of blind date. 'Not at all,' said Rico. 'Loretta had a bad break-up with her ex a week ago and Marika's helping her through it. They said they would meet us in the restaurant at eight this evening. We can go for a beer first. There's a bar just around the corner from the restaurant.'

The men had talked nonstop since meeting at the rugby club and that evening in the bar in Auckland was no exception. Rico wanted to know more about how the police could have dismissed Nathan on medical grounds, without giving him more time to recover. Nathan explained that at the time it was hell, like the end of the world, but he was over it now and moving on.

Rico also asked what Nathan's plans for the future were and Nathan explained that Millie wanted him to move to New Zealand and that Chris had offered him guidance on working the world stock markets. Rico knew Nathan well enough to know that he hadn't made his mind up. What Rico didn't mention was the death of Nathan's mum and dad. There was no point in going over old ground; it was too upsetting for Nathan, but Rico did still wonder what had happened to the perpetrator of the crime. The way he had just disappeared was very odd. Not that he suspected Nathan, but someone must have got to him.

The two of them made their way to the restaurant and were shown to their table. Marika and Loretta were being fashionably late. Nathan was feeling quite apprehensive, which he quite often did when meeting people for the first time but it normally only took him a couple of minutes to become comfortable.

Before long, two extremely attractive women, casually and with confidence, glided into the restaurant. Both looked about the same height, five seven in their heels, with long brown hair that passed the shoulders. One wore a little black dress and the other a little red one. They were both stunning.

Rico nudged Nathan. 'They're here.' Nathan felt honoured that these two beautiful women had come to spend their time with them. Both men stood up as the women approached the table. 'Nathan, this is my friend Marika,' said Rico.

'Hi, nice to meet you,' Nathan greeted her.

'And this is her friend and mine, Loretta.'

'Hi Loretta, it's a pleasure.' Nathan extended his greeting to the other woman.

'Likewise,' Loretta replied rather coldly.

Rico gave Marika a hug and she pecked him on the cheek. Meanwhile, Nathan felt suddenly sceptical as to what sort of night was in store. However, the night turned out to be a great success. Marika was very humorous and Loretta had laughed along with Nathan and Rico. Nathan had taken a liking to Loretta, who was a beautiful woman, although maybe a little guarded, which was understandable considering she had just escaped from a bad relationship, but she did have a likeable, quiet personality.

At the end of the night all four of them jumped into a taxi. The first stop was at Marika's place where Loretta was staying over. Loretta gave Nathan a quick kiss and thanked him as she left the taxi. Nathan was delighted and hoped he would have the opportunity to meet her again. The taxi then went to Rico's house. Nathan was in such a good mood that he tipped the driver.

Once inside, Rico said, 'You two seemed to be getting on well.'

'Yes, we did, didn't we. I really enjoyed it Rico. Thanks for inviting me down.'

'No problem mate. It was great to see you so unexpectedly.'

'And how long have you known Marika?' asked Nathan.

'Only a couple of months. What do you think of her?'

'If you don't mind me saying, you're an incredibly lucky man having her on your arm. She's funny, she's pleasant and she's beautiful.'

'Cheers mate,' replied Rico. 'And what do you think of Loretta?'

'In all honesty Rico, I was really attracted to her the moment I saw her. She's stunning, but I'm not sure she's that keen on me.'

'I'll try to find out. I'm sure Marika will be asking her the same things that I've asked you.'

After a couple of beers and a movie, Nathan and Rico retired to their beds. The next morning, at approximately 9am, Rico opened Nathan's bedroom door. 'Nathan, I've got to go mate. I've just found out that there was a serious incident in Wellsford last night.'

Nathan was rubbing his eyes. 'How serious?'

'It could end up being a murder, and it was in my mum and dad's road.'

'Do you mind if I come with you?' asked Nathan.

'Of course not. I was going to take you home anyway.'

'I'll be ready.'

During the drive up to Wellsford, Rico received a phone call saying that the person in question, an eighty-year-old lady, had died after an attack in her home. It turned out that the victim lived in the house right next door to Rico's parents and she was a member of the Wellsford Ecumenical Church congregation. Rico rang his parents from the car just to make sure everything was alright and to let them know he was on his way. His mother was upset as she had seen the police cars and ambulance outside and knew something was wrong.

Rico was about to pull off SH1 to drop Nathan off at Fern Heights when Nathan asked, 'Rico, would it be possible for me to shadow you on this?'

'Well I don't see why not. I probably won't be able to let you see the crime scene though. Anyway, your interest is …?'

'I heard your mother say that the victim was a good church-going woman and that she went to the Ecumenical Church. I was in the same church yesterday afternoon after it was broken into.'

'I didn't know about that,' said Rico sharply.

'I didn't realise you paid such an interest in Wellsford concerns, especially with your domain being Auckland.'

'Wellsford is always my concern. It may not be on my patch but it's my hometown. It's where I was born, where my parents still live and I love the place.'

'Point taken,' said Nathan.

'Well, tell me about this break-in.'

'It was a bit odd; someone had forced open the vestry window, gained entrance and had gone through the documents and binders. They seemed to be particularly interested in the PCC minutes or Church Council minutes, which were left open on the vestry desk. I think they had set the alarm off when they decided to open the vestry door, then I should imagine with all the noise from the alarm they made a sharp exit back the way they came in.'

'This is all a bit strange,' said Rico. 'Wellsford's such a quiet place, in fact it's usually so quiet that quite often the patrolling officers end up elsewhere looking for work.'

'I think there must be some connection between the break-in and the murder. It makes me wonder whether someone broke into the church, found out the victim's address then went and committed this horrible crime,' said Nathan.

They pulled into Ford Lane, just off SH1. There was a taped cordon across the drive of a small house, where two police cars and a white van were parked, with an officer standing on the driveway. Rico pulled into the drive of his parents' house next door.

'Come in and meet the folks,' said Rico. He used a small key to open the front door and they walked in. Rico's parents were in the lounge in separate easy chairs, both looking concerned. 'Mum, Dad, this is my good friend Nathan from England. He's staying with his sister in Dome Valley.'

'Hello Nathan,' they both said together.

'I'm sorry to meet you under these circumstances,' said Nathan.

'It's shocking,' said Rico's mum. 'It really is. She was a lovely woman, you know; lived on her own for years. A regular at church every Sunday and a very good and kind neighbour. I don't know what's going wrong in this world, I really don't.'

'Listen folks, I'm just going to nip in next door at Brenda's to see what's occurred. Nathan, if you don't mind staying put.'

'Yes, that's fine.'

Rico was given access by the officer standing at the end of the drive after showing his identification. He walked down the side of the house towards the side entrance. There was another officer just inside who gave him a pair of covers for his shoes and a pair of blue latex gloves. 'Has the scenes of crime officer been?' asked Rico.

'Yes, he left about fifteen minutes ago,' replied the officer.

'Where did it happen?'

'In the lounge, second door on your left.'

'Okay, thanks.'

Rico walked gingerly into the lounge, where he could see blood splattered on the wall adjacent to where the woman appeared to have been sitting when she was attacked. There was also a substantial amount of blood on the chair. Three box files sat on the table next to the chair. Also on the table, Rico could see two stained, damp rings, the remnants of two cups of tea or coffee. He took a series of photos with his smartphone then carefully opened one of the box files. Skimming through the contents, he could see church magazines, orders of service for weddings, funerals and christenings, and other documents. The contents of the other boxes seemed to cover earlier periods.

'I would like to take these three box files. Have you got an evidence bag please?' Rico asked, and the officer handed him a large clear polythene bag. Rico then wrote on his list of exhibits what was being taken and by whom before carefully placing the box files in the bag and tying a large loose knot in the neck of the bag. He placed it on the floor by the door and said to the officer, 'I'll collect this on the way out.' The officer nodded in acknowledgement.

Rico walked into the master bedroom, where there was no evidence of any disturbance. He walked into a second bedroom, which was set out like a study. There was an old bureau with its lid down and some pens and paper on top. Next to the bureau was a small two-drawer filing cabinet. Rico opened the top drawer to take a look. The files were labelled gas, electricity, telephone, water, plumber, electrician, gardener. The drawer below held details of bank accounts, savings and insurance policies. Brenda was very well organised. He closed the drawer.

On the wall next to Rico was a sturdy shelf containing two box files, one labelled receipts and the other shopping lists. Both boxes contained exactly as they said on the label. He could see that the dust had been disturbed on the shelf and figured that the three box files that he was taking as evidence came from this spot and had been moved very recently. There didn't seem to be anything else out of place in the whole house.

Rico had another quick look in the lounge. The scene of the crime gave him a shiver, the sheer brutality of the attack on an elderly woman. He could feel the anger building inside. A murder right next to his parents' house, and he knew the victim, eighty-eight-year-old Brenda Massey.

Rico turned to the officer on the door. 'Can you tell me what other exhibits they have taken?'

The officer passed Rico a list, which showed the main items as an ornamental chrome swan, two mugs, a rug that was in front of the chair, the cushion from the chair, two embroidered armrest covers from the chair, and some fingerprints and hair samples.

'Okay. Thanks for your help,' said Rico, handing back the list. On the way out he picked up the exhibits bag and when outside removed his shoe covers and gloves, discarding them into a box provided for that purpose. Before he returned to his parents' house, Rico called his senior officer at Auckland. As a result of the conversation, he was now in charge of the murder squad to be based at Wellsford police station.

Rico opened the front door of his parents' house, where Nathan was comfortable on the lounge sofa with a cup of tea and a plate of biscuits. Rico's mother didn't look quite as worried as she had when they arrived.

'Have you heard how Brenda is?' his mother asked.

Rico crouched down in front of his mother and took hold of her tiny hands in a show of compassion. 'I'm sorry Mum, she didn't make it.' Both Rico's parents cried. When the sobbing stopped Rico told them that he was going to be running the murder squad from Wellsford and asked whether he could stay at their house for the immediate future.

Rico's father said, 'You don't need to ask Son, you're always welcome to stay here.'

'Right. I'm going to have to take Nathan home, then I'll be going down to Auckland for clothes and essentials. I'll be back and won't be leaving until this bastard's locked up.' His mother looked at him in shock at his language. 'Sorry Mum,' Rico said apologetically.

In the car on the way back to Millie's, Nathan asked Rico about the crime scene, as Rico hadn't been that forthcoming. 'Come on Rico, from one copper to another,' Nathan said.

'That's the problem though, isn't it, you're not,' Rico replied. It cut through Nathan like a knife; and yes, it was true, but it hurt. It hurt a lot.

The rest of the short journey was in silence. Then as the car pulled up outside Millie's house, Nathan said, 'Well thanks for putting me up last night and taking me to meet your parents. I guess I can't be any use to you now, so good luck and I hope you catch whoever did it.'

Nathan was just about to get out of the car when Rico grabbed his arm. 'Look, I'm sorry if I was a bit sharp with you before but it upsets me when things happen so close to my folks. The fact of the matter is we may need your help, and if you don't mind, could you look through these box files from Brenda's house and see what you can find?'

'Give me a clue … what am I looking for?'

'Well, I can tell you what I think happened to her. I think she invited someone into her house. She sat them down and made them a drink of tea or coffee. Then either she or the visitor went into the study and pulled three box files off the shelf, took them into the lounge and put them on a small table near Brenda's chair. Or maybe it was the other way around; she could have made the drinks after the box files were brought into the lounge because two cups had been rested on top. Either way, the contents of the box files could be significant.'

'How did she die?' asked Nathan.

'A blunt force trauma to the head. Looks like it could be that she was struck with an ornamental chrome swan.'

'Are we saying that this could be someone she knows? Or could it have been a stranger putting her under threat?'

'It's hard to tell but I have a feeling it was the latter, but it's going to be difficult to find a motive.'

'Okay, I'll take a look,' Nathan agreed. 'I'll give you a call if I find anything of interest.' He got out of the car with the box files and his overnight bag.

'Cheers mate, speak later,' replied Rico.

Millie was in the kitchen as Nathan walked through. 'I wasn't expecting you back for a few hours, and what's with the box files?' she asked.

'I've just come back from Rico's parents' house. The lady next door was killed overnight.'

'Oh my god. Who was it?'

'Brenda Massey. Eighty-eight years old.'

'Oh no, that's terrible. She was one of the church stalwarts. What on earth has happened?'

'Someone appears to have been invited into her home or she allowed them in under duress. At some point they hit her on the head with an ornamental chrome swan, killing her outright. These box files were in the lounge so Rico asked whether I could look through them to see if there's anything of significance.'

'I'm shocked,' said Millie, 'I really am. Brenda was a lovely, pleasant woman who enjoyed life and was hoping to live until she was a hundred. She told me as much at church last weekend. I think she was the oldest member of our church and had been coming since it was built. I'm going to church for the eleven-o'clock service. Please come with me.'

'Okay,' replied Nathan.

~~~

Nathan and Millie pulled into the church car park. 'I've never seen that guy before,' Millie said, gesticulating to a black Holden parked in the corner at a strange angle.

'Could be police, looking to see who Brenda's associates were at church,' suggested Nathan.

'Wow, they don't hang about do they.'

'I said it *could* be.'

'Well, who else could it be?' Millie said.

'I don't know. It will be interesting to see whether he comes into church.'

'It's a shame if we start being suspicious of everyone though, don't you think?'

'Not at all. Not until this murderer's behind bars.'

Nathan parked the car and went into church with Millie. He looked through the net curtains from the entrance area to see the black Holden pulling out of the car park. After Millie had introduced her brother to everyone present, she had the unfortunate duty of informing the vicar that Brenda Massey had passed away in the early hours. There was much upset, sadness and crying, and people wanted details of how she had died. Millie informed them that she had died in her home and that she had heard that it was being treated with suspicion by the police. The vicar made alterations to the service to ensure that special prayers and a hymn were dedicated to Brenda.

Nathan took the opportunity to speak to the vicar after the service. The vicar was very thankful for the help that Nathan and Millie had given to Margaret at the church break-in. Nathan asked him whether there was anything missing and he said that as far as he was concerned nothing had been taken, although it looked as if a lot of the PCC minute books had been rifled through because several of the loose-leaf inserts were on the floor. Again, he stated that there didn't seem to be any missing and questioned why anyone would want to take a PCC minute book anyway.

Nathan decided that it would be pointless speaking to any of the other members of the congregation because Brenda was obviously highly thought of and many people were deeply upset. It seemed wholly inappropriate to start asking whether Brenda had any enemies or recent disputes. Anyway, it wasn't his job to ask such questions, so he waited in the car for Millie, who wasn't far behind.

Nathan could tell that Millie had been crying. 'It was really upsetting in there,' she told him. 'Some of the people had known Brenda for over eighty years and they were at school together. Can you take me home please Nathan?'

As Nathan drove back to Fern Heights it was noticeable that there were more police cars patrolling than you would usually see. With a murderer on the loose this was no more than the public could have expected. The bush telegraph is usually highly effective in towns like Wellsford and word would be getting around about poor Brenda Massey.

As they entered the house, Millie said, 'I would like to help you looking through those box files. I may be of some help, knowing all the regulars, so I would really like to try to do my bit.'

'I haven't got a problem with that Millie. I don't know what we're looking for but let's just keep an open mind.'

That afternoon, after a sandwich lunch, they looked at the first box. As Rico had noted, they contained church magazines and orders of service for any event that had occurred in the church since it had opened.

'Why didn't the police take these boxes away if they thought there might be something of significance in them?' asked Millie.

'They were taking them. Rico brought them out of the house. You can see by the residue on the outside that they've already been fingerprinted.'

'Well, why didn't the fingerprint officers take them away with them?'

'I don't know,' replied Nathan. 'They either do things differently here or the first detective on the scene didn't think there was any evidential value in them.'

'Maybe Rico's just given you these to keep you involved but out from under his feet.'

'That's possible, and if that's the case then at least I know where I stand. But there's always the possibility that the contents of these boxes could lead us down the path to locking up a murderer. And that's why we need to keep a positive outlook and be as thorough as possible. If Rico doesn't want me to be involved, then I'll step back. Okay, let's go through one file at a time, making a list of the contents and any relevant dates or maybe any disputes.'

They were very methodical. There were reams and reams of church magazines and *Pew News*, the church newsletter. The majority were just a folded piece of A4 paper giving four pages of writing with a sketch of the church on the front cover and weekly service times on the rear. The format since day one had hardly changed. Then there were orders of service for births, marriages and deaths, with the odd additional choir concert, band concert and Christmas and Easter concerts thrown in. There appeared to be nothing out of the ordinary, but a few hours later they had a list of the documents in date order.

'Looking at this list, I don't think Brenda ever missed a service. Surely she must have missed through illness or holiday?' said Nathan.

'I should imagine that if she didn't attend for whatever reason, she would have asked the vicar or someone else to hold a copy for her,' suggested Millie.

'Yes, that makes sense. Oh, that's a shame.'

'What have you found?' asked Millie.

'Look at the list for *Pew News* and the church magazine. Issue one is missing. This would be the one to celebrate the opening of the church.'

'Maybe they didn't print one. Maybe they didn't have time, with trying to set up a new church.'

'I would be incredibly surprised at that. The first edition you would expect to be the biggest and the best, in celebration of an achievement.'

'I agree,' Millie replied.

'So, according to the *Pew News* second edition, which was dated Sunday, 7 December 1969, the first service at the church and issue number one should have been the previous Sunday, 30 November.'

'So, what do you glean from this information?' asked Millie quizzically.

'Absolutely nothing Millie. Absolutely nothing, other than we know when your church opened.'

They looked through the complete list of documents but there was nothing that caught the eye. By now it was 6pm and Millie could see an anxious look on Nathan's face.

'Why don't you call Rico to tell him what we haven't found and see how the investigation is progressing,' Millie suggested.

'No, I'll leave it a bit longer. The first twenty-four to forty-eight hours are crucial and they'll be run off their feet. How about we go out for a beer and something to eat?' Millie looked unsure. 'Come on, my treat,' Nathan offered.

'Well okay, but I don't want to go to Wellsford, so let's go to Warkworth instead.'

'That's fine by me. Let's get ready and go.'

Warkworth, a pretty town of approximately five thousand people, was only a few miles south down SH1. Standing at the head of the Mahurangi harbour and the estuary that ran through it to the harbour, the town boasted a nice collection of shops and eateries and was home to several colonial-type buildings, such as the old masonic hall. This was timber-built in 1883 with two high Greek-style pillars adjacent to the front entrance door. The building had been maintained to a good standard and was now used as a general meeting place for community events. A few hundred metres away there was a small bar/restaurant that doubled up as a pizzeria. Nathan was able to find a parking place right outside.

Moments later they were sitting at a table by a small window that overlooked the main street through the town. Although as a rule early Sunday evening tended to be quiet, there was a resurgence of holidaymakers, New Zealanders and visitors, passing through and stopping for something to eat and drink on their journey. January in New Zealand was always a busy time as the schools were off for their summer holidays.

'I'm trying not to think about poor Brenda, so tell me how your night went last night,' said Millie. She could see that Nathan's mood was lightened in an instant.

'We had a really good night. We went for a meal with Rico's partner Marika and her friend Loretta.'

'Oh, Loretta is it?' said Millie as she elbowed him and smiled. Nathan amazingly could feel himself blushing. 'So, what's she like?'

'Mid-to-late-twenties, with long brown hair, and she's slim and exceptionally beautiful. She was a bit guarded at first, but when Marika started telling her jokes and funny stories, it was like having your own comedian at your table. So, in all honesty, we didn't get much chance to talk as we were too busy listening and laughing. I'm hoping Loretta will see me again though'.

'I hope so too,' replied Millie, resting her hand on Nathan's in a gesture of reassurance.

9

NATHAN AND Millie enjoyed their evening – pizza and a bottle of Peroni each. They were on the coffees when a group of men arrived and decided to have a drink at the bar before sitting down at a table. Nathan and Millie overheard one of the men saying that an elderly woman in Wellsford had been raped before being shot through the head. One of the other men appeared confident that his version of events was correct and that the woman had been gang-raped then had her throat cut.

At this point Millie stood up and was about to approach the men and give them a ticking off. Nathan took hold of her arm and they left the restaurant, having already paid. The manager came running out after them. 'I'm so sorry. I could see your reaction to the men at the bar. I hope it hasn't spoiled your evening.' Millie ignored him. She was still annoyed.

'It's okay,' said Nathan, 'but please let the men know that both of their versions of events are incorrect. They'll know what you're talking about.'

Nathan and Millie travelled back to Fern Heights with little being said. Just as they were about to get out of the car, Millie said, 'I really enjoyed this evening until those men came in.'

'Same here,' Nathan replied.

'It's great to have you here Nathan.'

'Thanks, I'm really enjoying it. I know that sounds bad after what's happened to Brenda but I'm settling in,' Nathan said with a smile.

'Well, keep me informed about Loretta.'

Nathan was blushing again and changed the subject. 'I meant to ask … how's Chris getting on with his mum?'

'I think I'll ring him now,' Millie replied. As soon as they got into the house, she picked up the landline phone to call Chris's mobile. Meanwhile, Nathan left her to it and went into the kitchen.

Five minutes later, Millie reappeared, looking very sullen. 'It's awful,' she said. 'So sad. She's going into a hospice in Melbourne tomorrow. She's too ill to be looked after at home.'

'Then you should be with Chris. He'll need your support and I'm sure his mum will be glad to see you.'

'Oh, I feel awful,' Millie said. 'Inviting you over then us both leaving you.'

'Look Millie, your mother-in-law is dying and your husband needs you. I'm a fully-grown man and I can look after myself. If you can find a flight that suits you, I can take you to the airport. And please don't worry about me.'

'Thank you,' Millie replied and kissed him on the cheek.

Later that evening, Nathan drove Millie to Auckland airport. The traffic was noticeably quiet, so he was there within thirty minutes. Millie was now eager to go. She was worried that she wouldn't get the opportunity to speak to her mother-in-law again or be by her husband's side when he most needed her. Nathan dropped her off right outside the terminal building, got her case out of the boot and watched her walk into the departures building.

On his way back to Fern Heights, Nathan received a message on his mobile. It was Rico, who wanted to know whether he had found anything significant in the documents from the box files. Nathan told him that Brenda Massey had been very thorough with her record keeping and the only discrepancy he could see was that the first issue of *Pew News* and the church magazine was missing.

Rico texted sarcastically:

Wow, well this is going to blow the case wide open.

Nathan didn't feel like replying to Rico's sarcasm and he still couldn't understand the hostility Rico was showing towards him. Eventually he just suggested that Rico should come to collect the boxes when he was free. Rico replied with a thumbs up symbol.

When Nathan arrived home, he went straight to bed. However, his mind was too active, so he picked up a paperback and it took about thirty minutes before he finally fell asleep.

He was awoken the next morning at 8.30am by his mobile, which was on silent but was vibrating on the bedside unit next to him. It was Millie. She was delighted to have spoken to her mother-in-law, although she was extremely ill. Millie wasn't sure when she would be back and told Nathan to help himself to anything he needed.

Nathan replied, 'Okay, but I'll pay you back for everything. I'm not here to live for free.' They agreed to talk about it when Millie got back.

As soon as Millie hung up, Nathan's mobile rang again. It was Rico, who said he was passing in about fifteen minutes and asked whether he could call in to collect the box files. Nathan said he would have the kettle on.

Nathan was sitting outside on the patio when Rico's car came sweeping up the drive. The box files were on the table ready for collection. Rico walked up to the patio and sat himself down.

'How's the case going?' asked Nathan.

'So-so,' replied Rico.

'And what does that mean? Or aren't you prepared to tell me in case I get too close?'

'No, not at all. I'm sure your help will be invaluable as the case develops. We just have to follow our early leads, and if they take us nowhere, we may need outside help.'

'And have you got any early leads?'

'Actually, yes, we have some very grainy footage of a male leaving Brenda Massey's house in the early hours and driving off in a car. It's the next door but one neighbour, who has one of these courtesy cameras above her front door. It not only gives her a view of who's at her door but also a view up the street. It's practically useless in the dark but you can definitely see someone leaving Brenda's house. Probably her murderer.'

'Is there no way the footage can be enhanced?'

'I'm reliably informed it can't because the quality is that poor.'

'What about the car?'

'Not sure but it looked like a Commodore.'

Nathan poured two cups of tea from a large pot.

'Where's Millie?' asked Rico.

'She had to go to Melbourne to be with her husband, Chris. His mother's not very well and has to go into a hospice.'

'Sorry to hear that,' said Rico. 'I do have a small piece of good news that I think you may be interested in,' he added.

'I'm quite partial to a bit of good news, particularly when there isn't much about.'

'I'm forwarding a message to you from Marika.'

Nathan's mobile pinged and a message appeared on the screen:

Please pass this number on to Nathan. It's Loretta's mobile.

Then a series of digits were displayed.

'Now that's what I call good news,' said Nathan, touching fists with Rico over the table. 'Please thank Marika for me and tell her I'll call Loretta later.'

'Okay,' replied Rico casually.

'So, are you taking the box files away?' asked Nathan.

'Well, I think I should while I'm here. I'm trying to keep all the exhibits together in one place. They've already been dusted for fingerprints but they only found Brenda's prints on the box lids.'

'So, are you any closer to finding out whether this could be someone she knows?'

'No closer, but my own feeling is that she was under duress. Let's be honest about it, you wouldn't call at an elderly lady's house in the middle of the night if you knew her. And the chances of her answering the door, never mind letting you in, would be low. But maybe if you were brandishing a knife and threatening to break in ...'

Nathan nodded in agreement with Rico's theory. 'Is there any indication whatsoever that the break-in at the church is maybe connected with Brenda's murder?' he asked.

'None whatsoever unless you can prove otherwise.'

'Would you like me to look into the possibility?'

'Well you may be able to find something out that we can't, seeing as you're on the inside.'

'Hardly,' replied Nathan, 'but leave it with me.'

The two of them parted company on better terms than previously and Nathan was happy that it also seemed as if he had been given carte blanche to look into the church break-in for any possible connection. Even better, the fact that he had Loretta's mobile number made him smile and feel good inside.

After Nathan had showered and finished his breakfast, he decided to go for a drive. He couldn't help but drive through Wellsford. All seemed normal as he approached the church, where he noticed there were a couple of cars in the car park. He recognised one as belonging to Margaret, so he decided to pull in to make sure everything was okay.

Nathan entered the front door of the church and walked into the small corridor, spotting Margaret as she appeared in the vestry doorway. 'Hi Margaret, I was just passing and I saw your car. I wanted to see that everything was okay after the break-in.'

'Oh, please come through,' Margaret said, then gesticulated into the vestry. 'This is Reverend Martin, our vicar.'

'I know, we met yesterday,' Nathan replied. As he walked into the vestry he was surprised. Martin looked younger than he had the previous day, maybe in his late thirties. Perhaps it was his church robes that aged him. Today, he was clean-shaven and wore a dark suit with a clerical collar. He wasn't as tall as Nathan, but it appeared as if he looked after himself.

'Hi Martin, nice to see you again,' said Nathan.

'Likewise,' Martin replied. 'Thanks again for the assistance that you gave Margaret after the break-in.'

'I'm always happy to help a damsel in distress.' Margaret smiled and looked rather embarrassed. 'Actually, I'm an ex-police officer,' continued Nathan, 'and I'm a friend of the detective in charge, Rico Manu. I said I would offer any help I could to try to catch Brenda's killer. Are you sure that no documents went missing during the break-in here?'

'So, you think the break-in is connected to the murder?' asked Martin.

'I don't honestly know, but we have to keep all options open.'

'It's an awful situation, it really is. Things like this don't happen around here. People are terribly upset and worried,' added Martin.

'I understand,' said Nathan, placing a hand on the vicar's shoulder.

'Were there any documents in particular that you were interested in Nathan?' asked Martin.

'Well, I'm looking around the time that the church opened in 1969. Would you happen to have a copy of the very first *Pew News* or church magazine?'

'That's a strange request. Is it relevant?'

'I'm just dotting the i's and crossing the t's.'

'I'll have a look. You would expect there to be a special edition to commemorate the opening of a new church, so I would be looking for an edition that's slightly thicker than the others maybe,' suggested the vicar. He started to thumb his way through a series of lever arch files until he came across the church magazines that looked older and more faded through time.

'Here we are,' said Martin hopefully. He extracted a magazine from the prongs of the lever arch and handed it to Nathan. As expected it was a bumper edition with contributions from the Bishop of Auckland, the Diocese of Auckland and the vicar of the day. It also included several advertisements – a builder, plumber, electrician, painter and decorator, plasterer, carpet fitter, guttering company and a civil engineer. Nathan wondered whether all these businesses were just advertising or were involved in the building of the church. There was a lot of other information in the magazine; too much to read right then.

'Could I possibly take this home, Martin, and go through it at my leisure?' Nathan asked.

'Of course, not a problem. There should also be a *Pew News* in this file … they should all be here.' This second file didn't seem to be in order, but the vicar found *Pew News* No. 1 and handed it to Nathan.

'These were scattered all over the floor after the break-in. It's all very strange,' said Margaret.

The front cover showed a sketch of the new church and the details of the service were enclosed. As well as notes from the vicar and a prayer for the day there was a section relating to what looked like major benefactors to the building of the new church. There was a list of names and a mention of gratitude to persons who wished to remain anonymous.

'Could I take this as well?' asked Nathan.

'Of course,' said Martin. 'Just give them back to one of us when you've finished with them.'

''Thanks, I really appreciate that. If you don't mind, while I'm here, would you have records of the old Church Council meetings?'

Martin became rather guarded and looked uncomfortable. 'They should be here too. They're usually handwritten minutes in hardback A4-sized lined notebooks, but some of the information in the minutes can be extremely sensitive and is only really for the eyes of the PCC members.'

'Well, if I give you my word that no one else will see them and that all the information enclosed will be treated in the strictest of confidence, would it be possible to take the book that relates to the same period, 1969?'

'I have to trust you Nathan. It's not in my make-up not to. Your sister has been a member of the church for several years and there's no reason why I should doubt your integrity.' Martin handed over the notebook entitled 'PCC MINUTES 1969–70', which he slid from beneath several others on a shelf in the filing cabinet.

'Would you like me to write a receipt to say that I've taken these documents?' Nathan offered.

'No, that won't be necessary, but if you don't mind, I'll just make a note of which records you're taking,' Martin suggested as he picked up a pen from the desk and scribbled on a piece of paper before putting the paper into his pocket. Nathan thought the vicar was trying to show efficiency with the church records but that's all it was, a show. Martin seemed upset, which was understandable. Brenda's death seemed to be weighing on him heavily as it was on the community.

After Nathan had said his goodbyes and exchanged contact details with Reverend Martin and Margaret, he opened the boot of his car and placed the documents in one of the elasticated pouches. As he pulled out of the car park and headed towards SH1 there was a small coffee shop on the corner, so he decided to pull over, as there was a parking place immediately outside.

Nathan walked in, ordered a flat white, then went over to a small table at the rear of the coffee shop, which had a view overlooking SH1, including the Wellsford police station.

A few moments later, a young woman with a stained apron walked over to his table carrying his flat white. 'There you go,' she said with enthusiasm. 'Is there anything else I can get for you?'

'No thanks,' replied Nathan with a smile, but he noticed that she seemed to be hovering.

'I hope you don't mind me asking but are you a cop?' the woman asked.

'No, why do you ask?'

'It's just that when the cops do come in here that's how we find things out, particularly with this murderer on the loose. It's a need-to-know basis and us women need to know.'

'I'm sorry, I can't help you,' said Nathan and looked away. The woman walked back to the kitchen area without another word.

A short while later, when Nathan had finished his coffee, he decided to have another word with the young woman, who miraculously appeared from the kitchen just as he stood up from his table. 'Can I just ask,' he said, 'what you've heard about the murder?'

The woman suddenly looked interested and Nathan could tell that she was wringing her hands in her large front apron pocket. 'Well, I heard that she had been sexually assaulted and battered. It's shocking. A lovely old lady. She was a regular churchgoer too.'

'Did you know her then?'

'Brenda? Yes, everyone knew her. I think she had lived here her whole life. Went to school here, worked here, got married here. Her husband fought in the Second World War you know. They're doing a thing about her in the museum. I heard it had just been finished and that they've put it on hold because of her death.'

'A thing? What do you mean, like a history?'

'Yes, exactly. They have a student from Auckland who's helping with their family research.'

'Interesting,' said Nathan. 'I'm going to call in at the museum later, so I'll ask them about it. Anyway, must go. Thanks for the coffee.' Nathan made for the door.

'Please call again,' the young woman shouted after him, but he had already left.

Nathan had intended to return to Fern Heights. He wanted to look through the documents from the church but he changed his mind and decided to go for a drive up into the Dome Valley Forest hills. Situated just off SH1 there was a café and a viewing area called Dome Valley Lookout but this tended to be where holidaymakers visited and could on occasion be quite busy. He knew an old loggers' route that Chris had shown him on a previous visit where the view from the top of the hill was amazing because the loggers had cleared an area that gave a fantastic vista of the surrounding wooded hills.

It was a steep climb on a narrow road through dense radiata pine trees, forested on a large scale in New Zealand. Like many roads off the beaten track, it was gravelly and unfinished but the heavy-duty tyres on the SUV made short work of it. As Nathan expected, he reached the top without seeing another vehicle or person. The view was better than he had previously thought, no doubt enhanced by a crystal-clear day with no clouds, bright sunshine and little humidity.

He jumped out of the car and leaned against it as he inhaled a deep breath of pine-fresh air and looked out over rolling and densely covered tree-topped hills. There were a pair of hawks undulating on the thermals above, and apart from their high-pitched screech it was deathly quiet. No traffic, no people, just nature. It was invigorating. Then Loretta sprung into his mind, interrupting his thought pattern like a bolt out of the blue. He wasn't afraid to admit that he was excited about the prospect of seeing her again.

Things were starting to feel better for Nathan. For years he felt he had been in a dark place surrounded by work, evil things and downright bad luck. He was looking forward to speaking with Loretta later. He had only met her once and now he seemed to be suffering from what felt like a schoolboy crush. He hardly knew her but he needed to see her again and he desperately hoped that she felt the same way.

Suddenly, Nathan was disturbed by a rustling noise in the brush behind him. He couldn't see anything but walked a little closer. There was another rustle. He hesitated for a second. He had heard about the wild boar that lived in the forest and that they were overly aggressive. He decided to go no further; in fact, he started to retrace his steps, walking backwards without taking his eye off the brush.

Suddenly, something shot out, looked at him and ran down the hill, throwing pine needles into the air as it ran. Nathan was shocked but immediately recognised it as a cat-sized marsupial, the possum. Chis had told him how these animals had arrived in New Zealand in 1837 from Australia, introduced by the fur traders but were now considered as pests, eating and killing native plants and birds. Nathan watched as it approached a large tree at speed and ran up its trunk with great aplomb. He knew for a fact that Chris had set several traps in the vast acreage of Fern Heights and caught on average two possums a week.

Nathan returned his attention to the beautiful view before him, laid out like a canvass masterpiece. He took his mobile out of his pocket and took a couple of photos then decided to go back to Fern Heights. He got into the car and started downhill. Although going at a slow pace he still kicked up a substantial amount of dirt and left a large plume of white dust in the air behind him. Before he knew it, he was back on SH1 and only a matter of minutes from Fern Heights.

As he drove up the long sloping driveway, Nathan noticed that the temperature outside was already showing twenty-eight degrees and it wasn't yet midday. He planned to sit outside on the patio under the huge parasol with a large glass of fresh orange juice with ice and scrutinise the church documents. He pulled up outside the house, opened the boot and extracted the documents, but then his mobile started ringing. It was Millie and she was upset. Her mother-in-law had been taken to a hospice but died the same day. Millie was going to stay with Chris to arrange the funeral. Nathan offered his condolences and assured her that all was well at Fern Heights and that they didn't need to worry about rushing back.

A short while later, Nathan had settled himself on the patio as planned. He couldn't help but feel sorrow for the loss of Chris's mother, but decided to compartmentalise his feelings. He sat back and admired another spectacular view.

Sipping his cold orange juice, he relaxed back into the reclining chair. A light breeze drifted across his face. He sniffed the air and caught the slightest hint of pine aroma, then closed his eyes …

He was walking across an open field. It wasn't yet dark but would be in another hour. Behind him was a pig farm where the animals were bred for best pork. He was walking away from the farm and he had blood on his hands. He knew this part of the world. He was born only a few miles down the road in Cheltenham …

Nathan awoke from his daydream with a start. His shoulders felt tense, as he had moved from his original relaxed posture and was now partly on his side in a strange half-foetal position. He looked at his watch and realised he had been asleep for about ten minutes. It felt as if he had been asleep for hours after a heavy night and a bottle of wine. He took a gulp of his orange juice. Although the ice had melted, it was still cool. Despite sitting in the shade, the sweat was rolling down his back and down both sides of his face. This was the same nightmare he'd had back in the UK many times, but not recently. He didn't know why they should start again, nor did he understand their meaning.

He got up and made his way through the kitchen into the laundry room, picking up a towel and heading back outside. After a good towel down, he sat at the patio table and picked up the church magazine. He read through every word with the intention of recording anything that may be of interest but found nothing. He looked at the *Pew News* and again the only thing of interest was the paragraph relating to the list of benefactors:

Wellsford Council

The Anglican Diocese of Auckland

Mr William Dennis

Mrs Hannah Ross

With a special mention of gratitude to persons who wished to remain anonymous.

Why would a person wish to remain anonymous? Nathan wondered. Perhaps because they were very wealthy and didn't wish to draw attention to themselves? Could it be perhaps a controversial character who maybe didn't always agree with the hierarchy? Maybe someone who didn't want to be inundated with further charitable requests? Someone who had perhaps inherited a large amount and wanted to give some of it to a good cause? By the same token it could be money that was made illegally that someone was trying to wash their hands of. The possibilities were endless and there was no indication that it was anything to do with anything.

Nathan recorded these thoughts on a notepad then picked up the minute book. The cover stated that it was the PCC minute book of 1969–70. The book wasn't in particularly good condition but it still had its hard blue cover. There was no evidence that any of the pages were missing. Nathan opened the book and the first thing he noticed was the date of the first meeting recorded as 10 December 1969. This was a couple of weeks after the church had been officially opened. So, the book contained only one set of minutes for 1969 and the rest were for 1970.

Nathan read through the minutes, where there was mention of a successful opening, with the church building works being completed and paid for on time. There were other references to a few snagging difficulties with the building in general, but the rest was run-of-the-mill minutes. This wasn't the book he needed; it was the previous one 1968–69. Frustrated, Nathan threw the book on to the patio table and went into the kitchen to top up his glass. He would need to go back to the vestry to see whether the previous minute book was there.

As he opened the fridge, Nathan noticed a book standing on its end on the kitchen unit along with other documents such as cookery recipes and party planning. He picked up the book, which was entitled *Maori Rituals, Mythology and Traditions*. He filled his glass with fresh orange juice and an ice cube and closed the fridge. He went back outside with the drink and the book, hoping that it would take his mind off church documents and poor Brenda.

As Nathan began to read the book, he found that it was nothing like he had read before. It was a compilation of the history of the indigenous people of New Zealand – how they arrived, their migration and settlement traditions. Their coming together with European settlers, their fighting with European settlers and the Treaty of Waitangi, the first agreement between the tribes and the British. There was a section that particularly caught his imagination relating to Wednesday, 5 February 1840:

> From early morning Maori tribes had been arriving
> at Waitangi. The bay was alive with waka [canoes]

some with thirty or more paddlers who amazingly kept time with the stroke. They joined the stream of settlers' boats and ships all converging together to land at the British Governor's house. The lands around the house were being set up to sell refreshments, such as pork, other roast meats, pies, bread, ale and spirits. Special provision was made for the Maori guests: half a ton of flour, five tons of potatoes, thirty pigs and other foods. On the lawn in front of the Governor's house a huge marquee had been erected. It was made from ship sails and was said to be forty to fifty metres in length.

Nathan was totally captivated, so much so that he sat there all afternoon only drinking bottled water and eating a family bag of crisps for his lunch. He folded over the corner of the page as his marker and put the book down on the table. He had been sitting there for quite a while and had become very stiff, so he stood up, stretching his long arms above his head.

The sun was still extremely hot and Nathan could feel it burning his scalp through his hair. He decided it was time for a swim. This would be his first on this visit. He ran upstairs, put on a pair of swimming shorts, grabbed a towel and ran back down. The pool was covered in a large, plastic, air-bubbled sheet connected to a rolling mechanism at one end. This was designed to retain the sun's heat and warm the water. He walked to the far end of the pool and started to wind the mechanism that rolled in the pool cover.

His feet were burning as the tiling underfoot was so hot. He wound the cover in quickly then jumped into the water to relieve the burning sensation on the soles of his feet. The water was very warm. He swam down to the opposite end of the pool where there was a thermometer dangling in the water on a piece of string. He picked it up and looked at it — thirty-one degrees, the same temperature as the outside air.

It was lovely and warm in the water and after a few lengths of breaststroke Nathan lolled about on his back and relaxed. He felt good but there was one thing niggling away in the back of his mind. Why had the nightmare returned? He wasn't going to dwell on it though. He had done that too much in the past and had made himself ill. He was of the mindset now that he had moved on from his past and wanted to build a future. He wasn't in a rush, but he had moved on.

Nathan stepped out of the pool and dried himself with a towel, then quickly nipped into the kitchen and grabbed a bottle of Heineken from the fridge before returning to the patio to sit under the cover of the parasol. He checked his mobile for any messages that he may have missed while in the pool. There was a missed call from Margaret, so he immediately rang her back.

'Hi Margaret, its Nathan, is everything alright?'

'Yes, I had a call from the lady that lives near the church to say that the alarm had gone off again, but I've just had a call from Reverend Martin to say he's had a call too, so he's going up there now. So I'm sorry to bother you.'

'Not at all.' Nathan could hear a child's voice in the background. 'Have you got visitors then?'

'Yes, I'm looking after my granddaughter with it being school holidays and all that. She can be a bit of a handful.'

'I'll leave you to it Margaret. See you soon no doubt.'

'Okay, thanks Nathan, and thanks for calling me back. Bye then.'

'Bye,' replied Nathan and hung up.

He sat back in his chair and took a swig of beer, but he was unsettled. Another alarm activation at the church and the vicar was attending on his own. He took another swig of his beer, put the bottle down on the table and rushed upstairs to get changed. He was going to the church just to make sure the vicar was okay.

In a T-shirt, shorts and trainers, Nathan jumped into the SUV and ten minutes later was pulling into the church car park. He pulled up next to what he assumed was Reverend Martin's car and jumped out. It was quiet, so Martin must have turned the alarm off on his arrival.

Nathan pushed open the front door of the church and stepped into the small corridor. 'Martin, is everything okay,?' he shouted. There was no reply, so he walked up to the vestry door, which was closed, and turned the handle. It was dark inside because of the boarded-up window. Nathan reached to his left and found the light switch on the wall, turning it on.

A tubular fluorescent light flickered and slowly hummed into life. Nathan was horrified at what was in front of him. As the light flooded the room, he could see that Reverend Martin was sitting in one of the sturdy wooden vestry chairs. He was in his suit with the clerical collar. His arms had been bound with rope to each of the chair arms and his legs were also tied. His head was to one side and he had what looked like a large cloth stuffed into his mouth. Both his eyes were blackened and his face was covered in blood. His clerical collar was trickled with two lines of blood, which were running from his mouth. Nathan looked at Martin's hands, which were bleeding profusely. It looked as if two fingernails from each hand had been extracted. The floor was covered with a huge pool of blood.

'Martin! Martin!' shouted Nathan as he rushed towards the vicar. He thought he saw Martin's eyes flicker just for a moment, then he heard a light groan. Nathan carefully pulled the cloth out of Martin's mouth and a couple of his front teeth fell out on to the floor. Martin gave a weak cough and nothing more.

'I'm just going to get my mobile from the car. Hold on,' Nathan told him, then ran out of the room to his car, grabbed his mobile and called the emergency services. He then went back inside to be with Martin. He crouched low in front of him and took his head in his hands. As he straightened Martin's neck, he was sprayed with blood. He could see a large deep gash in the side of Martin's neck, probably through one of the main arteries, which explained the large amount of blood on the floor.

Nathan allowed Martin's head to fall to the side then went to the wardrobe behind him and pulled out one of the cloth robes. He twisted it around in his hands as if he were trying to make a rope, then placed it in the crook of Martin's neck to act as an absorbent padding to try to stem the flow of blood.

'Martin, hold on please, help's on its way.' Nathan watched as the alb slowly turned crimson red. Who could do this to another human being? Nathan had been involved in many murder squads when he was in the Met Police, but he had never experienced someone who had been the victim of torture. It wasn't hard to see that this man of the cloth had been through hell. For what purpose? Somebody wanted information and by the look of Martin's body it was probably information that he couldn't give rather than wouldn't give.

Nathan was suddenly conscious that he was in the middle of a crime scene but before he went out of the room he checked Martin's pulse in his left wrist. Unfortunately, there wasn't one, so he tried the right wrist – nothing. Nathan walked out of the room and sat on the floor with his back against the wall in the corridor. He felt like he was in a nightmare again. But he looked at his blood-soaked hands and he knew he was living this one right now.

10

THE POLICE arrived first and confirmed that Reverend Martin was showing no signs of life. An ambulance then arrived and the paramedics confirmed that Martin was deceased upon their arrival. Nathan had then been taken into custody for questioning and was now in the police cells at Wellsford police station, wearing white fabric-type overalls. All his clothes had been examined, swabbed, DNA-tested and he had been fingerprinted and orally swabbed. He had been interviewed briefly about his presence at the church and the interviewer seemed to be happy with his explanation.

The murder weapon had not so far been found. The church and the car park were still cordoned off and would be for a while as the police looked for further evidence. A witness had been interviewed, who described seeing a man dressed like Nathan running out of the church. What she hadn't seen was Nathan going to his car, making a phone call and then running back into the church. The fingerprint officers were busy in the vestry extracting fingerprints from the door handle, the light switch, the wardrobe door, the blood-soaked chair and anything else that they felt like dusting.

The press were starting to gather. Already aware that this wasn't the first murder in this small town, they had become more active. News company researchers and reporters flocked and gathered on street corners, stopping members of the public and questioning them to see whether they knew the victims and, if so, what they were like. Soon, the camera crews started arriving and were moving between the church, Brenda Massey's house and the police station.

~~~

Nathan's cell door was opened and he was taken into an interview room. The room was very bright and had two windows that were heavily barred and partly covered by vertical blinds. There was a CCTV camera in the corner of the room at ceiling level looking in his direction and a recording device on the desk. He was invited to sit by the man already at the desk, who was in a dark blue suit, white shirt and what looked like a golf club blue-and-grey-striped tie, complete with a flamboyant crest.

'My name is Detective Inspector Tim Broadwell. I'm from the Criminal Investigation Branch currently working with the murder squad,' the man in the suit said.

'You've made a big mistake arresting me. I was there to help, to see that Reverend Martin was okay. I had received a call from the churchwarden, Margaret Mills, to say that the alarm had gone off, so I just went to the church to make sure that he was okay, not to murder him. Can you please call my friend Rico Manu?'

'I already have. He's on his way down from Northlands. He told me all about you.' DI Broadwell didn't elaborate. Nathan, waiting for something further, held his silence. The two men looked at each other across the table. Broadwell broke the silence first. 'I don't agree with DI Manu.'

'What do you mean?' Nathan asked.

'I don't agree with having civilians working alongside the police in an active investigation.'

'Look, I had a call from the churchwarden informing me that the church alarm had activated. When she told me the vicar was on his way to deal with it, I thought he shouldn't be on his own, so I went to the church and found him in that terrible state.'

Nathan closed his eyes and tried to block out the sights, the sounds and the smells of the vestry and poor Martin, then continued, 'I'm no expert with regards to torture victims but in my opinion he looked like he was being asked a question that he was unable to answer, and because he didn't, they just left him to die.'

'I wasn't asking for your opinion,' said DI Broadwell in a brusque manner.

Nathan thought he would play Broadwell at his own game. 'Then don't ask me any questions because you're not going to get any answers.'

With that, DI Broadwell stood up from his chair. Nathan, for a split second, thought he was going to be struck, then Broadwell said, 'Come on back to your cell.'

When Nathan stood up, he realised they were about the same height, but Broadwell was particularly wide around the waist and his shirt buttons were struggling to keep his shirt closed across his stomach. He took Nathan by the arm and escorted him back to his cell.

'I'm sure Rico will come to see you when he arrives,' said DI Broadwell, then he slammed the heavy metal door shut with great force and Nathan could feel the floor vibrate beneath him. He shook his head and wondered whether Broadwell spent his days in a bubble of anger and unhappiness, because if he did, he knew how it felt.

It was a couple of hours before Nathan's cell door opened again, and when it did, Rico stood there. 'I believe you came to the aid of the vicar,' Rico said.

'I did, although I'm not sure your colleague Broadwell believes me.' Rico stepped forward and Nathan stood up from his bench. They shook hands. 'I'm glad to see you,' said Nathan.

'That must have been an awful thing that you walked into.'

'Well I've seen a few murders, but nothing like that. It was cruel, brutal. Whoever did this is dangerous and there's no reason to think that they're going to stop now. It's something to do with the church and, as such, all the members of that church are now at risk.'

'That could include you,' suggested Rico.

Nathan looked at him and he nodded in acceptance. 'Can you arrange to get me released? You know where I'll be, and before you ask, yes, my fingerprints will be all over the vestry. I just wanted to help Martin, but he was too far gone.'

'We'll sort something out but don't leave the country,' Rico said and smiled.

'And I'll need some clothes too.'

A couple of hours later, Nathan was on his way back to Fern Heights. The SUV had been driven to the police station from the church car park and thoroughly searched. Nathan made his exit wearing a Wellsford Rugby Club tracksuit and an old pair of trainers, which Rico had produced from the rear of his car.

There were several TV crews on the wide pavement immediately outside the police station. Nathan was aware that it was common practice for reporters to record every vehicle that left a place of interest, whether the crime scene or in this case the police station, and attempt to follow the vehicle and add to their story. For this reason, he was extra careful on his way back to Fern Heights. When he was happy that he wasn't being followed, he turned off SH1 to Fern Heights.

It was pitch black as he drove up the winding track to the start of the driveway. As he passed the gateposts his headlights briefly highlighted the two small black plastic boxes that were fitted one on each post. It was an infrared beam system that notified whoever was in the house that someone or something had just passed through the gate by activating a small alarm in the kitchen. The system had been turned off a couple of years ago because it used to frighten Millie when it activated at night. And it was usually a false alarm. Nathan thought he might turn it on again, and he knew it was turned off by a fused spur switch in the kitchen.

He drove up the driveway, parked up and entered the house. He ran upstairs and changed out of the musty clothes that Rico had kindly loaned him. Back in shorts, T-shirt and a pair of Chris's flip-flops, he grabbed a beer from the fridge and, mobile in pocket, opened the door and walked out on to the patio where there was still a beer bottle on the table from that afternoon.

It was now 10.15pm and Nathan wanted to call Loretta but thought it may be too late. He decided to text her, giving his apologies for not calling her earlier. She replied after about ten minutes.

> I've had an early night. Perhaps you should after your busy day. Call me tomorrow night, if free to do so x

Nathan assumed she was up to speed on the day's events. Rico must have told Marika and she would have told Loretta. Loretta perhaps wasn't impressed, having just come out of a bad relationship with a man who also ended up in police custody.

Nathan looked at the message again – 'if free to do so x'. There was only one positive thing he could glean from it and that was the kiss at the end. He would call her tomorrow night and try to improve the opinion that she must be forming of him.

It was peaceful now apart from the constant cricket-type noise from the cicadas in the trees. It was a particularly warm evening and with the things that Nathan had seen earlier in the day he was doubting whether he would get any sleep that night. The flashbacks to the fingers, the teeth as he pulled the cloth out of Martin's mouth, the laceration to his neck and so much blood …

The moths and other flying insects were now starting to gather, attracted by the kitchen light shining through the windows. Nathan went inside and grabbed another beer and a can of insect repellent. He also flicked the switch that operated the gate infrared beam. It beeped intermittently for a few seconds then went quiet.

He returned to the patio and sprayed his arms, legs and the back of his neck with the repellent, although he suspected he had already picked up a couple of mosquito bites. He tried to relax but DI Tim Broadwell came into his mind, then Brenda Massey, then Reverend Martin. A mixture of thoughts and sights were all swilling around in his head, so he decided to call it a day. He picked up the beer bottles and took them inside for recycling. He then turned the kitchen light off and went upstairs.

At the last minute, Nathan decided that a shower would be a good idea, as he had only been able to get washed at the police station after the photo samples and swabs had been taken. He still felt grubby. He jumped into the shower and was deluged with warm water, standing there for a good ten minutes as it massaged his scalp and shoulders. As he applied some shampoo to his hair he became unnerved. He thought he heard the bleeper in the kitchen from the gate infrared beam system. But how could he hear it from up here, through a concrete floor and numerous doors?

He turned the shower off immediately and through the dripping noises from the shower head and his body, there it was again. 'Shit,' he said as he scrambled out of the shower, grabbed a towel and turned off all the lights before opening the curtains just a fraction and lifting the blind. He looked in the direction of the drive and there was just enough moonlight to see the gateposts at the bottom, but it was a long way off and, in the darkness, you wouldn't know whether someone was lurking around. In the daylight they would be easily spotted.

Nathan decided to go outside to take a look. Using his mobile as a torch he quickly pulled on his shorts and flip-flops and made his way down to the kitchen. There was a large flashlight fitted to a bracket on the wall, so he took that with him but didn't turn it on. He sneaked out on to the patio and made his way around to where his car was parked at the top of the drive. He walked with stealth, keeping his back to the house, his eyes searching for any movement.

Nathan stopped for a moment to listen. An owl in a tree nearby screeched, causing him to jump. He was surprised at how nervous he felt. He was on his guard. He thought there could be someone there waiting in the shadows to pounce. He looked down the driveway, but it was too dark, so he decided to turn on the torch. Flicking on the switch, the whole area seemed to illuminate, so he turned the head of the torch to narrow the beam and shone it down the driveway, but all he could see in the beam were flying insects. There was no one on the driveway or at the gate, although there were plenty of places to hide in the surrounding woodland.

Nathan thought about walking down to the gate to see whether there were any footprints or tyre marks, but he quickly dismissed the idea as it would leave him too vulnerable out in the open. He would take a look around in the daylight to see whether he could see anything. He made his way back around the house and entered through the kitchen patio door, making sure to lock it behind him. It was something Millie and Chris only did when they remembered to. Nathan went to bed shortly after and lay there listening for a while until he fell asleep.

He woke up early the next day and made his way down to the kitchen. He prepared himself a bowl of nutty muesli, added some milk and raspberries and poured himself a glass of fresh orange juice, before unlocking the door and going out on to the patio. It was another beautiful day – very warm, very still and a brilliant clear blue sky.

Nathan sat down at the table and looked at his mobile to update himself on the latest world news. There was a virus coming out of Africa, there was one coming out of China, there was talk of a world war over oil, there was mass immigration from one continent to another, there were more terrorist attacks in the UK and US. He concluded that he was probably in one of the safest countries at the moment, but even the slow lifestyle of the Kiwis was under attack as recent events had proved. The images of Reverend Martin bound to the chair would live with him for the rest of his life.

He was crunching away on his muesli when his mobile rang. It was Rico. With a mouth full of muesli, Nathan picked up the phone.

'Hi Rico.'

'Good morning. Any chance of calling in for a coffee?'

'How long will you be?'

'About ten minutes.'

'Okay, see you then. Bye.'

Nathan got up and went into the kitchen, where he spooned coffee into the cafetiere and filled the kettle. He poured the boiling water on to the coffee and took the cafetiere outside with two mugs. Within minutes, he heard the bleeper in the kitchen and Rico drove up, got out of the car and sat down at the patio table.

'A bit of a dramatic day for you yesterday,' said Rico.

'Yes, and one that I would rather forget, although I have a feeling the memories may be with me for a long time.'

'Look Nathan, Tim Broadwell is kicking up a fuss because of your involvement and helping me out.'

'I thought you were in charge of the murder squad Rico.'

'I am but he's the same rank as me and I know back at HQ he's said a couple of things and raised a few eyebrows, so much so that somebody has already done a thorough background check on you.'

'I don't care. I've got nothing to hide,' said Nathan.

Rico now looked serious and Nathan noticed that he seemed to be uneasy all of a sudden and started to fidget. 'Look Nathan, there's something in your file that—'

'Something in my file?' interrupted Nathan angrily. 'Can I remind you that I left the police on medical grounds with a certificate of exemplary service, so there can't be anything in my file that's detrimental, otherwise I wouldn't have been recognised for the award.'

'Look, and I'm sorry to mention this, but after your parents were killed the file says that you were affected badly.'

'Well wouldn't you be if a druggy came along in a car and mowed your parents down while high on whatever?'

'Yes, I would, but I don't think I would take matters any further.'

'What's that supposed to mean?' asked Nathan.

'Well, it's rumoured that you may have caught up with the murderer and issued summary justice.'

Nathan managed to keep his cool, although inside he was feeling terribly angry. 'There was never any evidence that I was involved, and I was never suspected.'

'I've got news for you Nathan; you're not going to like it, but you were suspected, but because it was only a theory and you were ill and grieving at the time, it was never followed up.'

'Oh, aren't I the lucky one, being given the benefit of the doubt but being left with a huge question mark over my head for the rest of my life. It's all bollocks. No wonder they couldn't wait to get rid of me.' Nathan banged the table with his fist, resulting in two mugs of coffee spilling over their rims and leaving two small puddles on the table.

'It's not like you to feel sorry for yourself Nathan.'

'I don't, believe me I don't. It's these question marks about me. Can I be trusted? Did I murder someone in the past and get away with it? If I did, prove it; if not, leave me alone.'

'Nathan, can I remind you that I'm on your side, but I'm being squeezed by HQ. I've always been on your side, you know that. Look, the end result is your services are no longer required by the New Zealand police, but I want to stay friends. I know we fall out occasionally but when we're on good form you have to admit we have a laugh.'

Rico could see Nathan softening as the stern look turned into a smile. 'I'm sorry mate, I shouldn't have offloaded on you,' Nathan said apologetically. 'I appreciate your friendship.'

'Well let's see if we can't arrange another night out with the girls,' said Rico.

'I'm not sure that Loretta is overly impressed with me. I think she knows I spent some time in the cells.' Nathan glared at Rico.

'Hands up, I admit I did mention it to Marika, but I told her not to mention it to Loretta. Sorry, I should have known better. Thick as thieves they are,' Rico said sheepishly.

'I'm going to call her later, so I'll mention the weekend,' suggested Nathan.

'Okay.'

'Just changing the subject ... the gatepost here has an alarm on it, one of those infrared beams. The damn thing activated last night while I was in the shower. Frightened the life out of me it did.'

'Were you worried you had been followed?'

'Yes, followed or someone just snooping around. I was going to have a look to see whether there were any tyre marks on the verges or any sign that someone had been hanging around.'

'Everyone's a bit twitchy at the moment. In fact, most people are really scared. As you know, little usually happens around here, so it's understandable. There's nothing wrong with being extra vigilant though. But don't become a vigilante. Call us if you need us,' said Rico.

'Are you any nearer catching the perpetrators?' asked Nathan.

'We're still gathering evidence and that's hard enough. Do you know there's basically no CCTV in this town? Just the odd house or shop that have had them fitted privately. There's no town centre scheme, as they've never needed it. We've had a couple of people in helping with our enquiries though.'

'Don't I know!' said Nathan sarcastically.

Rico ignored him and continued. 'Two horrific murders and a break-in at the church doesn't make sense. I can't see any motive.' Rico suddenly looked drained. He was clearly under considerable pressure from HQ to get this drawn to a conclusion and that pressure was building by the minute.

'I'll have to go Nathan. There's a team briefing in thirty minutes. Keep in touch and let me know about the weekend.'

'You keep in touch with me too. I would like to know how the case is coming along … that's if you're allowed to.'

They both stood up and high-fived. 'I'll have a look around the gate on the way out to see if I can see anything.'

'Thanks Rico.'

Nathan watched Rico as his car went slowly down the driveway. He saw him stop at the gateway, get out of the car and have a quick walk around, looking at the floor as he went. He then jumped back in the car and drove off.

Nathan sat down and finished his coffee. Rico's comment based around the rumour that he may have issued summary justice to his parents' killer was one that he hadn't heard in a while, although at the time he knew what people were saying about him. But how it had come to light when someone had done a check on him from the other side of the world was a mystery. As damaging as such a rumour potentially was, he had moved on now to a new life. But then it served him right. If he hadn't become involved in police work here it would never have come to light. He couldn't help wondering whether Rico already knew about the rumour or had he only found out as a result of the background check on him?

Nathan finished his breakfast and went upstairs for a shower. When he had finished, he had a wet shave then slapped on the factor 30 sun cream. He had read somewhere recently that the sun in Australia and New Zealand had a much higher UV index. It certainly felt stronger, particularly on his head, so he was going to wear his baseball cap. It was one that Chris had given him on his arrival – beige, with a running deer on the front, with the name John Deere in capital letters below it. Chris had mentioned that they were a tractor manufacturer but Nathan was none the wiser.

He went down into the kitchen and poured himself another glass of fresh orange juice, then went back outside and sat under the parasol. He sat there in solitude; the only sound around was bird song. The cicadas hadn't yet kicked off with their cacophony from the trees but the parakeets were busy coming and going from tree to tree in their usual pairs. A new arrival on the scene were a pair of large dragonflies sailing past with a hint of blue on their bodies and amazing transparent-like wings. Spectacular and graceful.

Nathan decided he was going to go to the Wellsford museum. His interest in history had been rekindled by Millie's book about the Maori people and he was particularly interested in the early British settlers. He had found a folded leaflet in the back of the book, just an A4 sheet but it listed all the historical sites that could be visited in the area. There was a Maori heritage centre just outside Wellsford at Te Hana, and there were other museums at Warkworth, Puhoi and Dargaville, as well as many other historic houses and sites. This should be a good distraction from recent events.

Nathan's mobile rang; it was Millie. She had heard on the news about the murder of Reverend Martin and was terribly upset. On top of the death of her mother-in-law it was a difficult time for her. Nathan filled her in on the basics but spared her the gory details. Through her tears and quivering voice, he could make out that Millie wanted him to make a welfare call to Margaret. This he said he would do. He just wished he could give his sister a big hug and tell her that everything was going to be alright. But then he remembered she had a husband who could do that for her, and he was sure he would.

Nathan came off the phone to Millie and immediately called Margaret. She too was upset and couldn't understand why all these terrible things were happening to the church and their folk. She cried and cried and said she would never be able to go into the vestry again, knowing what had happened in there. Like with Millie, Nathan spared her the gory details and offered to go around to her house to see her but she said she was okay and just wanted some quiet contemplation time.

But Nathan was determined not to just sit around wringing his hands, worrying about what was going to happen next. He grabbed his things, locked the doors and jumped in the car. As he drove down the driveway, he stopped by the gateposts and got out to have a look around. No tyre marks on the verges, no cigarette butts – nothing to indicate that anyone had been hanging about. Must have been a false alarm, so now he knew why Millie didn't like it. All the same it would be great if there was a CCTV camera on the gate. He had been spoiled in London, where there were cameras everywhere and they were great evidence gatherers. Nathan was battling with himself. He had to stop thinking about police work and he had to stop now.

A short time later, he pulled into the museum car park. The museum was on the same road as the church and he could see up ahead that the police still had the road by the church cordoned off. He walked into the museum and was pleasantly surprised. There was a nice atmosphere. The man on reception was extremely helpful and took time to engage Nathan in conversation. When he realised that Nathan was English, he thought he may have come to the museum to carry out research as a relative of a past migrant to the colony. Nathan pointed out that he wasn't but he was interested all the same.

He was told that there was a student in the back room who was doing a thesis on the Albertlanders. This was a group of migrants from England who had settled in the area in the 1860s at a time when the coastal areas were covered by bush and scrub. To make matters worse there were probably occasional skirmishes between them and the local Maori people.

Nathan walked into the main body of the museum and was surprised at the size and quantity of items on display. There were models of sailing ships of the type that the early

Albertland settlers arrived upon after their horrific journey from England. There were everyday domestic items from the period, some pieces of kauri wood and some of the famous kauri gum, the resin extracted from the trees and used for crafts such as jewellery and ornaments. The gum, being highly inflammable, was used as a fire starter. It was also used commercially in varnish. For these reasons it became a much-sought-after commodity and was one of Auckland's main exports in the latter half of the nineteenth century.

There was an array of photographs featuring different pioneering families from the early years in Albertland and a significant amount of documentary evidence relating to their everyday lives. There was a large centre section of a flag, which was flown on one of the early settler ships all the way from England.

Nathan was in his element, then his heart sank. He came across a display for the Massey family. It was a display case showing the regimental uniform of Victor Massey and there was a series of photographs of Victor, who had died of his injuries many years after the Second World War. There was a photograph of his dedicated wife, who had looked after him and his injuries for nearly ten years. Then there was a photograph of his wife in later years – the recently deceased Brenda Massey.

The man from reception suddenly appeared next to Nathan. 'This is a sad business,' the man said, pointing at the picture of Brenda. 'This lady was killed in her home recently.'

'I heard,' replied Nathan. 'The lady in the café mentioned that you were doing a display on the Masseys. It was just a bit of a shock and incredibly sad that—'

'We weren't sure whether we should take it down or not,' the receptionist interrupted.

'Well it's not for me to say but I wouldn't. They were obviously an amazing couple and that hasn't changed. They're part of the history of this town.'

'If you don't mind, I'm going to make a note of your comments and forward them to our curator, who's looking for feedback on the Masseys.'

'Of course, no problem.'

The man walked back to his desk in reception. Looking back at the display, Nathan saw several medals, awarded for bravery and service. There was an old Golden Virginia tobacco tin and an old sewing kit wrapped up in a lint-type cloth with Victor's name and number printed on it. It looked as if it had been issued as part of his kit. Nathan now knew what Brenda Massey and her husband looked like. He had to remind himself again to move on and not dwell on the murders.

Immediately next to this display was a small bookcase that had several books for sale. Nathan scanned through them and sampled the writing styles before he settled on two books: *The Origins of the Treaty of Waitangi* and *The New Zealand Pioneers*. There was also a small brochure with a photograph of a very quaint church, which had the title *Minniesdale Chapel circa 1867, Shegadeens Road, Wharehine. An Historical Record*. Nathan flicked through the pages and found that it was talking about the early pioneers, the Albertlanders.

The opening paragraph read: 'This beautiful little chapel is more than just a building. It's a testimonial to the faith and courage of our pioneering forebears, men and women who sought to make for themselves and their children, a home in the wilderness.'

This was definitely of interest to Nathan. Seeing as he had plenty of time on his hands, there was no time like the present, but maybe after a coffee. He walked back to reception with his leaflets and books. Having paid what was due and exchanging pleasantries, he left the museum.

11

TRENT ALLEN was a career criminal. Originally from Darwen in the Northern Territories of Australia, he had served several years in prison for deception, burglary, robbery and credit card frauds. He had arrived in Auckland a couple of weeks after his release from prison and wanted to follow his younger brother Lachlan by making a new life and being successful. He didn't know how he was going to do it, but he was going to try.

The problem with Trent was that while in prison in Australia he had developed a taste for drugs, and anything and everything was available behind bars. Now that he was free, he was desperate for money and drugs and had been in touch with his brother as soon as he had landed in Auckland. Lachlan loved his brother, but because of his past indiscretions he didn't want to associate with him.

Lachlan had never been in trouble with the law, so it follows he had never been incarcerated. The thought frightened the life out of him. Besides, Lachlan was a successful restaurateur and had eating houses in Auckland and Wellington, where he lived. He had a clean-cut and quiet image and that's the way he liked it. But when Trent called, he could never say no. He had transferred five thousand dollars into Trent's account and told him to go and look for a job.

Lachlan had done some research and found a couple of bedsits in Manukau, south of Auckland and near the airport. Trent had taken one of the bedsits and in no time at all had a job with a cleaning team at Auckland airport. But he was running out of money. He had been buying marijuana, which had quickly moved to other narcotic concoctions and now he was using cocaine.

With a week to go before his first pay cheque and desperate for a fix, Trent had entered a jeweller's shop in central Auckland and while viewing a watch placed it on his wrist and tried to make a run for it. Unfortunately for Trent, the security guard had been watching and had pressed a button by the door, which not only called the police but closed and secured the front door.

Trent, on seeing this, had panicked, picking up a fire extinguisher and throwing it at the guard, who managed to fend it off and in doing so smashed one of the shop's display cabinets. As the guard stepped forward to grab Trent, he had picked up a large piece of glass from the floor and lunged at the guard. The guard hadn't been quick enough and Trent pushed it deep into his neck, cutting the main artery. The guard had died almost immediately.

Trent had then picked up the fire extinguisher and used it as a hammer to smash the glass in the front door and made his escape. He hadn't gone far before he was challenged by three police officers and gave himself up. Found guilty at court a few months later, he had been sent to Auckland prison to serve eighteen years without parole at just thirty-two years old.

Trent had accepted that he was better off in prison. He had really struggled to manage outside. How do you hold down a job when you're under the influence of narcotics or going cold turkey? How do you pay your way? The bills, the rent, food and his habit – he was never going to earn enough money to pay for it all. Any money that he earned in prison could go towards his next fix. And on top of all that he had no bills to pay.

Lachlan had been upset but not surprised. He knew the state of his brother's mind. He knew how he thought and he knew that Trent would probably blow all the money that he gave him. But he was still his brother and he would help him whenever he could, regardless of what crime he had committed. As long as he kept his distance.

~~~

Eighteen years later and Trent was almost ready for his release. His appearance had changed considerably. He was now quite muscular through hours and hours spent every week in the gymnasium in the yard. His hair was cropped short and speckled silver, grey and black. He looked every day of his fifty years. His arms were covered in what looked like DIY tattoos, culminating in what appeared to be a swastika in a circle on the side of his neck.

Lachlan had once again been Trent's saviour. He had purchased an old camper van that was on a site near Pakiri Beach on the north-east coast. He had even bought him a second-hand car and insured it for a year. Lachlan had arranged for five hundred dollars a week to be paid into his account, but for six weeks only, then Trent was on his own.

Trent had managed to obtain some travel books and a couple of maps. He had never been any further north than Auckland and he was lying in his cell wondering what the area was like. He had a map sellotaped to the wall on which he had circled Pakiri Beach and had made a note of some of the nearby towns. His final days in prison were spent researching the area that was to become his home. This included towns such as Wellsford and Warkworth. He was looking forward to his day of release, when Lachlan was coming to meet him with a friend to hand over the car and the keys for the camper van.

12

NATHAN WALKED down the steps from the library. He could see the café on the corner, so he left his car where it was and walked over. As he walked through the door there were about six or seven men sitting at three tables, who all turned their heads to look at him. It was very unnerving. He had already made up his mind that they were all cops, Criminal Investigation Branch probably.

Rather than walk into the main seating area, there was a small bar with stools to the side, so Nathan perched himself on one of the stools. The young woman who had served him the other day suddenly appeared from the kitchen.

'Hello again,' Nathan greeted her.

'Hello again. Great to see you. What can I get you?' she asked.

'Just a flat white please.'

'Okay, be right up.'

Nathan couldn't help noticing that two of the men at one of the tables were chatting very quietly, then they turned to look at him. They were either talking about him or trying to intimidate him. Nathan turned away just as the flat white appeared on the bar in front of him.

'I see you've got the cops in,' said Nathan.

'Yes, I told you this is where they come for a break. Isn't it shocking about the vicar? Everyone is so scared. I heard he had been tortured. What type of person is it that's running loose on our streets? And why torture a vicar?'

'I take it they haven't caught anyone yet then?' asked Nathan.

'Don't think so. They're playing their cards pretty close to their chests these days. I heard they've had a couple of men in for questioning over the last few days.'

'Yes, I've heard the same,' said Nathan, not wanting to mention that he was one of them. 'Can I ask you,' he added, holding up the booklet for Minniesdale Chapel, 'have you ever been here?'

The young woman glimpsed at it briefly. 'No, I haven't but I believe it's a gorgeous place. I'm not a churchy person so I've never bothered. I've driven past it a couple of times though; do you want some directions? It's about twenty minutes away, that's all.'

'That would be fantastic, thank you.'

Fifteen minutes later Nathan left the café with his directions to Minniesdale Chapel. He crossed the road and made his way to his car in the museum car park. It was another hot day and once again a cloudless sky. A beautiful day to go out and please yourself and enjoy it.

As Nathan approached his car, he couldn't help but notice that further up the road it was still cordoned off. He jumped in and turned on the air conditioning. The images of Reverend Martin strapped in his chair surrounded by blood made him feel sick. He rubbed his temples and breathed in the cool air from the directional blower in the dashboard.

Meanwhile, in the café, the cops got up from their tables to leave. On their way out, one went over to the waitress and asked, 'Where did he say he was going?'

She knew who he was talking about. 'Minniesdale Chapel,' she replied. The cop pressed a banknote into her hand.

'Thanks. Have a nice day,' the waitress simply replied with a smile.

Nathan left the car park and followed his instructions on to SH16. The views were spectacular, with partly forested rolling hills and fields full of cattle. He turned off at a junction heading for Port Albert, and before he knew it he was on a dirt road. He passed another junction for Port Albert, now heading south. After approximately ten minutes he saw a sign with an arrow for 'Historical Minniesdale Chapel'. Turning right at the sign, he was now on a single-track road.

After a couple of minutes, Nathan could see the building on the left-hand side, so he pulled up on to the grass verge. As expected, the chapel was absolutely stunning. It sat there on the side of a hill in all its shining glory, surrounded by a white picket fence. In the backdrop, the hills were covered by radiata pine trees and in the foreground was a large expanse of water, the Oruawharo river, which was an inlet from Kaipara harbour.

The chapel was a brilliant-white timber construction with a small bell turret on the roof at its front elevation. It had a single arched front door and two arched windows on each side. It was by far the smallest and prettiest church that Nathan had ever seen. He walked down the short narrow path to the front door and tried the handle, not expecting it to be open. As he turned the ring handle the latch opened, as did the door.

Nathan stepped inside. It was breathtakingly simple but beautiful. The beams, the structure and all the timbers were on show. A light oak in colour, they matched the pews and the timber floor. There was a carpet runner from the front door to the tiny altar at the far end of the chapel. The wall behind the altar had two large arched windows, one to either side of it, then at high level there was a triple window consisting of three arches in one frame.

The chapel was light and airy and some of the windows had a stained-glass section within them. As the sun poured through, reflections of different colours settled on and warmed the timber pews. It was noticeable that the windows were small and in keeping with the stature of the chapel. This probably helped to keep the temperature a few degrees cooler in the summer months.

On display there was a black-and-white photograph of a splendid looking Reverend Edwin Stanley Brookes, the founder of the chapel, who had it built at his own expense and served there as minister for thirty years. On the opposite wall was a photograph of Jemima Hovey Brookes, his wife and the matriarch of the Brookes family.

Nathan took several photos on his mobile then stepped outside just as another car drove past, leaving a cloud of dust behind it. He couldn't help wondering how the building looked so clean with a dusty road right outside, unless it had recently been repainted. He walked over to a bench and sat down to enjoy the view of the chapel and its surroundings.

Looking across at his SUV, Nathan noticed that it was covered in a light-coloured chalky powder, which reminded him of his mother sprinkling flour on to her rolling pin and board before rolling out some pastry. Then he noticed that the front passenger window looked as if it had been partly wiped clean, as if someone had taken a look inside and given the window a wipe with their hand. He left the bench and walked over to the SUV, suspecting that someone had taken a look inside his car while he was inside the chapel.

Nathan was now dragged out of his solace and enjoyment of the venue and its location into an environment of suspicion and a need to know what was going on around him. Was someone watching him? Perhaps the police weren't satisfied with his explanation and were keeping tabs on him. He thought about ringing Rico. Then he changed his mind, as he needed more to go on and didn't want Rico to think he was paranoid.

Instead, he had a casual look around the SUV. As he walked around the rear of the vehicle, he noticed about a car's length away, a small dark puddle just on the edge of the grass verge and the limestone road. It was no more than the size of an apple. He bent over and touched it with his forefinger and thumb, rubbing it between his fingers and sniffing it. Definitely engine oil.

As he stood up, Nathan noticed a cigarette filter in the middle of the road with the remains of ash and paper still connected, as if it had just been thrown out of a car and not stubbed out. It was obviously fresh as it hadn't been flattened by a passing vehicle. But there had been one other vehicle. Just as he came out of the chapel, a dark car and a cloud of dust. Had they seen him coming out of the chapel and left quickly? Or was it just passing by?

Nathan got into the SUV and was heading back the way he had come when he decided to take a detour via Hoteo. The car's sat nav showed a road that travelled around the West Dome hills. It was a single-track road with the occasional passing place and signs for 'logging route'. He couldn't believe that these roads were suitable for logging trucks and hoped he didn't come face to face with one.

Some of the farm buildings he passed looked as if they should be in the Wild West – large timber buildings, barns and outbuildings that were heavily weathered and grey in colour. There was an abundance of cattle and sheep pockmarking the hillsides. Nathan was enjoying the view when yet again the image of Reverend Martin came to mind. It seemed that ever since he had arrived in New Zealand everything had gone wrong. There were the murders, the death of Chris's mother and his own detention by the police. A potential new girlfriend, who had found out about his detention and wasn't impressed. And to top it all off, he now had a feeling that someone was watching or following him.

He continued his journey through Hoteo and Kaipara and joined SH1 at Kaipara Flats Road. He took a left, heading north and was approaching the turn-off for Fern Heights. He constantly checked his rear-view mirror and decided to drive past the turn-off and do a U-turn further on, then approach from the other direction.

This he did, then turned right into the entrance to Fern Heights, stopping on the wooden bridge. He kept his eyes on the mirror. He waited there for a good ten minutes just to see whether anyone dared to follow him. There was nothing but traffic heading north and south, so he drove over the bridge and noticed there was a metal gate that he hadn't spotted previously. He stopped the SUV, got out and closed the gate. At its centre, the gate had a red-and-white sign saying 'Private, No Entry'. He then drove on and made his way up to the house, closing the gates at the foot of the drive in passing.

Nathan entered the house with his morning's acquisitions – the books and leaflets from the museum. He quickly poured a large glass of orange juice and made himself a ham sandwich before walking out on to the patio and sitting down in his favourite spot to enjoy his late lunch and the view.

He thought about how things might be going in Melbourne for Millie and Chris, trying to organise a funeral for Chris's mother. Then out of the blue his thoughts turned to much nicer things, Loretta. How was he going to win her around? He decided to send her a quick message asking how her day was going. He waited for a reply, but when one didn't come, he started to make excuses for her, like she was in a meeting or she was driving. As time went on, his thoughts changed to perhaps she doesn't want to know me, and he became despondent.

His mood was lifted, though, the more and more he read the book, *The New Zealand Pioneers*. The locating of land, the purchasing of land from the indigenous people – it was obvious in the early days that some land had been taken from people who were already settled, causing ructions all over the country. So, the British government organised the Treaty of Waitangi, a meeting between the indigenous people and the European settlers, to try to thrash things out or at least get to a starting point. Tribes from all over New Zealand flocked to the Bay of Islands in the north-east of the country. The bay was awash with Maori waka canoes, each with thirty or more occupants using paddles.

Nathan was captivated, so much so that the time slipped by, and before he knew it, he was thirsty. It was getting on for four o'clock. He stood up and went to the kitchen for a beer but then heard his mobile ping, indicating a message. Typical. He had sat there for a couple of hours in silence, and as soon as he left his seat, he got a message. He returned with a cold beer, unscrewed the lid and took a gulp as he looked at his mobile. It was Loretta.

> Hi Nathan, I've just left my final meeting of today, a bit later than I expected but never mind. A good day today, a lot of driving, just leaving Whangarei. How was your day? Have you been keeping out of mischief?

Nathan smiled at her last comment. Maybe she wasn't taking yesterday's incident too seriously after all. No mischief today unless you count a museum and chapel visit as bad behaviour. He texted a reply:

> If you're travelling back to Auckland from Whangarei why don't you stop of here on the way. I'm just off the SH1.

He cringed as he sent the message. Did he sound too pushy? Why would she stop off here when we've only met once before? Loretta replied pretty quickly:

If you send me your postcode or some directions I'll see if I have the time, I guess it all depends on traffic etc.

Nathan was pleased and he hoped that she could. He messaged her the postcode and some specific directions of where to turn off SH1, ending the message by saying he hoped to see her later. Again, he had the feeling he was being a bit pushy. She replied:

Thanks and likewise x

This time he was even more pleased. He got a kiss.

Whangarei was probably about an hour and a half away, depending on the traffic. Nathan thought he had better try cleaning the kitchen, so he loaded the dishwasher and did a general tidy up. Then he remembered he had closed the two gates, so he jumped into the SUV and drove down the drive, opened the gate, then drove to the wooden bridge and opened the 'No Entry' gate.

On the way back but before he had reached the bottom of the drive something caught his eye at the side of the road. It looked as if someone had emptied the ash tray of their car on to the grass. He stopped the SUV and jumped out. There were a lot of cigarette stubs and a handful of pistachio nut shells. *Nobody should have been here as it's a private road*, thought Nathan.

He had a further look around the area, checking for anything else, such as a small oil leak, but there was nothing. Then he looked up towards the house and realised there was a clear line of sight through the trees to Fern Heights. He remembered that Chris had mentioned that the electric company had had an issue with one of the overhead lines. Chris had to clear a line of trees so they could install a new line. It could be that someone from the electric company had decided it was a good place to clean out their ash tray. It was as good an explanation as any. Or was he being paranoid again?

Nathan made his way back to the house and decided to unroll the cover on the swimming pool to make it more attractive to look at when he showed Loretta around. He went back into the kitchen and completed his tidy up, then went back outside with a fresh beer. He picked up the book and started reading. Once again, he became totally engrossed, allowing his beer to get too warm.

Suddenly, the bleeper went in the kitchen and he stood up to see a small red Audi slowly making its way up the drive. He waited until it got closer, then he could see Loretta's long chestnut hair through the window. Nathan was delighted, not only because it was Loretta but also because he needed some company. He walked around to the front of the house to meet her on the driveway just as she was getting out of the car.

Loretta looked very professional and attractive in her navy-blue trouser suit. She had the jacket draped over her arm and she wore a brilliant-white blouse and black high-heeled shoes. She looked and smelled like a million dollars. Her hair had a slight wave and her make-up was immaculate. Nathan felt under-dressed in his T-shirt, shorts and flip-flops.

He walked up to the car and said, 'Welcome to Fern Heights,' then kissed her lightly on the cheek.

'Thank you, that's a nice welcome. Wow, what a place.'

'I know, it's pretty amazing. I did tell you it was my sister and brother-in-law's didn't I?'

'Yes, you did. How are they?'

'I'm afraid they're not here at present. They're in Melbourne for Chris's mum's funeral.'

'Oh, I'm sorry to hear that.'

'Yes, it was a bit unfortunate. Shortly after I arrived they had to leave to move her into a hospice, and the day they moved her she died. So now they're busy organising everything for the funeral. Anyway, how was the journey down? Not too much traffic I hope.'

'No, I've seen it much worse,' she replied.

'Let's go and have a drink on the patio and get out of this sun,' Nathan suggested, taking her hand and walking around the house to the patio.

They sat down at the table. 'Looks like you've been having a party,' Loretta said, pointing at the beer bottles. Nathan pointed out that they were all half full as he kept getting too engrossed in the book that he was reading.

'Would you like a drink, Loretta?'

'I would love a black coffee.'

'Right, I won't be a minute. Is a Nespresso alright for you?'

'Perfect,' she replied.

Nathan made two black coffees and re-joined her on the patio.

'This view is amazing, so relaxing,' Loretta said.

'I know, I've been spending a lot of time out here, reading and letting my beer get warm.'

'Amongst other things,' she replied with a wry smile.

'Well, I would like to explain to you what happened.'

Loretta had a serious expression on her face as Nathan continued. 'I won't give you the gory details, but I had been speaking with Margaret the churchwarden at the Ecumenical Church in Wellsford. It's the church that my sister goes to. They had a break-in a few days ago. The alarm had activated and Margaret was too frightened to go into the church on her own, so she rang Millie and we both went to the church to help her out. Then the other day the alarm went off again and Margaret rang to let me know that she had got hold of the vicar and he was on his way out there. She couldn't go because she was child-minding.

'I decided to go to the church to see that the vicar was alright, and he wasn't. He had been bound to a chair and severely attacked. I ran to my car and called the police, then ran back inside to look after him. Then when the police arrived, they arrested me because I was there and had a large amount of blood on me. I was trying to help the vicar. He was barely alive and died a few minutes later. That's why I was taken into police custody. I guess they were just doing their job.'

'Spoken like a true ex-police officer. But it must be an awful experience seeing what you had seen and then being accused of carrying it out.'

'It was and I keep getting flashbacks of the poor vicar. It was shocking, absolutely shocking. You know, it's something you never get used to. I attended many murders in London when I was in the police and they all have that same lingering effect. Anyway, I've been wanting to explain that to you because I didn't think you seemed too impressed when you found out, presumably from Rico via Marika.'

'I wasn't but I am now. It's so easy to form the wrong impression. When Marika told me what had happened, I immediately thought the worst. My ex is to blame for that. He became regularly involved with the police, so I'm sorry for tarring you with the same brush.'

'It's easily done and, to be honest, I thought you were going to wash your hands of me.'

'I nearly did, but I'm here now.'

They smiled at each other. 'Seeing as you're in real estate, how would you like me to show you around my sister's house?'

'Well, to be honest, under normal circumstances I wouldn't, but because this house looks like it's something special, I would love you to, as long as your sister wouldn't mind.'

'She wouldn't,' Nathan replied.

He proudly walked her around, including the granny flat, the garages and the outbuildings. He left the pool and barbecue area until the end. Loretta was suitably impressed.

'I was thinking of firing up the barbecue later,' Nathan said. 'I've got some nice king prawns on skewers if you fancy them.' He had taken them out of the freezer that morning. They were huge, typical of New Zealand.

'Sorry,' Loretta replied, 'I can hear my mobile ringing. I left it on the table on the patio.' They walked through the house. The mobile had stopped ringing before they reached the table. Loretta checked it. 'Sorry, I just have to make a call.'

Nathan wondered whether it was from a boyfriend, but whoever it was seemed to ask her a lot of questions. When she finished the call, she put down her mobile. 'It was my dad. He's checking up on me.'

'Ah … are you a daddy's girl?'

'No, not at all,' Loretta smiled, 'but Daddy's my boss.'

'Oops,' said Nathan.

'Perhaps this is a good time to find out more about each other, seeing as Marika stole the show last weekend. We didn't really have the chance to talk did we,' Loretta said.

'No, but boy did we laugh.'

'We certainly did. Marika's the life and soul of the party. We became best friends about two years ago. I met her at one of the yacht clubs in Auckland. She was part of a team that regularly went out fishing and I was there with my dad, meeting a client.'

'Tell me about your dad and your business.'

'Okay. My dad owns a real estate company based in Auckland called Mykanos Estates. He came over here from Cyprus because he didn't like the way the country was being partitioned by the Turks, who invaded in 1973. I think he lost a lot of land as a result. But we still have a business in Cyprus. Mykanos NZ is an extension of the original business and continues to be successful.

'So is it a fair assumption to make that you're a Mykanos?'

'It is,' she replied. 'Anyway, after school I went to college doing business studies before joining the company. I never fancied university.'

'So, do you have any brothers or sisters in the business?'

'No, just me. I'm the natural heir.'

'So how do you feel about that?'

'Excited. I love the business, always have from the day I started work. Now it's your turn,' Loretta said.

'Okay, if you'll excuse me just a second.' Nathan walked into the kitchen and pulled a bottle of white wine from the fridge. He grabbed two glasses and returned to the table. 'I know you're driving but will you join me in a glass of Chardonnay?'

'Do you need a drink to tell me about yourself?' Loretta said, teasing him.

'No not at all, but it helps,' he replied, smiling.

Nathan poured two glasses of wine from the bottle, which was now dripping with condensation on its outer surface. He started with his time in the police, the death of his mother and father and then the incident playing rugby.

'And somehow, I ended up here, thanks to Millie. To think, I could still be at home in my flat and repeatedly going out every day to museums and libraries to keep myself entertained. If I sound like a sad person Loretta, I'm not. I just went through a bad patch. I was taking everything I said and did too seriously. Well, not anymore.'

'Good for you. So this is like a fresh start for you over here?'

'Well, yes. I still have my flat in London. A neighbour's looking after it for me, but yes, I'm going to try to forge a new life over here.'

'What about a job and earning a living?' Loretta enquired.

'I'm lucky that I inherited some money when Mum and Dad died and I have the compensation from my injury, so I'm in no desperate hurry. But Chris works from home on the world's stock markets and he's offered to show me the ropes to see if I fancy gambling some of my inheritance for a quick profit.'

'I take it by the look of this house that he's good at his job.'

'Either that or he's a particularly good criminal,' replied Nathan. Loretta laughed and he noticed that, when she did, she had a small dimple in each cheek that was extremely attractive.

'So, I guess at some point you're going to need a place of your own, or are you going to be staying in the granny flat?'

'No, I'm lucky that I know a particularly good real estate company and I know the boss's daughter.'

'Is that so? Well I hope you get a good deal when the time comes.' Nathan noticed Loretta watching him over the rim of her wine glass as she took another sip.

It was early evening now and the temperature had dropped ever so slightly.

'I've made a big mistake,' said Loretta out of the blue. Nathan's heart dropped with disappointment.

'What's the matter?' he asked.

'I've had too much to drink, so I can't drive. I never leave myself in a vulnerable position like this.'

'I'm sorry Loretta, I didn't mean to—'

Loretta interrupted him. 'It's not your fault, I was enjoying myself, relaxing and chatting.'

'I'll pay for a taxi for you to get home, it's not a problem,' Nathan offered.

'It is because I'll be at home and my car will be here. I have appointments in the morning. I should have stayed in the hotel at Whangarei. That was the plan for tonight.'

Nathan wasn't sure what to say. He was worried about inflaming the situation. 'Well, stay here. There are plenty of rooms, so you can take your pick. It will be nice to have some company.'

Loretta thought about Nathan's proposal for a few seconds. 'I'm sorry. This obviously wasn't planned,' she said, looking rather embarrassed, but the alcohol in her blood was giving her more confidence. She picked up the bottle of wine and topped up both glasses. 'Thank you, I'll accept your kind offer. I've got an overnight bag in my car. I'll go and get it.'

'I don't suppose you have a swimming costume with you?'

'Of course I do, I'm a New Zealand girl,' Loretta replied as she walked off towards her car.

Nathan felt really happy, a feeling he didn't recognise as having had for many years. When she returned, Loretta had a small black cabin-type case with a handle extending from the top.

'This contains my life-support system. Whenever I travel up north or down south, this case always comes with me to enable a stay over in a local hotel. I would rather do that and get up early the next morning and travel then.'

'That makes sense. Now let me take you up to your room.'

Nathan took Loretta upstairs and she chose a room at the back of the house that overlooked the swimming pool. 'I'll be down shortly; I'm just going to freshen up,' she said.

'Okay,' Nathan replied as he made his way back downstairs. He went back down to the patio area and sat down to enjoy his wine. A few minutes later there was a loud splash from the swimming pool. Nathan rushed around to see Loretta just stepping out of the pool. She threw her hair back into a temporary ponytail and squeezed it to wring out the water.

She was wearing a red costume. She had a beautiful figure and looked to Nathan as if she kept herself trim but was by no means skinny. The pool water glistened on her olive skin as she walked towards him. She kissed him on the lips gently and quickly took his hand and walked towards the swimming pool. As they got close to the edge, she caught him off guard, kissed him again then immediately pushed him into the pool. She jumped in after him and Nathan removed his wet T-shirt, revealing his muscular frame. He took her in his arms and they kissed passionately.

After their swim, Nathan fired up the gas barbecue and cooked the skewered prawns. They sat there in damp towels enjoying the skewers, caressing each other and drinking a second bottle of Chardonnay.

Later, after Loretta had made her way up to bed, Nathan remained downstairs doing some last-minute tidying up. He then made his way up the stairs and walked quietly past her bedroom door. He heard the door open behind him, so he turned around and Loretta was standing there in a vest top and knickers. He walked over to her and took her head in the palms of his hands and kissed her. 'Thank you, I've really enjoyed this evening,' he said.

'So have I.' Loretta took his hand and pulled him into her bedroom. He closed the door behind them.

~~~

The following morning, Nathan awoke to no sign of Loretta, then he heard her coming out of the en-suite. She walked over to him. She was dressed for work in her suit and a blue stripy blouse. 'Good morning,' she said, 'did you sleep well?'

'Very well, thank you,' Nathan replied.

'I'll have to go now. The traffic will be building on its way into Auckland, but I just want to thank you for a great night.' Loretta leaned over and kissed him.

Nathan could smell her minty breath and floral perfume. 'Can we see each other again soon?' he said.

'Yes, call me. I have to go.'

Loretta left the room and a couple of minutes later Nathan heard her car going down the drive and the bleep from the kitchen as she passed through the gate alarm. He lay there thinking about the previous night and how good it was to feel a woman in his arms again. And how good it felt to have a woman in his life, a beautiful one at that. He hoped it stayed that way.

He must have dozed off, then he realised that his mobile was ringing in the kitchen downstairs. He got up and ran down but missed the call. It was from Rico. The mobile then pinged in his hand, Rico had messaged him:

Are you taking visitors?

Nathan replied:

Yes, how long?

Ten mins

Okay

Nathan went for a quick wash and brushed his teeth. He then went downstairs to the kitchen to make coffee and heard the gate alarm go off as Rico drove up the drive.

Rico appeared on the patio and Nathan opened the kitchen window and passed out two mugs of coffee. 'Good morning Rico.'

'Good morning,' Rico replied.

'I won't be a second.'

'Okay.'

Nathan had placed a couple of pieces of bread into the toaster, which had now popped up. He buttered the toast, grabbed two plates and went outside. 'How are you?' he asked Rico.

'Just the same. Stressed and unable to get any breaks with these murders. Just not having any luck. I can't see a church connection other than they both went to the same church. The murders and the way they were carried out ... there just aren't any similarities, there's no method.'

'But there doesn't have to be a method Rico. That's what you look for in a serial killer. Two murders carried out by the same person doesn't make them a serial killer. I agree with you that they were both totally different the way they were carried out. Brenda's murder to me looked like the murderer was searching for past church information and, when unsuccessful, finished her off so she couldn't testify.

'Whereas Martin looked to me as if he was tortured for information, and again, when the murderer didn't get the information they wanted, and in fear of being identified later, felt the need to take the vicar's life. And don't forget, previous to all this was the break-in at the church. It's almost as if the attacker had maybe taken some information at the time of the break-in, maybe names and addresses of people that could potentially help to achieve their goal.

'They could have been to the vicar's house previously, but when they realised he was out of town, picked one of the other people on the list, and unfortunately for Brenda, she was next. Whoever's doing this, I think is still looking for information, which leaves Margaret the churchwarden and all the other members of the congregation vulnerable, particularly if their names and address details were stolen.'

'As good as your theory is, it's all supposition and we don't even know what the hell this person's looking for.'

'Whatever it is, I don't think they found it. The answer could be in the church documents at our disposal but that's all we've got at the moment,' said Nathan. Rico remained quiet, looking tense with worry.

'I've spoken to Margaret. She's absolutely terrified already without knowing that she could be on some sort of hit list,' Nathan continued. 'She isn't fit to be interviewed and I don't think she will be for a while. If you want, I could go to see her on a welfare visit and see if I can gently prise anything out of her. If Millie were here, she would want to go and comfort her.'

'Well you know I can't authorise you to do that,' said Rico.

'Yes, and I know I don't have to do it, but like I said, it's a welfare visit and I'm genuinely concerned for her.'

'Okay, but if you find anything out, I'll need to know immediately.'

'You're just using me for coffee and information aren't you Detective Inspector?'

Rico thought about it for a few seconds and said, 'Yes, that's very intuitive of you Nathan.' Both men smiled and shook hands before Rico stood up and left.

Then Nathan remembered he hadn't mentioned about last night, so he caught up with Rico just as he started down the drive. Rico lowered the passenger window. 'There's something I forgot to mention,' said Nathan. 'I had a visitor last night. Loretta on her way back from Whangarei.'

'Oh, really? And how did that go?'

'We had a brilliant evening.' Nathan was beaming now.

'Don't tell me she slept over.'

'She did.'

'You're an incredibly lucky Englishman to have one of our fine New Zealand women on your arm.'

'I know,' said Nathan, banging the roof of the car. Rico drove off. *Isn't that one of my sayings – a woman on your arm?* Nathan thought. He hoped it was true.

Later that morning, Nathan called Margaret to see whether he could drop round to see how she was. She was a bit hesitant but she gave him her address and he made his way to her house, on the same road as Brenda Massey and Rico's parents. On arrival, Nathan parked his car and approached the rather smart-looking wooden-clad bungalow painted in white, which was typical of the town.

The front door opened as Nathan approached the bungalow and he was shocked by Margaret's appearance. He immediately felt sorry for her. Towering over her, he put his arms around her and gave her a big hug. Margaret sobbed deeply then invited him into the lounge. 'Would you like a tea or coffee Nathan?' she asked.

'Only if you're making one. Please don't make it especially for me.'

'I'm making tea,' she replied.

'That will be fine.'

Margaret walked into the kitchen and Nathan heard cups and saucers being taken out of a cupboard. Looking around the lounge he could see some old photographs of Margaret and what he assumed to be her husband and daughter. There were some nice glass ornamental figures on a shelf above a free-standing log burner with a flu, which went up through the roof. He noticed a small wooden cross that could fit into the palm of your hand, which was positioned on a bible on a small table next to what appeared to be Margaret's chair.

Margaret walked into the room with a tray loaded with a teapot, two cups and saucers, milk and sugar bowls, spoons and a plate of digestive biscuits. 'I'm sorry for letting my emotions get the better of me,' she said apologetically.

'You've done nothing wrong and there's no need to apologise.'

'You know, when you've worked together like me and Reverend Martin for so long, you do become best friends and we genuinely liked each other. He used to say that I should be on the payroll for everything that I do. Of course, I would never take a cent; that's the accepted role of a churchwarden. He was a loving, caring man Nathan, he really was.'

'And that's how you'll remember him.'

'I will.'

'Changing the subject,' Nathan said, 'I noticed the old photographs. Is that you with your husband and daughter?'

'That's right. Great memories. Unfortunately, Arthur died twenty years ago this year. Lucy was only seven when he died, but it was expected, as he had suffered from cancer since his early thirties.'

'And when I spoke to you the other day, you said you were babysitting.'

'That's right, I have my granddaughter, May. I look after her before and after school and during the school holidays. She's a good child and has recently started at the Sunday school at our church, but now I don't know what's going to happen.'

Margaret started to pour the tea. 'Would you like to put your own milk and sugar in?'

'Yes, that's fine. It's just milk for me anyway.'

'I've had the police around asking me whether I know of any reason why anyone should want to harm Martin,' said Margaret. 'But as soon as they asked the question I just broke down. Thinking of him in the vestry, an innocent God-loving man who did his best for the community, confronted by some crazed maniac. He must have been so frightened. I even said a prayer for you because I know that you found him.'

Nathan hoped that Margaret wasn't going to ask him how Martin had died or what condition he was in. 'You don't need to worry about me Margaret. Unfortunately, when I was in the police in London I used to come across death on a weekly basis and I learned to compartmentalise the things I saw. Those thoughts never go away but it's a structure that I have, to deal with such things. The main issue for all concerned is that the perpetrator is captured and put behind bars.'

'I know,' Margaret agreed.

Nathan thought this may be as good a time as any. 'Margaret, do you mind if I ask you some questions?'

'As long as it's not about Reverend Martin.'

'Well actually no, it isn't. Would you know whether there was a record of all your church members in the vestry?'

'What do you mean by record?'

'A list or a series of documents showing their names and addresses.'

'Let me just think for a minute.'

'It's okay, take your time.' Nathan had a drink of tea and a biscuit.

'There really shouldn't be any names and addresses in the church,' Margaret said. 'There's an electoral roll with a list of names and addresses of regular givers to the church. They're also allowed to vote on any church issues. But I keep that here.'

'Do you think I could see it?'

'Well, it is confidential.'

'I understand, but just a quick look.'

Fresh tears appeared in Margaret's eyes but Nathan waited. He felt as if he was being harsh on Margaret but it was the only way to find out what he needed to know.

'Okay,' Margaret said as she got up from her chair and went out of the room. She reappeared very quickly with a small hardback book. 'This is it,' she said. 'There are years and years of electoral roll information in this book. Most of these people are dead.' The tears ran down her face.

'I'm sorry Margaret, I shouldn't be asking you these things not so soon after—'

'It's alright,' she interrupted him, and turned to the current page in the book. She then turned the book around to show him. He saw a list of names and addresses and an amount written in a column at the end of the page.

'There aren't many names,' said Nathan.

'I know, only sixteen in total. Most people like to pay in cash and only when they attend. Most love the church but don't want to be involved with the running of it or making any decisions that may affect it.'

'I notice Brenda isn't on the list,' said Nathan.

'I know. She had been saying for years that she wanted to set up a standing order to the church but she never got round to doing it I suppose. And she never seemed to want to have to vote on any issues within the church. She just loved attending and loved the people.'

'I notice that your name and Reverend Martin's aren't on the list either.'

'No, I know. It's just a given that we're automatically on the electoral roll.'

'Margaret, could I please take a photograph of the list? I promise you I'll keep it to myself, in confidence.'

Margaret hesitated and looked Nathan in the eye. 'In strictest confidence,' she said.

'I promise,' he replied.

'Then I place my trust in you Nathan.'

Nathan took her hand briefly and thanked her. He then used his mobile phone to take a quick photo before she changed her mind. 'Thanks Margaret, I've taken up enough of your time.'

'You're always welcome.'

'I know that you have my number, so if you feel the need to call me, please do. Remember, I'm not a police officer, I'm here as a friend. In the meantime, if you think of any other records that were or may still be in the vestry that contain names and addresses, will you please contact me?'

'Yes, I will Nathan, but I have to ask, is this anything to do with the two murders?'

Nathan was struggling to reply when a cat walked into the room, allowing him to divert the conversation. 'Who's this little fellah then?'

'This is my cat Lucky, and she's a girl,' said Margaret in disgust as if Nathan should have noticed.

'How old is your kitten?' Nathan asked.

'She's not a kitten, she's fourteen years old.'

Nathan had difficulty keeping a straight face. This was a cat with a kitten's head and a kink in its tail. He picked the cat up. 'I've got to say this Margaret, your cat has got an exceedingly small head.'

'You think I don't know? Everyone comments when they see her. I don't think her head has grown since she was about four months old and that kink has been in her tail since she was born, poor thing.'

'I don't think she's poor,' said Nathan. 'I think she's the luckiest cat in the world.'

'She is. She's my friend and my companion,' said Margaret.

Nathan put the cat down and took the opportunity to say his goodbyes before any more difficult questions came his way. He thanked Margaret for the tea and biscuits and reminded her that he was at the end of the phone if she needed him.

Nathan drove back to Fern Heights, where he went into the room where he and Loretta had spent the night. He could smell her perfume on the sheets and the pillows. He smiled to himself and hoped he would see her again soon. He then removed the pillowcases and the bed linen; he couldn't leave them until Millie got back. He didn't know how she would react when she found out that Loretta had stayed over. He took the bed linen downstairs and loaded the items into the washing machine and turned it on. It was normal for him to do his own washing, but he always asked Millie to do the ironing. Maybe this time he would have to do his own.

After pouring himself a glass of cool orange juice, Nathan walked out on to the patio and sat down at his usual seat. There was something bothering him, something at the back of his mind niggling away at him as if he had forgotten something. He looked at the photo he had taken at Margaret's of the list of sixteen people but it didn't mean anything to him. He recalled the initial break-in at the church. Everything had happened since that original break-in when paperwork and box files were strewn all over the vestry. The intruder hadn't been anywhere else in the church. It was as if they were looking for a document or documents. And the murder of Brenda Massey occurred after the break-in at the church. The intruder must have got her personal details from the vestry, so must have taken something or written something down. They could have written on one of the many Post-it note pads that were in the vestry and left an imprint on the note below.

His mobile was ringing. It was Margaret. 'Hi Margaret.'

'Hi Nathan, I'm sorry to bother you but there was one thing that I thought of regarding names and addresses.'

'Okay, that's fine, carry on Margaret.'

'There was a small box of church collection envelopes on top of a filing cabinet. On the lid of each box there's a name and address window that we always fill in because if someone can't make it to church, we drop them off at their homes.'

'Sorry, just to clarify, there were several church envelopes individually boxed and addressed to members of the church?' enquired Nathan.

'Yes, that's correct.'

Nathan could feel something building. Could this be the platform he needed to build a case to hand over to Rico? 'Margaret, if you don't mind, I would like to come round and borrow your church keys. I would like to have another look around the vestry.'

'That's all right. I presume the police have finished in there?'

'I'll find out when I get there,' Nathan replied.

Nathan immediately drove to Margaret's, collected the keys and arrived at the church a few minutes later. The car park was empty so the police had obviously done their thing and left. He got out of the SUV and walked towards the church doors. He was reminded of the sight that greeted him the last time he entered the vestry but this time he pushed the door open slowly and was greeted by a chemical odour, which he presumed was something to do with the forensics people or cleaning products that had been used.

He switched the light on as it was still dark due to the boarded-up window. The first thing he noticed was that the room looked totally different. The majority of the carpet tiles had been removed, one of the chairs and the desk were missing. Documents and binders were just piled up on top of the filing cabinet or on the floor in the corner of the room. He was pleased to see that all the blood-soaked items were gone, and no doubt being scrutinised by the police.

The first thing Nathan looked for was a small cardboard box containing individually boxed collection envelopes. He could see such a box on top of some box files on a wooden shelf. He managed to reach the box and lifted it down. It was full of part-used candles. He noticed on the same shelf a small box that had been crushed up against the wall by a heavy box file. He moved the box file first, which contained some small brass candle holders. He reached for the crushed box from the rear of the shelf, lifted it down and opened the lid.

He had found the boxes of collection envelopes complete with names and addresses. Slotted in a gap down the side of the envelope boxes it looked as if there was a small notepad. Nathan stopped for a moment and put the box down. He realised that there was a good chance that this box and the notepad had been touched by the murderer. He rang Rico on his mobile.

Rico answered quickly and sounded harassed. 'I'm just going into a meeting with the chief.'

'I may have something of interest in the church vestry.'

'Okay, I can't come now but I'll send someone else.' Rico hung up.

A short while later, Nathan heard the gravel crunching beneath the wheels of a car as it pulled into the car park. He could hear two men talking as they got out of the car and approached the church. The first man entered.

'Hi, I'm Detective Mike Lima. I believe you called us.'

Nathan was about to reply when DI Tim Broadwell walked in behind Detective Lima. 'You know who I am Mason,' DI Broadwell said sternly.

Nathan immediately felt deep animosity towards this man, remembering how he had treated him when he was in custody. He thought he would reply in kind, 'Unfortunately, Broadwell, yes I do.' The two men locked eyes for a few seconds.

Broadwell walked up to Nathan. 'Have I done something to upset you or are you like this with everyone?' said Nathan.

'I don't like Poms coming over here sticking their noses in,' said Broadwell. Detective Lima shuffled on his feet and looked embarrassed.

Nathan didn't know what to say. He had never been called a Pom before. He didn't find it very offensive but knew it was supposed to be. 'Do you always upset people that try to help you?' he asked..

'You're not helping; you're a hindrance. A jumped-up failed ex-cop who thinks he's god's gift because he was in the Metropolitan Police in London.'

It took everything that Nathan had to control himself. Broadwell was goading him, and as much as Nathan wanted to take him down, he knew that was what Broadwell wanted him to do.

Detective Lima intervened. 'Why did you call us?'

'I called Rico Manu.'

'Is there something that you want to tell us or show us?' asked Lima.

'No, I've changed my mind. I've been insulted by your boss enough.'

'I've a good mind to take you in for wasting police time,' said Broadwell. Nathan knew he was right, but he was now determined more than ever that he wasn't going to help the police, especially anything that involved Broadwell. He kept quiet and just glared at the DI.

'I'm watching you Mason, you useless time-waster,' warned Broadwell, and with that both men turned, walked out of the vestry and left the church.

Nathan was still angry but breathed a sigh of relief. Broadwell's last comment was spinning around in his head: *I'm watching you Mason, you useless time-waster.* Nathan picked up the box and on his way out to his SUV he locked the church doors behind him. He then called at Margaret's to drop the keys off but she had gone out, so he left them in her mailbox, as he expected she would soon be back.

It was noticeable as Nathan drove through Wellsford that the number of police cars on SH1 had increased. There were two parked up by the road to the rugby ground and one near the service station. Another appeared in Nathan's rear-view mirror as he approached the golf club turn-off. As it overtook him it seemed to slow for a second and he had the feeling that they were having a good look at him. He expected to be pulled over, but the car just raced on ahead.

He switched the radio on to the local news channel and the newsreader was giving a bulletin on the Wellsford murders. There had been no significant breakthroughs, although an Englishman from the Dome Valley area had been held and released without charge. Nathan was amazed that information such as his detention should make the local news. *Are they going to advertise every time they detain someone for questioning? They must be really struggling with this case.* He needed to make sure he stayed away from Broadwell at all costs.

Driving South on SH1, Nathan drove past his turn-off to Fern Heights then turned around further down the road and approached from the south before turning in. He was still very conscious of the possibility of being watched, particularly by Broadwell and his sidekicks.

He made his way back to the house and placed the box on the patio table, then went into the kitchen and came back with a pair of latex gloves from the cleaning cupboard. He slipped them on and carefully took out the notepad from the box. As he suspected, there was an imprint on the notepad of what had been written on the page above it before it was torn off.

The person who had written the note must have been heavy-handed because the imprint was plain to see. It was a perfect bold impression of Brenda Massey's address in capital letters. Nathan felt a rush of blood that reminded him of when they had made a breakthrough in a Crime Squad enquiry. It was a feeling he liked and one that he never thought he would experience again in his life. But here he was in a foreign country carrying out his own enquiries and the feeling was back. It was all-consuming and he knew it.

Nathan went into the kitchen and made himself a coffee. He went outside and just sat there enjoying another beautiful day, watching two dragonflies buzzing each other like two Second World War aeroplanes. His mobile rang. It was Rico.

'Hi Rico.'

'Nathan, what the fuck are you doing?'

'Why? What's up?' replied Nathan.

'What's up!' Rico shouted. 'My chief has just had me by the balls in his office and in front of Broadwell, saying that you've been wasting police time … fucking Broadwell about. He's talking about bringing you in for some trumped-up charges, and I'm taking the shit because you're my friend.'

'Well that Broadwell is an offensive bastard,' replied Nathan.

'That may be the case but he's gunning for you, and the chief is gunning for me. It's like a pressure cooker in here. I've got to warn you to stay away from anything to do with this case, otherwise you're going to screw it up for all of us, and unlike some, I can't afford to lose my job.'

'It was you that sent Broadwell out to the church.'

'I asked Lima. He works for me directly, but Broadwell must have overheard, or Lima told him.'

'Okay, I'll stay away as long as you take surveillance off me.'

'Surveillance? What are you talking about? This is Wellsford not London. We've got better things to do with our time.'

'What, like catching murderers you mean?' said Nathan.

'And what's that supposed to mean?'

'Well, you're obviously struggling for suspects because I heard on the radio before that a man from England living in Dome Valley was arrested and released. Would it not be better keeping stuff like that confidential for the sake of me and the enquiry?'

'I'm sorry but I didn't release that information.'

'I'm sorry too,' replied Nathan, 'but before you completely hang me out to dry, there's something here that I picked up at the church vestry and I would like to hand it over to you.'

'Can you drop it in at the police station?' said Rico.

'No, I'm not going anywhere near that place. If you want it, come and get it. If you don't, that's fine. And by the way, what exactly did you mean when you said that unlike some you couldn't afford to lose your job? I would like to point out that I didn't lose my job, I was medically discharged and paid an amount equivalent to about five years' pay. I'm allowed to live the life I please because my parents were murdered when I was twenty-seven years old and I'm living off my inheritance.'

'Right, okay,' replied Rico and hung up.

Nathan was upset, annoyed, angry and he realised that his friendship with Rico was over. After a few minutes he started to wonder whether he had overreacted. He decided to write everything down about the visit to Margaret's and the church and what he had found out so far about the murders. He wrote his theory down in full and in longhand. As far as he was concerned, he was drawing a line under the issue and he was no longer helping Rico or the police.

Dear Rico

This is a record of my findings on the Massey and Martin murders.

There was a break-in at Wellsford Ecumenical Church. There is no evidence that anything was taken, and it appears that a person or persons unknown entered the vestry by breaking a window. They systematically went through several church documents held in ring binders, box files and hardback books. It appears that the alarm system activated when they opened the inner door to the corridor, so they made their escape back through the broken window.

1. Brenda Massey, a church elder, was murdered in her home soon after. I am not aware of the information relating to this incident.

2. I suspect that, due to the proximity timewise of the break-in at the church and the murder of Brenda Massey, they may be connected. There is a possibility that the address of Brenda Massey was obtained from the vestry. When it became apparent that Brenda was not privy to the information required by the attacker, he/she killed her. The next victim was the vicar, who while being tortured

was unable to provide the information required and died as a result of a slashing cut to his neck. I believe the vicar would have been the first victim and that the alarm activation at the church was to try to lure him in. Unfortunately for Brenda, the vicar was out of town and couldn't attend and, for whatever reason, the attacker chose her as victim number one.

3. As a rule, there are no details of the church members' names and addresses in the vestry. But it has come to light that there is a box containing several smaller boxes that contain empty church envelopes. These boxes were due to be hand-delivered to the recipients' homes and, as such, their names and addresses were written on the lid of each box. One of the boxes had Brenda Massey's name and address written on it. Working on the possibility that the attacker could have gained this information and written it down on a pad of paper, leaving an imprint on the page below, I looked for a pad and found one in the same cardboard box. There was an imprint on the pad showing Brenda Massey's address. I therefore believe it to be a copy of the murderer's handwriting. There is also the possibility that the attacker may have made a note of the other eight addresses, one of which is where I am staying at the home of my sister. So, the occupiers of all these addresses are potential victims.

4. The box and notepad is in my possession. The contents of the box have not been contaminated by my fingerprints and are ready for collection at Fern Heights.

Nathan Mason

Leaving the completed letter on the writing pad, Nathan walked through the kitchen and into Chris's study. It was the first time he had been in the room and it was nicely kitted out with a large brown Chesterfield-style revolving chair, which sat behind a large desk with three monitors, a desktop computer and a laptop.

The study looked directly out on to the drive and the garages. Nathan spotted a pair of binoculars on the windowsill. He knew Chris liked to know who was flying over in their private aircraft and quite often could identify who it was through an app on his tablet that displayed the aircraft's identification.

Nathan picked the binoculars up, finding that they were quite heavy, despite their small size. There was a small symbol on the side that had been worn out. All he could read was 'FLI' and underneath was 'IR bin'. He looked at the lenses and they were a shade of red. He realised that they must be FLIR thermal-imaging binoculars to see at night and would have cost thousands. He put them up to his face and focused them in. They worked as normal during the daytime, the zoom operating electronically with the push of a small toggle. He was looking forward to giving them a try in the dark.

Looking around the study, Nathan noticed a gun cabinet in the corner. He knew that Chris liked his shotguns and had been a licence holder for many years, but Nathan thought that leaving the key in the lock wasn't good practice. He turned the key and placed it in the top drawer of the desk.

With the feeling that he had intruded enough into Chris's study, Nathan saw a box of envelopes on the top of a filing cabinet, along with a ream of copier paper. He took one of the envelopes and left the study, closing the door behind him. He went back through the kitchen to the patio, tore his letter to Rico off the pad and placed it in the envelope. He wrote 'DI Rico Manu' on the front of the envelope and sealed it.

Nathan decided it was time for a swim and a cool down, so he grabbed a pair of his spare swimming shorts that had been left out to dry, got changed in the kitchen and went back outside. He had forgotten to cover the pool over so there were a few moths, leaves and other bits and pieces floating on the surface. There was a net on a long pole lying by the pool, so with a few scoops he removed most of the flotsam. After banging the net on the perimeter fence so that it emptied itself on to the grass away from the pool area, Nathan put the net down and allowed himself to just fall into the water. It was a perfect temperature – warm but not too warm as to not refresh the body.

Nathan's immediate thoughts reverted to the last time he was in the pool, with Loretta. The way they had held each other in the water and kissed, the softness of her skin and the sweetness of her breath. He was in Utopia and he hoped that she was too. He was lying on his back with his eyes closed, the sun beating down on his chest, face and stomach. The water just lapped over him, cooling the skin.

Suddenly, Nathan was distracted by a very slight burning smell. He adjusted his position so he was standing in the pool, looked around and carefully sniffed the air. He thought he could smell cigarette smoke. He looked at the hilly slopes around the house. On this side they were covered with radiata pine as far as he could see. There was only a slight breeze so there was a possibility it was drifting over from the drive or the private road.

Nathan jumped out of the pool and dried himself off. He slipped on his flip-flops and wrapped the damp towel around his waist. He walked around the front of the house, looking at the drive. He couldn't see the bottom end of the drive until he reached the other side of the house, but as he walked further round, he could see the drive was clear. He looked through the clearing in the trees and couldn't see anyone, then all of a sudden, a man appeared on the private road. He appeared to be having a leisurely stroll and a smoke until he saw Nathan standing by the house, at which point he did an about turn.

A couple of seconds later Nathan heard a car start and drive off from the private road. Unfortunately, it was hidden by the trees. There was no way he could run down there quickly enough. It was too far and the car would be well gone. He wished he had closed the gate on the bridge, not that it would stop anyone opening it. Suddenly he felt vulnerable.

Paranoia was creeping in again. What if he was being watched from the trees as well? If it was the police, why were they doing it? Could it be the murderer? If so, the chances were that whoever it was had obtained his address from the church envelopes in the vestry. He couldn't call the police for help anyway, not after this morning. He was on his own and he had to look after himself and his sister's home.

~~~

Later that afternoon, Detective Lima called at Fern Heights. Nathan invited him on to the patio and offered him a cold orange juice, which he accepted.

'Is this the stuff from the vestry?' asked Lima.

'Yes, there's a box with items in it, which I've put into this large polythene bag. And can you give this envelope to Rico please?'

'Sure, no problem.'

'How's the murder case going?' asked Nathan.

'You know I've been told not to say anything to you and to treat you like a member of the public.'

'That's okay. Is that by Broadwell or Rico?'

'Broadwell has been in the chief's ear. Personally, I think he's miffed because he's not in charge of the case and has to answer to Rico. I think world war three is going to break out pretty soon.'

'What about suspects?' enquired Nathan, trying his luck.

'We're still pulling people in, but in all honesty, it doesn't look good. We don't have any prints or DNA from Mrs Massey's. And in the church vestry we only found fingerprints belonging to the vicar, the churchwarden, a paramedic and you.'

'Well, you were always going to find mine. I arrived after the break-in and after Reverend Martin's murder.'

'I've said far too much already,' said Lima, then his mobile phone rang. From what Nathan could glean from the conversation, there had been a break-in at a house in Wellsford and the patrol officer on the scene was asking for a detective. Nathan passed Lima a notepad and he wrote down a name and address before tearing off the page and saying, 'Sorry, got to go, a domestic break-in. Thanks for the drink.'

'Just before you go, can I ask you another question? And if you don't mind, a simple yes or no would suffice,' said Nathan.

'Go on then,' said Lima with a sigh.

'Are the police following me?'

'Not that I know of. Mind you, I'm just a dogsbody; I'm not sure I would be told anyway. Why what makes you think we are?'

'Oh, I keep getting visitors, but they never come to the door. This is a private road, so there shouldn't be anyone coming up here but there is.'

'Maybe it's people just taking a wrong turn.'

Nathan knew that Lima was making light of it and probably didn't know anything, so he thought he would go along with him. 'Yes, you're right, it's probably nothing. Sorry, I'll let you get on your way,' he said as he handed Lima the bag and the envelope.

As soon as Lima had gone, Nathan went straight to the notepad that the detective had written on when he had taken the call on his mobile. He could see an imprint on the paper, so he went through to Chris's study and held the paper underneath the desktop light. Using the same method as he had with the note from the vestry, Nathan angled the paper so the bright light left a shadow. Although it was in longhand it looked as if Lima had written 'John Smallwood, 47 Lacly Lane, Wellsford'.

Nathan made a note of the name and address and made his way back to the patio. Surely this couldn't be connected to the church; it was too good to be true. He consulted the list he had made of the names and addresses on the church envelope boxes. Looking down the list he came across John Selwood, 42 Lady Lane, Wellsford. He couldn't believe what he was seeing; it had to be the same person. If it was, this was the murderer striking again. He picked up his mobile and called Margaret.

'Hi Margaret, sorry to disturb you again, its Nathan.'

'Hi Nathan, is everything okay?'

'Yes, all okay thanks. Listen, I've just had a visit from the police and I've handed some information over to them. While he was here, he took a phone call about a house break-in that had occurred in Wellsford today.'

'Oh right. Anyone we know?' Margaret asked.

'That's why I'm ringing. Who's John Selwood, 42 Lady Lane?'

'Oh no, that will be John, the church treasurer, but he's in an old people's home now, in Warkworth.'

'I'm relieved to hear that. So the house was empty?'

'Yes, he only moved out a couple of weeks ago, so I assume all his things are still in there.'

'So, if he's the treasurer, who's doing the accounts now?'

'Well, I said I would do them when nobody else volunteered. I could do without it really, but we had no choice. Oh, I do hope they haven't done too much damage. He would be so upset.'

'Are you very friendly with him?' asked Nathan.

'Oh yes, we've known each other for years. I only went to see him the other day, to see that he had settled in the home.'

'And had he?'

'Yes, he seemed fine.'

'Does he have any other visitors?'

'I don't think he has any relatives. That's why I went to see him, and to ask him what needs to be done with the accounts on a weekly basis. Otherwise they just wouldn't get done. Do you think it would be wrong of me to go around to his house just to see if everything is okay?'

Nathan was hoping she would say that. 'Not at all,' he replied. 'I think it's a good idea, and if you want to go to see him afterwards, I'll take you to the home if you direct me.'

'Okay, I'll call you later.'

~~~

Later that afternoon, Margaret called Nathan back. She had been to John Selwood's house but had to wait while the forensics people finished their investigation. She told Nathan that she hadn't been able to tell how much was missing but the spare bedroom that John used as a study had been ransacked. He also had a small combination safe that Margaret knew was bolted to the floor under his desk. It looked as if someone had used a lot of force to remove it.

She said that she needed to go to see John and had rung ahead to make sure it was okay for her to visit.

A short while later, Nathan picked up Margaret and they were on their way to Warkworth to give John the bad news. They arrived at the home, which was a low-level two-storey modern building made of brick with tiled roofing. Margaret told Nathan that it had thirty rooms and was home to people over the age of 70. It was a privately-run organisation and as such was well maintained and cared for by the owners.

Margaret pointed to a window at the front on the ground floor. 'That's his room,' she said.

Nathan parked the car almost directly outside. 'I think I should perhaps stay in the car,' he suggested. 'We don't know each other, and I don't think he would appreciate a stranger in his room.'

'If you give me five minutes with him, I'm sure that when he realises that Millie's brother is outside, he'll want you to come in. He's as sharp as a pin and has all his faculties. You'll see. Keep your eyes on the window. It will be either a thumbs up or thumbs down.' With that, Margaret got out of the car and walked towards the entrance door.

Nathan kept his eye on the window and sure enough Margaret appeared to give him the thumbs up. He got out of the car and made his way through the entrance. It was very smart, a bit like a high-end hotel reception. The receptionist asked him who he wanted to see and then called the room before allowing him through an electrically operated secure door to the accommodation facility.

Margaret was waiting in the corridor and waved Nathan through, then he followed her into a large lounge area where

John was sitting on a chair in the corner. Nathan walked up to him and introduced himself. 'Hi, I'm Nathan Mason, Millie's brother.'

John held out a long bony hand. 'Nice to meet you. I'm John. Please take a seat.' Nathan sat down on a sofa next to Margaret, positioned directly opposite John.

The room looked wonderfully comfortable. One wall was completely lined with books. From what Nathan could see from where he was sitting it looked as if there were many religious and historical books. He thought they looked to be an interesting collection.

'What brings you to New Zealand?' asked John. Nathan was surprised at his confident and strong voice.

'Well, I'm staying with Millie and Chris with a view to a permanent move.'

'So is this your first visit?' John enquired.

'No, I've been a few times before.'

'So, what's the hold-up? You've seen what a beautiful country this is.' John burst into a loud hysterical laugh. 'I hope you don't mind but I can be rather frank at times and it's got me into trouble in the past.'

'Not at all. Why beat around the bush when you can get straight to the point.' John laughed loudly again and Nathan couldn't help but join in with this jovial pleasant man.

'What do you do for a living?' John asked.

'I was medically discharged from the Metropolitan Police in London,' Nathan replied.

John's face changed from jovial to caring in a second. 'That's awful Nathan. What happened? If you don't mind me asking.'

'Not at all. I was playing for the police rugby team when the scrum collapsed. I was trampled and suffered a clot to the head. That night I had a stroke and was never able to recover to the satisfaction of my bosses.'

'That's terrible, it really is. But what's good is that you've recovered to the point where nobody would know what has happened to you.'

'I know but unfortunately it wasn't enough to satisfy my bosses. I've lost a lot of my memory. Many years' worth in fact. That was part of the problem. I couldn't remember certain laws or legislation or even people and cases that I had worked on in the past.'

'And what was your role in the police Nathan?'

'I was a Detective Sergeant in charge of the Crime Squad, expecting a promotion to Inspector this year.'

'I feel for you Nathan, I really do. What are your plans now?' John asked.

'Millie's husband Chris works on the world stock markets from home, and he said he would introduce me to the markets, show me how things work to see if I would be interested in investing and making money.'

'Well I know he's worth a bob or two, so it sounds as if he may know the secrets of making money.' John laughed loudly again.

Margaret interrupted before they could continue. 'John, there's been a break-in at your house.'

'I know, I had a call from the police. What's the damage?' John said nonchalantly.

'I had a quick walk around but it looks as if they were more interested in your spare room, the one you use as a study. It was mainly church invoices from years ago. They just seem to have spread them everywhere as if they were looking for something. And John, I'm sorry, but they've taken your safe from under the desk.'

'Oh, I did give you last year's accounts, didn't I Margaret? They were in the large plastic box with the lid.'

'Yes, you did,' Margaret assured him.

'Thank goodness,' John said, then he looked pensive all of a sudden. He dropped his head and put his hands to his face. Nathan thought he was about to cry.

Margaret rather unsensitively said, 'I hope there wasn't much in the safe.'

John looked at her and said, 'Well there was, but fortunately for me I emptied it before I moved here.' He laughed out loud.

Nathan thought John had played them a treat, pretending to look concerned when really he didn't seem to give a damn about the safe, the house or anything. He wondered what medication he was on because whatever it was it was good.

John suddenly changed the subject and now looked seriously at both of them. 'What on earth is happening to the church?' he said. 'What's the world coming to when innocent people are murdered in their homes or in a place of worship? Who's doing this and why? The poor vicar and Brenda Massey … it's like something you read from a gangland murder scene or a mafia dossier. The police should be doing more. They should be pulling people up from Auckland to work on this. They should be flooding the place with cops, both uniform and plain clothes.'

'They are doing,' Nathan assured him. 'I have a friend, Rico Manu, and he's running the investigation. He's come up from Auckland.'

'Yes, I know Rico and his family. They're good people,' said John. Is that how you got involved in this mess?'

'Well I got involved through Millie after the first break-in at the church. We went to help Margaret. They had trashed the vestry looking through documents.'

'I wonder whether they found what they were looking for. What could be so valuable to them?' John asked.

'I'm not aware of what if anything was taken apart from possibly names and addresses of the congregation through their gift envelope boxes. And I know there's an old Church Council minute book missing from when the church was built in 1969, which referred to all the benefactors of the church.'

'I remember,' John said. 'I wasn't on the Church Council then but we all used to talk about the mysterious person who had supposedly donated a bar of gold to the church to complete the build. He or she wished to remain anonymous. In fact, the previous treasurer handed the plastic box to me; you know, the one I gave to you Margaret.'

'Yes,' Margaret replied.

'If my memory serves me correctly, the bottom of the box is lined by an old minute book,' said John. 'It's jammed in there. I've tried on numerous occasions to get it out but didn't want to damage it in the process. It's probably still in there beneath the lever arch files.'

'I can't say I've looked,' said Margaret. 'I'm just the caretaker for the treasurer's role. I have too much to do already as the churchwarden.'

This was music to Nathan's ears. The missing minute book could be at the bottom of a plastic box in Margaret's house and she didn't even know. 'Perhaps we could have a look later if it's alright with you Margaret,' said Nathan in anticipation.

'Okay,' she replied.

'Margaret, I have a favour to ask,' said John. 'I'm putting the house on the market and I was wondering whether on occasion you could call in to see that everything is alright. You still do have keys, don't you?'

'Yes, I do, and I'll do as you ask.'

'Thank you Margaret, you're a good woman and I don't know what I would have done without you over the years. The same goes for the church; you're a stalwart of the community.'

'As you still are,' Margaret replied, standing up and going over to John to stroke his hand. These were two old friends comforting each other and Nathan was quite touched and briefly felt as if he was intruding on a private moment.

As Margaret sat down, John asked, 'Now how's that sister of yours doing Nathan?'

'Unfortunately, she's over in Melbourne. Her mother-in-law died on the day they moved her to a hospice, so her and Chris have been busy planning and doing all the legal stuff. She probably won't be back until after the funeral, maybe the back end of next week.'

'Please send her my regards. I've not been able to get to church since my legs went. Damn bone cancer.'

'I have a feeling that she may want to come to see you when she gets back. When she realises that I've been to your new home, she won't want to miss out,' said Nathan.

'I would love that,' John replied. 'A good-looking woman is Millie. A bit too young for me though I fear.' He gave a cheeky wink before changing the topic of conversation yet again. 'By the way Margaret, I've arranged to have the window boarded up and reglazed. It was a company the police recommended so you don't need to worry about that. Everything else that's in the house is going to be removed and put into storage. They'll come here and get my key and then return it to me when they're finished so that I can sign all the documents and so on.'

'You're very organised,' said Nathan.

'Yes, I suppose I am; always have been. I guess it's the accountancy background. Everything has to be planned and in its place.'

Before Margaret and Nathan left, John exchanged mobile numbers with both of his visitors in case there were any further incidents at his house. When Nathan expressed an interest in the history books in the room, John said he must return soon, then he could have his pick of the books to borrow. Nathan was delighted and agreed to stay in touch.

On the way back to Wellsford, Margaret was clock-watching because she had to collect her granddaughter May from school. So, when they arrived at Margaret's house, she invited Nathan in and showed him a large transparent plastic box with its lid. It was very heavy and had been placed at the back of the hall cupboard, so Nathan pulled it from its place.

He could see the minute book at the bottom of the box, so he excitedly emptied the box of its lever arch files and placed them back in the cupboard. The minute book was well jammed in at the bottom. Nathan took the box away with him and was looking forward to getting back to Fern Heights to see what the book contained.

On his way home, he did his usual drive by and U-turn to approach from the other direction. He drove slowly across the wooden bridge then closed the gate behind him. He did the same with the drive gates. He couldn't see any evidence of any further visitors.

He carried the box into the kitchen and placed it on the worktop, then turned the box upside down and banged it on its base. The book wasn't budging so he went to fetch a hacksaw from Chris's toolbox in the garage and slowly began to cut through the box. He ended up with the book stuck in what looked like a plastic tray. After cutting a slot in each corner with the saw, he was able to bend the plastic, which shattered like a piece of brittle Perspex. The minute book was loose.

Picking the book up, Nathan noticed on the front that someone had written '1968 to 1969'. He went to the very last meeting in the book. He recognised the names listed in the meeting from the minutes that he had already read. There was a long paragraph from the vicar relating to the finished church and how delighted he was with the progress and the fact that it had been completed on time. He went on to give thanks to the many people involved and stated that without the donation from the mystery benefactor the project couldn't have gone ahead.

Nathan noticed at the end of the line that someone had written the letters C. W. in feint pencil. He went back to the top of the minutes to see the attendees and again at the end of the line in pencil were the letters C. W. Maybe these were the initials of the mystery benefactor. They could possibly have attended this meeting by special invitation. The vicar had written the initials down to perhaps remind readers in the future who had made the donation. This was, of course, totally disrespecting the benefactor's right to remain anonymous, other than to the Church Council members. But then again, the vicar probably never expected these minute books to see the light of day again, just to sit at the back of a dusty cupboard or in this case the bottom of a plastic box.

This could be a big breakthrough. *C. W. could be the person the murderer is looking for*, Nathan thought to himself. This was just a hunch and he could be wrong. There was also the chance that C. W. could be dead and buried, but Nathan was determined to find out. He knew that Margaret was in possession of the electoral roll book, so he decided he would give her a call first thing in the morning.

13

ONE WEEK earlier Trent Allen had been at his camper van. He was sitting outside on a fold-up chair with a small, white plastic table in front of him. On the table were a few local history books, travel books and a couple of photocopied documents, including a copy of a microfiche of a newspaper cutting from 1969.

Trent was very noticeable, with his baseball cap, dark sunglasses and a myriad of tattoos on his legs, arms and neck. He was watching all the time, aware of what was going on around him.

After his years of incarceration, the sight of young mums wandering around in their swimming costumes was very appealing but he knew he had to restrain himself and keep his mind on the job at hand. This was no time to be sidetracked. He believed he was on a path that would lead him to endless riches, so everything else would have to wait.

Through extensive research, Trent had become interested in a particular story covered by the local press about a mystery benefactor who had supposedly given a gold ingot towards the cost of completing the building of the Wellsford Ecumenical Church. It was reported in one of the local rags that the ingot was believed to be one of several that had been found locally. This had occurred in 1969 and Trent had become infatuated by this story and was determined to find who the mystery benefactor was and to see whether he could extract any further riches for himself. Maybe there would be no more need for any petty crimes. Just one big haul that would do him for the rest of his life.

His research had been meticulous but still he hadn't put the final pieces together. He was relying on other people to do that for him. Unfortunately, there may be some who had to fall by the wayside as he went along his path but that was the way it had to be. He was prepared to do anything to reach his final goal.

Trent didn't feel sorry for the old girl. He didn't believe she knew anything but he couldn't afford to let her live. The vicar must have known the answer to his questions but was prepared to protect one of his parishioners at the risk of his own life. Trent had hoped that he wouldn't have to resort to torture techniques. Maybe the vicar didn't really know after all.

Trent had several people to visit but time wasn't on his side. He needed more money as his habit was engulfing him. He seemed to need more every day just to keep himself on the level. He had found someone not far away who appeared to have access to almost any illegal narcotic but at an extortionate price. Fear of being stopped by the police meant that Trent couldn't afford to go near any major towns and cities. He had also reduced his food intake so he could buy more alcohol. He looked forward to the day when he could buy as much of the stuff as he liked. He wasn't going to be foiled by the police or the Englishman who seemed to be working for them. His time would come.

14

NATHAN SETTLED down to a quiet evening. He had barbecued a couple of beefburgers that he found in the freezer and was planning on going for a swim. However, he decided to open a bottle of wine instead and to call Loretta.

It was lovely to speak to her. Her voice was like a breath of fresh air and immediately Nathan's mind was taken away from the case and the murder. 'Is there any chance that we could meet up tomorrow evening,' he asked.

'Sure, if you don't mind coming to Auckland.'

'No, not at all. It would probably be better for me to get away from this place for a bit.'

'But it's beautiful there.'

'I know, but there's only so many beautiful trees and rolling countryside views that I can take. I'll be glad to be back in a city. Plus, everything's getting a bit heavy around Wellsford after what's been going on.'

'Yes, it sounds horrendous. What's the latest?'

'I think Rico's the person to answer that question,' Nathan said with distaste.

'Oh, have you fallen out again?'

'Yes, I'm afraid so.'

'What about this time?'

'It's a long story but I think the fact that I abused one of his colleagues was the final straw. Anyway, tomorrow evening …'

'Yes, I'm looking forward to it. I'll send you my home address. Is 8pm okay?'

'Yes, that's fine don't forget to message the address.'

'Don't worry, I won't. Bye. See you tomorrow.' Loretta hung up. A minute later, she messaged through her address. Nathan was happy and was looking forward to seeing her the following evening.

He decided to give Millie a call to see how things were going in Melbourne. She informed him that the funeral was the following Tuesday. After that they were hoping to come home, although she said Chris may have to return on occasion to tidy up some loose ends.

Nathan could tell by the tone of Millie's voice that it was difficult for her, but not as difficult as the time when they had lost their own parents. She was shocked by what she had read of what had happened in Wellsford while she had been away. Nathan promised to tell her all about it when she returned. They ended the call.

Nathan picked up the *Origins of the Treaty at Waitangi*, one of the books he had picked up at the museum. He became engrossed, and before he knew it, he had finished off a bottle of wine and it was nearly dark. He felt really groggy and the worse for wear, so he collected everything off the table and took it into the kitchen. He made sure that all the doors were locked, poured himself a glass of water and went up to bed.

Sometime in the early hours he awoke with a start. Had he just heard the gate alarm go off in the kitchen? He rubbed his eyes then got out of bed and made his way downstairs. He felt tired and hungover. He also had a gut feeling that something was wrong. As he got to the bottom of the stairs, he heard the gate alarm again. He scampered into Chris's study to get the best view of the drive.

Outside the house was a plain dark car, and a police patrol car was on its way up the drive. Nathan then saw the uniformed officer get out of his car to speak to two men in suits who looked like detectives. He then recognised one as DI Broadwell. Something must have happened.

Nathan opened the front door before they had chance to reach it. Broadwell and one of his sidekicks walked up to the doorway. 'Mason, we meet again,' said Broadwell.

'And what can I do for you this time?' said Nathan.

'Well, you can accompany us down to the police station for some questions.'

'What about this time? And why in the middle of the night?'

'There have been some developments,' said Broadwell.

'With regards to what?'

'Don't make this difficult Mason.'

'Well at least let me get some clothes on. Surely you don't want me to come down in my boxers.'

'Very well,' Broadwell conceded. The two detectives walked into the house while the uniformed officer waited outside. They followed Nathan up to his bedroom.

'What were you wearing last night?' asked Broadwell.

Nathan pointed at a chair in the corner. 'Just the T-shirt and shorts,' he said.

'What about footwear?'

'My flip-flops. They're in the kitchen.'

Broadwell gesticulated to his colleague, who immediately walked over to the clothes and sealed them in a clear plastic bag. 'Pick the flip-flops up on the way out Joe,' Broadwell instructed the other man.

'Okay Boss.'

Nathan pulled out a clean pair of combat shorts from the drawer and grabbed a clean T-shirt from a hanger in the wardrobe. He also grabbed an old pair of beige deck shoes that were in the bottom of the wardrobe. He turned to Broadwell, saying, 'You know this is ridiculous.'

'I'll be the judge of that,' replied Broadwell.

'Am I under arrest?'

'No, just helping with our enquiries.'

'But you've already said you don't want my help. Your words were that I'm just a jumped-up failed ex-cop from London, or something like that.'

'The situation has changed. Don't make it any worse.'

Nathan was conveyed to Wellsford police station and taken straight into an interview room. Detective Mike Lima joined him.

'I would really like to know what this is all about,' said Nathan.

'Okay, just bear with me,' replied Lima. 'Nathan did you go to see John Selwood in Warkworth yesterday afternoon?'

'Yes, I did.'

'Why did you go there?'

'I went with Margaret to inform him about the break-in at his home.'

'How did you know about the break-in at his home?'

Nathan hesitated. He knew that what he was about to say was going to upset one or two who were probably listening in to this conversation. 'When you came to my house yesterday you took a phone call. During your call you wrote down a name and address on a writing pad. After you had removed the paper from the pad and left, I looked at the sheet of paper that was beneath and could clearly see an imprint of a name and address. When I compared this name and address to the list that I have from the church vestry, a copy of which is now in your possession, I noticed that John Selwood was on the list.

'I then called Margaret and asked her whether she recognised the name and address. She knew immediately that it was the church treasurer, who she meets on a regular basis and who had recently moved to a care home in Warkworth. Margaret went to his house as she's a keyholder, but the police were still there. She had a quick look around and could see that the spare bedroom, which he used as a study, seemed to have received the majority of the intruder's attention and a small safe had been removed from under the desk. So, Margaret and I went to the care home to inform John about the break-in.'

Detective Lima looked stunned and lost for words. 'Is it a bit of a habit of yours … searching through notepads for writing imprints?' he said.

'Detective training school stuff. I can't help myself,' replied Nathan sarcastically.

'John Selwood was murdered at the home in Warkworth last night,' said Lima.

'Oh my god. No, that's terrible.' Nathan was really shocked. He was probably one of the last people to see him alive. He now felt remorseful for being so flippant with Lima. 'I'm sorry, and Margaret will be so upset.'

'We've already spoken to Margaret.'

'Is she okay?' Nathan asked.

'Not really,' Lima replied. 'She's struggling to come to terms with everything that's happened.'

'What happened to him?' asked Nathan.

At this point the door opened and Broadwell entered the room, followed by Rico. Rico told Lima to leave. Nathan was then subjected to hours of interrogation. Rico remained pretty quiet while Broadwell went to town.

Initially Nathan went on the offensive, spouting about Broadwell's attitude towards him and the fact that he was being followed. He was informed in no uncertain terms that at the moment he was their number-one suspect based upon the supposition that wherever he went, crime seemed to follow or had already been committed. They did not admit or deny that anyone was watching or following Nathan.

Nathan pushed the point that John Selwood was on the list as a potential victim and that he had already highlighted this fact. He drew their attention to his report and the link to the collection envelopes, but Broadwell wasn't having it. 'None of this makes sense,' the DI said. 'You're saying that people are dying for a reason that we don't understand but it's something to do with the church.'

'Yes, and it could be to do with a mystery beneficiary to the church,' Nathan said.

'This is Sherlock Holmes bullshit,' said Broadwell.

'Okay,' replied Nathan with his hands up in submission.

~~~

At the Warkworth care home, the forensics officers were finishing their gathering of potential clues to an identification of John Selwood's murderer. He had been beaten about the head many times as he sat up in bed and had died from a slash to the side of his neck, which had resulted in him bleeding out and saturating his bed.

However, there was no evidence that anything had been taken. Everything seemed to be in order. There was also no evidence of a struggle. It was as if the attacker was trying to beat something out of John but in the end had given in. But did they get the information? And was the slash to the neck a mark of success or failure?

~~~

Nathan had been returned to his cell and was having a breakfast of scrambled eggs and tea when the door was unlocked and Rico walked in.

'You know I'm not responsible for any of this,' said Nathan.

'I know,' said Rico.

'Well why don't you help me out?'

'Because I'm no longer in charge, Broadwell is.'

'Since when?'

'Just now. Apparently the chief listened in to the interview. He wasn't happy with my contribution, or lack of it. I think Broadwell's been in his ear about our friendship. It's a conflict of interest. I'm off the case and going back to my daily duties at Auckland.'

Nathan could see that Rico was angry and upset. 'I'm sorry to hear that,' he said.

'It's my fault. I should learn to pick my friends more carefully.' Rico left the room and slammed the door shut behind him.

Nathan was flabbergasted. He felt extremely down and disappointed. He was sorry that someone should think so lowly of him. Perhaps in Rico's eyes he had never really been his friend, just an acquaintance.

Nathan was released without charge later that afternoon and taken back to Fern Heights. The first thing he did was to ring Margaret. 'Hi Margaret, it's Nathan.'

Margaret was tearful and sobbing but managed to say, 'Hello Nathan, I tried to ring you. I know that you were taken in by the police.'

'Well, they have released me now. I'm back at Fern Heights.'

'I don't know what we're going to do. Poor John. It's so horrible, and such a lovely person. The church is finished now. I don't know how it can recover from this. I'm going to stay at my sister's in Wellington. I have to get away from all this. I don't feel safe. It's like one big nightmare. There's a psycho on the loose and it looks like he or she is going to keep coming after us all until they get what they want.'

'I understand how you feel, and I don't blame you for wanting to get away, but when are you going?'

'My sister's husband is driving up to collect me. He's just called and will be here in an hour.'

'I really need to see you before you go,' said Nathan.

'Oh well, I'm just in the process of packing my bags and tidying the house before I leave, so I haven't really got the time at the moment,' Margaret insisted.

'Margaret, if you don't mind, I'll take a minute of your time, that's all.'

'What is it that you want Nathan?'

'I really need to look at the church electoral roll again. I know it's a private document but, please, I really need to take another look,' Nathan pleaded.

'Okay, I'll have it ready for you if you come round in about twenty minutes.'

'Thanks ever so much Margaret. See you then.'

Nathan felt dirty, having been in the police cell. He went upstairs and had a quick shower, then put on a change of T-shirt and shorts. He left Fern Heights, first making sure that everywhere was locked up. On his way out he stopped on the wooden bridge and closed the gate behind him. John Selwood was now on his mind. Such a lovely man. Such a sense of humour. Such a shame.

Nathan soon arrived at Margaret's house. He knocked on the door and it opened pretty quickly. Margaret looked hot and bothered and her eyes were red through crying. She quickly ushered him into the lounge and sat him down. She gave him the hardback book that he had seen previously.

There were years and years of names, addresses and amounts of money that people had donated. Nathan went to the year 1969 to see who was listed. There were many more on the roll in the early days. He looked down the list for anyone with the initials C. W. Realising that they were in surname alphabetically, he went to the end of the fourth page and was excited to find Catherine Wall, Fred Wall and Marlene Wall. They were all listed at the same address in Kaipara Flats Road. He swiftly wrote down the three names. Margaret had been busying herself in the kitchen as Nathan shouted, 'Okay, finished.'

'That was quick,' Margaret replied.

She walked into the room and Nathan handed her the book. 'Thanks Margaret. Just before I go, can I ask, do you know the Wall family from Kaipara Flats Road?'

She thought about it for a minute. 'The name seems to ring a bell but it may be before my time, sorry.'

Nathan employed a diversionary tactic before she started to ask questions about his interest in the Wall family. 'Don't be. I'm sorry to bother you at this awful time and I think you're doing the right thing by getting away for a few weeks. What are you going to do about your granddaughter May?'

'It's okay, my daughter's made alternative arrangements. I'll miss her so much though.'

'I'm sure she'll be waiting for your return Margaret. Have a safe journey.'

Nathan gave her a hug and left the house. He jumped into his car and made his way to Kaipara Flats Road. He couldn't believe his luck. He thought he may have found the mystery benefactor and he had to warn them, because if his theory were correct, they could be the next victim. *What if the murderer was one step ahead and had somehow found out about the Walls?* Nathan thought. *I could be walking into a bloodbath. Imagine trying to explain that away to the police.*

Nathan was very anxious as he made his way through the Dome Valley before turning right into Kaipara Flats Road. He pulled over at the side of the road. He needed to think. He had worked out a possible scenario of the murderer being one step ahead of him and the implications for the Walls. But now he was thinking about what if the murderer was just one step behind him and was in search of the electoral roll for 1969. He or Margaret could be the next victim.

Nathan decided to give Margaret a call. 'Hi Margaret, Nathan again. Sorry to bother you again but I have a strange request and I wouldn't bother you if I didn't think it wasn't important.'

'Oh well, you were here only twenty minutes ago. You should have asked me then to save you the bother.'

'I know, but please listen to me. I want you to pack the electoral roll book in your case and take it with you.'

'But why would I want to do that?' Margaret replied in astonishment.

Nathan decided to just come out with it. 'I believe there's some information of evidential value in that book that could be detrimental to the Wall family if it falls into the wrong hands.'

'This is all very confusing Nathan. But okay, if you insist, I'll take it with me.'

'Thanks Margaret. I'll explain all when you return.'

'Yes, that would be appreciated,' she replied.

'Have you heard any more from your lift?' Nathan enquired.

'Yes, he just rang. He's only ten minutes away. He made better time than expected.'

'Okay Margaret. Have a safe trip and try to enjoy the break.'

'I will, but I'll be coming back for any funerals. I have a friend who will keep me informed.'

'Okay, bye for now,' said Nathan.

He was now worried that Margaret's house could become a target, so he decided to message Detective Lima to inform him that Margaret had gone away for a few weeks and that her house could be a possible target. He wasn't expecting a reply and there was nothing more that he could do.

Nathan looked through the car window at his surroundings. The land to the left was relatively flat but on the right was the range of the tree-covered Dome Valley hills. He pulled away slowly. There weren't many houses at all. There were some lovely colonial-type buildings, some modern brick bungalows and traditional wooden bungalows, but they were very scarce and well-spaced. The majority of the properties were on the left-hand side where the land was flat and easier to build on. It was a beautiful area and very scenic but quiet and very isolated.

The houses had mailboxes at the end of their drives and Nathan decided to get out to have a look. Some of them had a house name, some a number and others a family name written on the box. They had a little red indicator attached and he knew that when the arm was out it meant that there was something in the box to be collected for postage.

Nathan expected that the Walls's home would be one of the large colonial type. It didn't take long before he came across a small timber bungalow set back from the road by about three hundred metres or more. The building didn't appear to be in a good state and the land around it was rather overgrown. He couldn't see a car on the drive and thought that perhaps it was no longer lived in. He looked at the mailbox, which was slightly rusted and corroded, so he couldn't make out the name. He licked his thumb and rubbed it across the name plate, then had mixed emotions when he saw the name WALL.

Nathan was having his doubts now. If this was the family that had given the church a gold bar, you would expect them to appear more prosperous. But he had learned to never judge a book by its cover. He didn't know what to think but walked up the driveway to the front door. The closer he got the worse it looked. With the door's flaking wood and mass of cobwebs Nathan wondered whether anyone lived here. He knocked hard on the door. Nothing stirred so he knocked again, harder this time. Still nothing. He waited a little longer then, dejected, he turned around and started to walk back to his car. Just as he got to the end of the drive, he heard a noise at the front door. It was a bolt being slid open, followed by a click, and the door opened a couple of inches.

Nathan walked back to the door, where he could see an elderly lady peeping through the gap. He was briefly unsure how he should handle the situation but decided to formally identify himself and drop a few church names to try to win her over. 'Hello, my name is Nathan Mason. I'm an ex-detective from the Metropolitan Police in London. I've been helping the local police with their enquiries into the recent Wellsford murders. I'm a friend of Margaret the churchwarden and my sister also attends the same church. It's the Ecumenical at Wellsford.'

'And why did you want to speak to me?' the old woman asked.

'Well are you Mrs Wall?'

'Yes, I am. I'm Marlene Wall.'

'Do you think I could possibly come in and speak with you?'

'Well I don't usually invite people in.'

'It's really important Marlene. If you don't mind me calling you by your Christian name.'

'No, it's alright.'

'I really need to speak to you about the church,' said Nathan.

'Do you mean the murders?'

'No, not specifically.'

'Like I said, I don't usually invite people in,' she insisted.

'Okay. If I can give you my telephone number—'

'Why would I want that,' Marlene interrupted.

'Marlene, I really need to talk to you about your family and your involvement in the Ecumenical Church in the 1960s.'

Marlene hesitated and Nathan could tell that she was thinking about what he had just said. Whatever she said next was going to be crucial in proving whether or not his lines of enquiry were correct. She opened the door ever so slightly.

He could see that she was wearing a grey cardigan over a blouse, and a flowery skirt. Her legs looked swollen and she was wearing a pair of slippers with a fur line around the ankle.

'What was your name again?' she asked.

'Nathan, Nathan Mason.'

'You had better come in then.' Nathan felt a sense of achievement, even though he knew he was nowhere near his goal yet.

They walked into the lounge and Nathan sat on the sofa, while Marlene sat on a chair in the corner. He was pleasantly surprised as the house appeared to be well equipped and in good condition. Marlene obviously looked after the inside of the house as well as she could but perhaps wasn't well enough to the do the external work. The lounge had a dining area to the rear with a rather attractive polished walnut table and chairs. The rear windows were dressed in fine curtains. Through the windows there was a spectacular view across large, tree-lined fields with a backdrop of wooded hills.

Marlene sat back in her chair, which rocked ever so slightly. 'It's a nice house Marlene,' Nathan said.

'I know. I didn't have the heart to move. It's been in the family for so long. Look, I'm prepared to answer your questions but on one condition: the moment I ask you to leave you must go. Will you promise to do that?' Marlene said firmly.

'Of course.' Nathan was now worried that this could be over very quickly so he decided to get straight to the point. He didn't believe that Marlene was going to be lulled into a false sense of security. This was a woman who was on her guard all the time. 'Did a member of your family make an anonymous donation to the church in 1969 to help for its completion?'

'There's no money here if that's what you're getting around to.'

'No, I'm not. I'm just interested to know if it was anyone from your family that made an anonymous donation,' said Nathan.

'If we did and I said yes, it would no longer be anonymous like my mother insisted upon at the time,' Marlene said, then started to smile, knowing that she had just said yes in her own way.

Nathan felt relieved and excited that he had found the anonymous benefactor. 'What was your mum's name?' he asked.

'Catherine.'

'Is that with a C by any chance?'

'Yes.'

The initials C. W. had been permanently emblazoned on Nathan's brain and now he had confirmed they belonged to Catherine Wall. But he needed to find out the story. 'I was wondering whether you would be prepared to tell me about the circumstances of how the donation to the church came about?'

Marlene hesitated. 'Well like I said, I presume it's no longer anonymous if you've found out.'

'Well I don't know if anyone else knows,' said Nathan. 'No one else knows about the research that I've carried out.'

'I still can't see what your involvement is and why you're here unless its connected to those murders in some shape or form.'

'In answer to your question, I don't honestly know. All I can say to you is that I was helping the police with their enquiries. And when we realised that the horrible events were connected to the church, I became involved in helping Detective Inspector Manu. Since I became involved, I'll be quite honest with you, I've been detained by the police on two separate occasions.

'I actually found the vicar in the vestry and was implicated. Unfortunately, since then I've told the police that I no longer wish to help them, and they have washed their hands of me. However, I still carried on the research and that's why I'm here. You see, it all started after I arrived from the UK. That's another thing that isn't in my favour, according to the police anyway.'

'So, you found the vicar. It must have been dreadful.'

'It was, and if you don't mind, I would rather not linger on the point. It was very distressing,' said Nathan.

'You know, I haven't been to church for years, so I have no current connection,' Marlene said.

'I know, and it's your past connection that I'm interested in, so could you please tell me the circumstances around your gift to the church?'

'Would you like a cold drink?' Marlene asked.

'Just a glass of water please.'

Nathan thought that Marlene was maybe giving herself some thinking time but when she returned with two glasses of cold water, she seemed to be a bit more upbeat, as if she had decided that she wanted to talk. 'How long have you got?' she said.

'As long as you,' replied Nathan.

She sat down and began to talk. 'In the sixties after my dad died, I was working in the shop in Warkworth and my brother Fred was working at the timber mill. The three of us used to go to church regularly then, every week if we could get a lift. Fred made a friend who was a Maori. I think his name was Tawera. He was a really nice man and a dedicated Christian.

'Tawera got Fred interested in geology; you know, rocks and stones and all that type of stuff. They used to go off into the hills. They would be gone all day sometimes. I know they were getting a collection together; you know, greenstone, kauri gum and other things but I can't remember their names … semi-precious stones. Then all of a sudden out of the blue, Tawera moved away with his family. Although Fred didn't show it, I knew he was absolutely devastated. You see, he didn't have any other friends.'

'So, what did he do?' asked Nathan.

'Well, he carried on with his hobby by himself. I know that they had a cabin up in the woods because I remember when Tawera was around they were doing it up; making it more comfortable. I think it was their base. Anyway, he seemed to be spending more and more time away from home. Then one evening, I think it may have been at the weekend, he came home on his moped.' Marlene began to sob and the tears just rolled down her face.

'Take your time Marlene. I must say you have an amazing memory,' said Nathan.

'I know,' Marlene said, composing herself. 'It rarely lets me down, even today. But the problem is that I remember all the sadness and bad things that have happened in my life, like it happened yesterday.'

Nathan needed to get her back on track. 'You were saying he came home on his moped.'

'Yes, he had been out all day and was absolutely exhausted, but more excited than I had ever seen him.'

'Why?'

Marlene hesitated and took a sip of water. 'I can see him now. In a right state he was, burnt to a crisp and covered in bites. He carried his backpack into this room, placed it on the floor in front of me and Mum, then pulled out two shiny gold bars from the bag. We were dancing for joy and Fred said there was more to come and that he had stashed another three bars. I remember picking a bar up. It was so heavy and so bright, and we were so, so happy.'

Nathan wanted to ask her some questions but decided to let her tell the whole story.

Marlene continued: 'That night, Fred insisted that one of the bars was for us to live off and the other bar was to go to the church to complete the new building. They were struggling. The church wasn't even half built and there just wasn't enough in the coffers. He also insisted that we kept it quiet, like an anonymous donor. I think he was worried about people coming around here and robbing us. So that's what we agreed – one bar of gold for us and one for the church.

'Unfortunately, Fred went to bed that night and never woke up. I remember knocking on his door the following morning, thinking he should be at the timber mill by now. But he just didn't move when I went in. The doctor came out and said he had a heart attack in his sleep. At the time it felt like the end of the world, one day so happy and the next so sad.' The tears rolled down Marlene's cheeks and her bottom lip quivered.

'It sounds like he was an awfully hard worker,' said Nathan, then realised it was a stupid thing to say.

'He was, too hard for his own good and ended up paying the ultimate sacrifice. Anyway, we stuck to our promise and my mum gave a gold bar to the church on the understanding that our names remained anonymous. We've lived off the sale of the other bar ever since. And now there's just me. Is that why you came to see me? Because you want the rest of the gold?'

'I can honestly say no, that's not why I came to see you. But I'm concerned that someone else may know about the gold.'

'I don't see how. I've never told a soul until today. This is something that happened over forty-five years ago.'

Nathan suddenly felt very guilty, knowing that he could be leading the killer straight to Marlene's house. But he convinced himself that he had been careful, and he hadn't been followed.

'My suspicion is that someone else has found out about a benefactor who gave a bar of gold to the church in 1969,' said Nathan. 'But there's no reason to suspect that they know it was the Wall family.'

'Well you found out, didn't you, so what's to stop anyone else from doing the same?'

'The only reason I found out was because the initials C. W. were written in pencil on the vicar's private copy of the Church Council minutes. And doing my research through the church electoral roll of 1969 I found out who C. W. was. So, your anonymity, aside from me, is still intact and that's the way it will remain. I have to ask you though, Marlene, have you never wanted to get the rest of the gold?'

'I always figured that one day I may be able to give it a try but as I got older I had no one to help me, so I sort of put it to the back of my mind. They say let sleeping dogs lie.'

'What would you do with the gold if you found it now?'

'I think I would want to do what Fred did. Find some good causes that need the money and share it out but keep some for myself and maybe Tawera if he's still alive.'

'How would you feel if I went and looked for the gold?'

'Well, I don't know; you might take it all.'

'What if I said I don't want any of it?'

'I would say let me think about it. I don't want any fuss or it to be in the newspapers or anything. I'll be wanting to carry on with my private and quiet life just how I like it.'

'Can I ask you another question?'

'Yes.'

'Where did the gold come from?'

'He said he found it on a beach near Tauhoa and that there was a box with five bars in but he could only carry two home on his moped.' He had to dig them out of the sand. I remember it like yesterday. He showed me on his map, but I couldn't make it out. I can't read maps, never could. Never really had much reason to.'

'I don't suppose you would still have that map?' asked Nathan, trying to remain nonchalant.

'I doubt it but if it were anywhere it would have been in his biscuit tin.'

Nathan couldn't tell whether Marlene was being deliberately evasive or she really didn't know. 'Would you still have his biscuit tin?'

'I suppose there's always the possibility that Mum may have put it in the loft years ago when she was tidying his bedroom. I've never been up there myself. Do you fancy a cup of tea Nathan?'

'Yes Marlene. That would be lovely.'

'See, I know you English love your tea.'

'We certainly do Marlene, we certainly do.'

Nathan felt as if he was making inroads, that Marlene was softening her attitude towards him and that she was actually a likeable person. She continued their conversation from the kitchen, so Nathan got up and joined her. It was a smart, modern kitchen with a large American-style fridge-freezer like the one at Fern Heights. It was immaculately clean.

'So did your sister come here from England?' Marlene asked.

'Yes, Millie and Chris, her husband, had a house built in Dome Forest. It's called Fern Heights.'

'I remember it being built. All the plans were displayed in the council building in Warkworth. I called in one day just to have a look. It was quite controversial at the time because of its location in the forest on the side of a hill if my memory serves me. They had to take a lot of trees down and certain parties complained. Nice location though.'

'It is Marlene, it's a beautiful spot, but very isolated.'

'You won't be used to isolation if you're used to London.'

'Exactly, it's a shock to the system, and I'm on my own at the moment because Chris's mother, who lived in Melbourne, has died, so they're both over there. I'm trying to keep myself busy.'

'Do you take milk?'

'Yes, please. No sugar.'

They sat down again in the lounge. 'Why would you not want any of the money if you found the gold?' asked Marlene.

'I'm not in it for the money. I suppose I'm in it for the adventure. I'm also interested in history and I would love to know where the gold came from.'

'I seem to remember an old, typed document. It was to do with a ship that was either run aground or had some sort of accident in Kaipara harbour. I think they jettisoned their cargo to save the ship. I think it was a common occurrence back in the day. The harbour is just as dangerous now and full of wrecks and sharks,' Marlene said.

'And where did you see this document?' asked Nathan.

'It was in his biscuit tin with a load of other papers and things.'

'Marlene, I could really do with seeing this biscuit tin.'

'Well, if you're prepared to go into the loft and have a root around, it could be up there. If it isn't, it's probably been thrown away.'

Nathan knew that this biscuit tin contained not only items that could direct him to the gold but may also be able to inform him of its history. This biscuit tin was the key. 'What colour and size is the tin?' he asked.

'I think it was a square, red metal tin, about ten inches.'

'Do you have any stepladders so I can climb into the loft?'

'Yes, just open the hall cupboard. There's a set in there. You may have to stand on the very top rung to reach into the loft and then haul yourself up. There will be a light switch on the beam above your head when you get up there, but I'm not sure if it works as the bulb must be that old.'

Nathan again tried not to be too enthusiastic. 'I'm going to enjoy this tea first, then I'll go up there to see if I can find it.'

'That's fine by me. It's nice to have someone to talk to. You don't realise how lonely life has been until you get a visitor. I'm sorry if I wasn't very welcoming at first. But no one ever comes here, and if they did, I wouldn't let them in.'

'So, it was my pig-headed stubbornness that got me across the threshold then,' said Nathan smiling.

'Yes, exactly.' They both laughed.

Nathan finished his tea then went to the hall cupboard and pulled out the stepladder. Placing it beneath the loft hatch he climbed up, pushed the lid and lifted it into the loft. He was then able to climb a little further and have a good look around before heaving himself through the hole.

Nathan switched on the light above him. The incredibly old and dim bulb flickered into life but it was enough for him to see what was lying about. There was a couple of cardboard boxes, two old tea chests and a lot of what looked like old and fragmented fibreglass insulation, which was lying between the wooden joists. Because the joists were revealed it enabled him to navigate his way around without falling through the ceiling.

Assuming that the joists were in good order, Nathan checked the cardboard boxes first. The first one contained an old pair of velvet curtains, and when he lifted them, there was a couple of decorative wall plates, but that was about it. The second box contained an old tea service with an ornate tea pot, cups, saucers and large dinner plates. He made his way across to the tea chests, which were full of men's clothing – shirts, shorts, a suit and a pair of shoes. He wondered whether they were Fred's old clothes.

There was a selection of old newspapers in an extremely poor state, and then as he lifted them, Nathan saw the red biscuit tin. He thought his heart had missed a beat as he picked the box up and lifted it out of the tea chest. He loaded everything back into the chest and placed the biscuit tin by the loft hatch. He then switched off the light before clambering down, picking up the tin on the way.

Nathan walked into the lounge. 'I presume that this is his tin?' he asked.

'Yes, that's it.' Marlene suddenly looked incredibly sad and solemn.

'Does it bring back memories?' said Nathan.

'Yes, but it was so long ago. But they were the days; nothing was complicated and, yes, we were poor until Fred found the gold. We were rich for a night and then when he died Mum and I felt poor again.'

Nathan put the tin on a small table. 'Shall we have a look through it?' he said.

'Yes, go ahead.'

Nathan prised the lid off the tin and was immediately struck by a strong musty whiff. The documents inside looked old and dog-eared. There was an assortment of lined paper covered with handwriting, some neat, some scrawled. There was also a strange pencil-drawn map.

'That's it,' Marlene said. 'That's the map I've seen before.'

Nathan opened the map out. It had numerous folds in the sheet and each fold seemed to be accompanied by a dirty stain along its length. He could make out the distinctive coastline along the Kaipara harbour area and he could see Warkworth, Wellsford and Tauhoa. The three locations formed a sort of triangle on the map.

In the centre of the triangle was written 'Dome Forest' and there was a small pinprick in the centre of the forest. There was also a similar, even smaller hole on the coast by Tauhoa. Nathan wondered whether the hole in the hills was where the cabin was. Maybe the hole on the coast was the find location. He pointed at the hole in the forest and Marlene instantly said, 'I think that's where the cabin is.'

'And what about this other hole?' Nathan asked, pointing to the one on the coast.

'I don't know. Maybe that's where he found the gold.'

Nathan sifted through the other bits of paper, some of which included descriptions of geological rocks and stones. Other documents contained what looked like a checklist of features to look for in stone. There was a list of individual stones, cross-referenced to a line of particular features to look for, such as colour, veins, density and weight.

There was another document, which appeared to be older and the paper was exceptionally fine, like tracing paper or the old air mail writing paper. It appeared to be a set of instructions.

> ON ENTERING THE FOREST AT TAUHOA FOLLOW
> THE EYE TREES.
>
> DO NOT VARY FROM THE ROUTE.
>
> MAKE SURE TO BE OUT OF THE FOREST BEFORE
> DARKNESS FALLS.
>
> WALK BACK USING THE SAME ROUTE AND DO
> NOT VARY FROM IT.

'Marlene, if you don't mind, could I possibly photograph all of these documents?'

'So that you can go in search of the gold?'

'Yes, there's no point it resting out there waiting to be found by a complete stranger when you and Tawera could reap the dividends along with your chosen good causes. I think if there is someone else after the gold, I feel almost duty bound to get it first and prevent it being spent on god knows what. You want to have a say on where the money is spent, don't you Marlene?'

'Of course, without a doubt.'

'Then let me photograph the documents. I'll then put them back in the loft in their biscuit tin and you can leave them up there or do what you want with them.'

Nathan was very tense. This was the crux of the matter. How much did she actually trust him to get the gold and return it to her?

'You've been honest with me so far Nathan, and I see no reason why I shouldn't trust you. It's my gamble at the end of the day.'

'It's no gamble Marlene. Thank you.' He then photographed every document using his mobile phone. 'When I get back home, I'll spend some time studying these. I'm so grateful for this information Marlene. I'm going to see whether I can find your gold.'

'Will you keep in touch with me then?'

'Yes of course I will.'

'Then I wish you well. Good luck in your hunt. It's like a wilderness up there. I remember Fred used to say that and I remember laughing at the time and thinking he was being overdramatic, but I think he meant it.'

Nathan took Marlene's hand and cupped it between his. 'Thanks for the drinks,' he said. 'I must admit that I've enjoyed sitting with you and chatting.'

'And I you,' Marlene replied.

'Oh, just before I go; let me leave my mobile number for you,' Nathan suggested.

'Okay.' Marlene directed him back to the lounge and gave him a pen and a piece of paper. He wrote down his mobile number and the number of Fern Heights before he left.

As Nathan drove away, he couldn't help worrying whether his visit may have put Marlene at risk. He was now very unsure as to what to do. If something happened to Marlene tonight, he would have been the last person to see her so he would be in the frame. If he told the police he had been to visit her, they would either do nothing, tell him to stop interfering with their enquiries, or maybe ask why he had been to see her in the first place.

Driving back along Kaipara Flats Road towards SH1, Nathan didn't see a single vehicle, just like when he had arrived. There was no traffic even when he waited by the roadside for a short while. He was confident he hadn't been followed, so joined SH1, which was busy, then turned off into the private road for Fern Heights.

Nathan was pleased to see that the gate to Fern Heights was still closed across the wooden bridge. He closed it again after he had passed through. There was no new evidence that anyone had been through but he had a feeling that he couldn't put his finger on. It but just a niggle but he didn't feel alone, and it was very unsettling.

15

TRENT WAS biding his time but the situation was deteriorating quickly. He had so far been unable to locate anyone who had any knowledge about the mystery donor of gold in 1969. If he went to someone for help and they wouldn't or couldn't assist, then they had to be eliminated. Yes, the risk was considerable now that the police were flooding the area but it was like tossing a coin. On one side was a life of untold riches and on the other a life behind bars. The second option wasn't one he was prepared to consider.

He was going to get rich quick or die trying. He had done his research. He had read the old news reports from back in the day about the mystery benefactor who had found a cache of gold. If he could just find out who they were so that he could pay them a visit and they could offload some of their riches on to him …

This Englishman seemed to be getting in the way. He would have to be dealt with accordingly. The churchwarden would be next to receive a visit but he had to do some surveillance first. There was a good chance that the cops would be watching her house and be ready to spring an attack.

Trent couldn't afford to be seen around in Wellsford during daylight hours. He would have to wait until it was dark. He had found some country lanes and logging routes that could get him over to Wellsford on the quiet. In the meantime, it was just a case of getting across SH1 to the area where the Englishman was staying. To kill a few hours before it got dark.

~~~

At Wellsford police station incident room, a group of senior detectives that covered all of the North Island were meeting to discuss their progress, or lack of it.

Nathan Mason was mentioned numerous times because he was always there or thereabouts whenever an incident occurred. It was pointed out that because of his background in the police, Nathan would be knowledgeable when it came to the transfer of DNA and the leaving of fingerprints, hair follicles and clothing fibres. There was no evidence that he had tried to remove or indeed prevent anything incriminating from being left in the first place. In fact, he had left plenty of evidence of his visits on three out of the four incidents, with the exception of Brenda Massey.

There was no evidence of anyone else's involvement other than those already known to the police. It was this lack of evidence that convinced them that they weren't up against a novice here, but a hardened professional who had no intention of being caught. Even so, the signs indicated that the murderer was possibly now taking more risks, maybe in desperation. This made him or her more dangerous.

16

IT WAS now early evening and Nathan was happy and excited that he would be seeing Loretta later and that he had to drive to Auckland. He decided to shower before slipping into a new pair of denims and a crisp white, button-down-collar shirt. It was a nice change from T-shirts, shorts and flip-flops.

He looked at his phone and realised he had a missed call and message, both from Loretta. She was cancelling for tonight. She apologised and said she would call him tomorrow. Nathan was deflated and disappointed. He was really looking forward to seeing her again, particularly after a day like today. Maybe that was the problem. Perhaps Rico had stuck his oar in again after Nathan's detention this morning. He would have told Marika, knowing that she would tell Loretta. It was his way of spoiling things for him and it was working.

Nathan didn't know whether to call or message Loretta. He decided to call her. It went to voicemail, so he messaged her and said he was sorry she had cancelled and asked whether everything was alright between them. She didn't reply. He took off his shirt and jeans and reverted back to a fresh T-shirt and his old shorts. He was at an impasse; he didn't know what to do or where to go. He was so disappointed, as he just wanted to see Loretta.

Nathan needed to keep busy and was aware that he would have to do some washing in the next day or two, or maybe he could try to stretch it out until Millie was home. He didn't think she would be overly impressed if he selected the latter. He went downstairs into the kitchen, pulled a beer from the fridge and went out on to the patio.

Sipping his beer, Nathan started to scroll through the biscuit tin photographs on his mobile until he came to the map. It gave the impression that Tauhoa was in close proximity to Kaipara Flats Road where the Walls lived but, in all honesty, it was miles and miles over hills on unmade roads. So, if the original starting point was the small pinprick on the map at Tauhoa and the finishing point was the pinprick on the map that was presumably the cabin in Dome Forest, this was a long arduous route. There was no evidence of any roads, tracks or even paths.

Finding a way from A to B looked an absolute nightmare, then Nathan was reminded of one of the other documents he had photographed. Scrolling through he came across the handwriting on a piece of paper.

ON ENTERING THE FOREST AT TAUHOA FOLLOW THE EYE TREES.

DO NOT VARY FROM THE ROUTE.

MAKE SURE TO BE OUT OF THE FOREST BEFORE
DARKNESS FALLS.

WALK BACK USING THE SAME ROUTE AND DO
NOT VARY FROM IT.

He wondered what eye trees were and why it twice mentioned not to vary from the route or the path. From what he could see, finding the cabin was going to be like finding a needle in a haystack but he was going to try, and he was going to try tomorrow.

Nathan fired up the barbecue and cooked some veal patties and opened a bottle of Shiraz for a change. He was sitting there in front of the covered pool, feeling lonely. He kept checking to see whether Loretta had replied to him, but she hadn't. He thought about ringing her but then dismissed the idea. They had been getting on so well. But he couldn't really blame her. What would he think if she were the centre of police attention? It was so unfair but he had to man up. He was going on an adventure tomorrow and it wasn't going to be easy.

That evening before settling down Nathan packed his backpack with some essentials: water, biscuits, torch, lighter, basic first aid kit and an ordnance survey map that he had found amongst the books in the bookcase. From Chris's study he had retrieved a Swiss Army knife and the night-vision binoculars, and from the garage he found Chris's walking boots, which fortunately were a size ten.

Leaving the backpack in the study, Nathan went back outside, sat by the pool and took another sip of wine. The Shiraz was too strong and a little bitter so he never even finished his second glass and was thinking of going up to bed. Then he had the same feeling he'd had earlier ... that he wasn't alone ... that possibly someone was watching him. He decided to turn off the outside light to make it look as if he was going to bed, then he just sat there, making sure he was in the shadow of the moonlight.

It was deathly quiet with the odd hoot of an owl in a tree and the odd cicada clicking away nearby. There wasn't even a breeze, and the stars were putting on a dazzling display. After approximately ten minutes Nathan was contemplating going to bed then he thought he could smell cigarette smoke just like before, so he waited and looked for the telltale sign of a burning glow as the smoker dragged on his cigarette. There was nothing, but he could definitely smell the smoke, even stronger now.

Nathan waited. If there was anyone in the trees at the side of the house, he presumed they would have a torch, otherwise they would never find their way in or out of there. He wished he had Chris's thermal-imaging binoculars to hand but they were at the other end of the house. However, he had a plan. He stood up from the shadows, turned on the outside light and made it look as if he had just come back out of the house. He walked up to the table, grabbed the bottle of wine and glass, turned off the outside light and went in, closing the door behind him. He rushed to the kitchen, left the wine and glass then ran down the hall to Chris's study, where he retrieved the binoculars, went back down the hall to the side door and sneaked outside, back into the shadows.

He turned on the binoculars and started to search the trees opposite. The view reminded him of looking at an old negative photograph but with colour. Any warmer objects glowed brightly. There was nothing glaringly obvious then something moved to his left, so he turned and focused in. He could see the image of a person walking away. The image disappeared briefly as they passed beyond the tree trunks.

It was very unnerving for Nathan, knowing there was someone watching him. As he put the binoculars down, he could see a very faint torch lighting the person's way. Presumably, they were making their way back to a car parked somewhere near SH1 or maybe in the private road.

Nathan decided he was going to try to intercept the intruder. He ran back into the house, grabbed his keys and ran down the hall and out of the door on the other side of the house to the drive and his car. He screamed down the driveway, his car headlights showing that the gates were closed, so he jumped out quickly and opened them. Turning right on to the private road towards SH1, he thought it wise to turn off his headlights in an attempt to apprehend the intruder. He was too late. As he approached the wooden bridge, Nathan could see the dark-coloured car pull out from the trees and drive through the exit on to SH1. He recognised the car through its shape and rear illuminated lights as an old Holden Commodore.

Suddenly, there was a huge crash to the front of the car then another on the side. For a split second Nathan thought he was under fire, then it dawned on him that he had hit the gate on the wooden bridge. He pulled the SUV to a halt and banged the steering wheel with his open palm. 'Shit, you idiot.'

Nathan turned around and drove back to Fern Heights to assess the damage. As he pulled up in front of the house, the security lights came on and he jumped out to look at the damage. The front didn't look too bad. The bumper moulding was cracked rather badly but it had done its job in protecting the front of the car. Looking down the passenger side of the vehicle, he could see a large indentation along the wing and the front door, caused when the gate bounced back after the initial impact. He knew that Millie and Chris wouldn't be too happy but he would pay to get the repairs done. However, he didn't know what condition the gate was in, so he would need to take a look in the morning.

Although he was on edge after the whole incident, Nathan was now feeling extremely tired. It had been a long day. He wandered into the house and sent a message to Detective Lima informing him of tonight's occurrence. Making sure all the doors were locked, he walked upstairs and went to bed. He fell asleep almost immediately, and the last thing he thought of was Loretta.

17

TRENT WASN'T happy. He couldn't believe how he had let the Englishman come so close to him. Did he get close enough to recognise his car or the registration plate? It was sloppy work but the Englishman was more alert than he expected; more on edge, as if he had something to hide or to protect. Why had he visited the churchwarden's bungalow? Trent needed to find out.

Margaret's bungalow was on the outskirts of the town. To the rear was a small industrial unit manufacturing agricultural feed, serviced by a small approach road. There were two men who worked the regular nightshift in the unit, bagging up and boxing up feed for distribution all over the North Island. As Trent approached, he noticed an unmarked car with two men inside, probably detectives. They were parked more or less outside Margaret's bungalow.

Trent turned left into the service road and pulled over next to the industrial unit. He noticed that one of the detectives had got out of the car and was looking in his direction. Trent made it look as if he was an employee coming to work. He got out of the car and casually walked around to the rear of the unit out of sight. He hoped that was convincing enough.

When he eventually looked back round the corner, Trent noticed that the detective had got back into the car, so he continued around the rear of the unit across a small patch of open land, then he was at the rear fence of Margaret's garden. He athletically leaped over the fence and approached the bungalow, which was in darkness. He pulled from his pocket a small metal torch and a fold-up knife. He was able to very easily slide the blade of the knife between window and frame to dislodge the holding arm of the opening part of the window. He then opened the window wide enough and climbed in.

He was in what appeared to be a spare bedroom at the rear. Fortunately, it was unoccupied. Trent thought it wise to deal with the churchwarden first, so then he could search the place without fear of compromise. He made his way through to the front of the bungalow to a closed door, where he believed the front bedroom to be. He slowly opened the door and thought it unusual that the curtains weren't drawn. Through the window he could see the detectives sitting in the car outside. He walked over to the bed. It was empty. He turned around and immediately, but with great stealth, searched the rest of the bungalow. There was clearly no one home.

Trent's search started in the lounge. Anything that was to do with the church, such as historical records, he was taking with him. He was conscious of using the torch, particularly with the police outside, but he had to see what he was looking at and that was a risk he was prepared to take. He was methodical and wouldn't be rushed. He finished his search but didn't think he had found anything of any relevance. However, until he got back to the camper van he wouldn't know for sure.

He went back out through the open window, across the garden, over the fence and waste ground and back to his car. He was going to casually drive past the detectives in their car. As he pulled alongside, he took a very quick glance into their car and noticed their heads were back against the headrests and their mouths were open. They were asleep. Once again, Trent stuck to the back roads and logging routes while making his way back to the camper van.

The following morning, he read the documentation that he had taken from Margaret's the night before. There was still nothing conclusive and he still hadn't found out who the mystery benefactor was. This was starting to get under his skin. He was leaving a trail of devastation in his path and he knew it was only a matter of time before someone came knocking at his door. The only viable option left was the Englishman. He had to kidnap him and make him talk. He needed time to formulate a plan. But time wasn't on his side.

18

NATHAN AWOKE and the first thing he thought of was his fear that someone else could have fallen victim to this sick killer. He was still unnerved from the night before. Someone was stalking him, and he didn't think it was the police. So, it could only be one other person, the killer and he could be next on the list.

Nathan showered and sat outside on the patio with his muesli and coffee, looking at the homemade map and the correct map of the Tauhoa to Dome Forest area. He didn't know how he was going to get from A to B on the map. It looked approximately four to six miles through dense forest. He was planning to use a compass, which was an app on his mobile phone. He had used it before and found it to be accurate, and he may need to rely on it if he couldn't find reference to the eye trees. He didn't know but assumed that at some point he would be crossing private land and probably forestry land. He was going to have to be careful.

Broadwell would love to have him on some trespass charges at the very least.

After breakfast, Nathan packed a few other items in his backpack: water, chocolate, biscuits, some fruit, binoculars and the maps. He had also decided to wear dark beige combat shorts and a green T-shirt to try to blend in with the environment and reduce the risk of being shot by some irate farmer. Chris's walking boots would also be an important part of his kit, along with his Bronco hat, which he had purchased in Australia a few years ago. After throwing his equipment in the back of the SUV, he went back inside the house to make sure that everything was locked up and secure.

~~~

Trent was also awake early. He too had packed his car with everything he needed to spend a few hours observing the Englishman before dealing with him, however he saw fit. He had watched as Nathan loaded his SUV. He was clearly on his way out and it looked as if he was going for a hike. Trent made his way back to his car, which was parked on a farmer's small track just by SH1 but wouldn't be seen by Nathan as he passed over the wooden bridge.

~~~

As Nathan left the house and approached the SUV, he looked at the damage caused by hitting the gate the previous night. It didn't look any better. Ignoring it, he jumped in and steamed down the drive, not forgetting to get out and close the gate. As he passed over the wooden bridge, he got out to survey the damage to the large gate. The whole frame was a bit out of shape but it didn't stop him closing it behind him.

He joined SH1, southbound towards Warkworth, then after a couple of miles he turned right into Kaipara Flats Road heading west. He passed the Wall family house on the left and continued towards Hoteo. Now on the limestone roads he was kicking up a considerable amount of dust behind him. The views were breathtaking. The sun was shining and he was on a gold quest. He was totally focused on achieving his objective, to find the lost gold.

Meanwhile, Trent followed Nathan all the way from Fern Heights at a good distance. When they reached the limestone road he felt a little more relieved as the dust kicked up by the car in front offered some visual protection. All the same, he stayed a good 200 yards behind Nathan. He had to be prepared to stop and pull his car out of sight if Nathan stopped up ahead. In fact, Nathan did stop at the side of the road but Trent was lucky because at the time he was just passing a large farmyard, so he was able to pull in behind some trees and wait until the dust rose again, indicating that Nathan was on the move.

Nathan had stopped to pull the maps out of his backpack. He was looking to see where he was in comparison to the cabin to the north and Tauhoa to the west. He was well on his way to the beach near Tauhoa and was looking for a small inlet that Fred Wall had marked with a pinprick on his original map, which Nathan had then transposed on to the main map. He had a rough idea where it was. If he had an approximate location of where the gold was originally found, he then had to go into the treeline to find the eye trees at the start of the path.

The closer Nathan got to the location the more he realised how difficult this was going to be. The alternative was to head for the cabin by the shortest route, which was probably from the Kaipara Flats Road. He realised, though, that this was probably the hardest option. He needed to find the path through the trees from Tauhoa. He reckoned he wasn't far away now.

He crossed over SH16, which was just like a quiet A road, meandering along the east coast before eventually joining SH1 at Wellsford. The terrain changed a little and the roads were more like rough unmade tracks surrounded by low-level mangrove, which indicated to Nathan that he was near water.

After a couple of hundred metres there was suddenly a clearing in the mangrove and a small sandy beach presented itself. It was like a Caribbean beach without the palm trees. Beautiful white sand and the water lapping on to the beach. There was a small pathway to the rear, which seemed to disappear into the mangrove.

Nathan moved the car on to the sand at the rear and got out. It was hot already and it felt as if he was in a little sun trap, the mangrove protecting the beach from any light breeze. He turned to look at the forest behind him. It was huge, it was dark and ominous and also very hilly. The levels of trees seemed to cascade down from the summit. The majority were radiata pine, which were the preferred type due to their phenomenal growth rate and strength qualities.

Trent had hung back. He was right to do so because he would have shown himself as he approached the clearing. He knew that Nathan had stopped. He stood on the roof of his car, which enabled him to see over the mangrove and spot exactly where the SUV was. He pushed his car off the track as quietly as possible to prevent any noise that would give him away. He felt that he was too far away and needed to get closer, so he went on foot, quietly approaching the car on the beach. He couldn't see the clearing yet, but as he got closer he could hear small noises like the rear of the SUV being opened and a door being closed.

Nathan had his backpack, boots and hat and was ready to go. He headed east towards the treeline across some open ground. Trent was still in the mangrove, not far from the beach. He certainly couldn't afford to move into the open ground before the treeline as he would be seen, so he decided to lie low and wait.

Trent saw Nathan approach the forest then halt, before starting to look around at the trees. Nathan began to walk in one direction then did an about turn and walked back. He looked towards the beach. Trent felt that Nathan was looking straight at him, but he couldn't see him as he was well hidden. Nathan seemed to be searching for something and Trent was curious and extremely interested.

19

RICO MANU was sitting in his office at Auckland Police Station when there was a knock at the door. 'Come in,' he said. A young detective walked in. 'What have you got for me Lydia?' Manu asked.

'These are the new releases from Auckland prison. Some of them go back quite a few weeks. Just thought you might want to take a look Boss.'

'Yes, thanks.' Manu took the documents from her and she walked out, closing the door behind her. Rico always liked to see who was coming back out on to the streets, especially if they were released to an address on the North Island. There were mugshots of inmates with release dates and addresses. He always liked to keep an open mind on these people as they had served their time and were allowed back on to the streets. These people should never be deliberately targeted or presumed guilty of a crime because it fitted their MO. They should be given the benefit of the doubt.

Then he came across Trent Allen's mugshot. He knew the name and the face. He knew he was a nasty piece of work who had been linked to but never successfully prosecuted for other crimes. Then he noticed the location of his release – Pakiri Beach. Trent Allen had been released to live at a holiday park.

Rico couldn't believe what he was reading, and when he noted that the release date was two weeks ago, he suddenly got a sinking feeling in his stomach. Pakiri Beach was about a fifteen-minute drive from Wellsford, where all these terrible things had been occurring, and all since Trent Allen had been released from prison.

Rico picked up his mobile and called DI Broadwell at Wellsford. 'Tim, it's Rico.'

'Hi, I wasn't expecting to hear from you.'

'I wasn't expecting to call you, but in the interest of fighting crime there's someone you need to look at urgently.'

'With regard to what?' asked Broadwell.

'The Wellsford and Warkworth murders.'

'Oh, right, and who might that be?'

'Trent Allen. I suggest you take a look at the new releases from Auckland prison.'

'Okay, will do … and thanks.'

'Bye,' said Rico, and hung up. He had come to despise Broadwell after what had happened but he wouldn't be able to live with himself if he hadn't notified him, then Trent Allen turned out to be the murderer.

~~~

At Wellsford, DI Broadwell acted on Manu's information immediately. He was desperate for a breakthrough in this case. One of his detectives got in touch with the prison and found out that Trent Allen's brother Lachlan had been his sponsor and provided him with a car and the mobile home at Pakiri Beach. Lachlan was spoken to and the details of the Black Holden Commodore obtained, plus the location of the site of the mobile home. All this had been forwarded to Broadwell.

Broadwell had no indication that Allen was in any way involved in the murders but he had to treat him as a suspect, so he made his way to Pakiri Beach with a unit of four armed officers and Detective Lima. As they approached the site it was noticeable how busy it was. Apart from people from the South Island who had come up north for some summer sunshine, there were several holiday rental camper vans. There looked to be people from Europe and the United States touring the country, and this was one of the preferred stop-off points.

Broadwell stopped his car outside the site office and Lima went inside, coming out a moment later and directing the following vehicle to the location that was shown on a small handwritten map. Fortunately, Allen's camper van was located at the rear of the site away from the beachfront and the majority of the holidaymakers. As the two vehicles approached, the first thing they noticed was that Allen's car wasn't there. But that didn't mean he wasn't in.

Broadwell and Lima jumped out of the car and the armed officers surrounded the camper van. It was quite a large vehicle, typical of the type that you see in the United States with a motorcycle strapped to its rear and a ladder to the roof. However, this one was old and discoloured, a kind of creamy grey, and it didn't have a motorcycle.

Broadwell walked up to the door at the centre of the camper van. It had a small step in front of it. He banged hard with his fist. 'Mr Allen, it's the police. Can you come out? I need to speak with you.' When nothing happened, he banged the door again and repeated himself. All the blinds in the camper van were closed except one at the front corner. He walked over and looked in, then turned around and said, 'Right, let's get in there now.'

One of the officers went to his vehicle and returned with a jemmy. He had the door open in a second and two of the other armed officers ran inside, shouting, 'Armed police, armed police.' Broadwell and Lima followed them in after receiving the all clear.

Broadwell walked up to the dining table, where there were documents laid out all over the place, the majority relating to Wellsford Ecumenical Church. As he looked closer, he saw that most of them were church documents that had presumably been stolen – details of church meetings from the 60s and church magazines. There were several documents that looked as if they had been printed from a library or similar resource. There were historical documents that talked about the early settlers and their confrontations with local Maori. There was information about shipwrecks, old and not so old. Then there were some that looked like handwritten letters.

But when Broadwell looked closer, he realised it was more like a diary or a plan of what to do next. There was a list of names and addresses, including Brenda Massey, Reverend Martin, John Selwood, Margaret Mills and 'the Englishman'.

Broadwell looked in horror at the list, knowing that the first three were already dead, leaving Margaret and Mason next on the list. 'Right, everyone out,' he shouted. Looking at Lima, he said, 'Right, call forensics out here. I want a full hit on this place. I'll get two from the investigation team out here to record everything and photograph this camper van. We'll leave two of the armed officers in their car here and the other two can come back with us to Wellsford. We've got to find this murdering bastard Trent Allen before he gets to the churchwarden and Mason. Send someone round to both their addresses and find where the churchwarden has swanned off to. And I want every officer who's out there to know the type, colour and number plate of Allen's car. Let's haul him in and let's do it fast.'

'Okay Boss,' replied Lima and got straight on to it.

20

NATHAN WALKED along the treeline in the vicinity of the cove. It was impossible to know where to start. The trees all looked the same. He was beginning to have doubts as to whether he had done enough research on this trail. He had miles and miles to trek through this forest on a route that he couldn't even find the start of. He had been too keen to start on this quest. Maybe he needed to go back and think more about how he was going to approach this with a view to success.

At the moment that he was feeling a lack of positivity, he decided to have one more try. This time he walked just within the first line of trees then walked up and down along the approximate width of the cove.

The watching Trent was ready to move off to follow Nathan but something told him to stay. It was a wise move because he noticed that Nathan was doing the same thing, walking up and down. He kept losing sight of the Englishman then he would reappear.

Nathan was about to walk away back to his car when he heard what he thought was a woodpecker tapping away on a tree nearby. It sounded like it was more or less above his head when it stopped and he saw the bird dart into a hole in the tree trunk. He stood there for a few minutes with his hand leaning against the trunk, looking up to see whether the bird would reappear. But it didn't.

Then he noticed a tickle on the back of his hand, and to his amazement a line of soldier ants were on the march from the ground all the way up the trunk of the tree and without deviation crossed over the back of his hand in a perfect line. He moved his hand away quickly and shook it to remove the insects, then he looked back at the trunk and the patrolling ants closed the gap in their line almost immediately.

That's when Nathan noticed the eye. A piece of bark had been removed from the tree many years ago by the look of it, but it was still identifiable. About six centimetres in height and the shape of a human eye, it wasn't particularly easy to see but this had to be it. There was a line protruding from it at twelve o'clock, so Nathan assumed that it meant straight ahead. All the doubt from a few minutes ago dissolved. He was sure this was the first marker to the cabin. Now he just had to spot the rest. It suddenly dawned on him how long this was going to take. He couldn't just march on with gusto. He had to take his time, observing the tree trunks and watching his footing as he went.

Nathan looked ahead and started walking, noticing the thickening canopy and the drop of temperature. There was little living on the forest floor. There was a host of old pine cones and pine straw, but the sun hadn't warmed this part of the ground for at least a quarter of a century. He could no longer hear the sea lapping on the shore. It was deathly quiet, quite dark and very eerie.

Trent was watching from his hide. He had seen Nathan walk forwards further into the forest but he was waiting just in case he reappeared. Once Nathan advanced across the open ground, he would be easy to spot, so Trent waited but had to go soon or he may lose him in the forest. He waited another couple of minutes then walked slowly to the treeline. He felt and was very exposed, but as far as he could tell Nathan didn't know he was being followed.

Trent reached the treeline and gave his eyes time to refocus. It was gloomy but he could hear up ahead someone walking, presumably Nathan, the odd twig broken underfoot. He heard him cough as he walked. He couldn't see him but he could tell which way he had gone by the disrupted pine straw that layered the floor. They were a bit of a giveaway, a bit like footprints in the snow. He had to hang back though. If he could hear Nathan, then Nathan could hear him.

Peering into the forest ahead, Trent could see that it was endless tree trunks leading to a dark uphill horizon of trees. It was noticeably quiet. He could hear the odd bird singing but what he noticed most of all was the insect life, particularly of the flying kind. He recognised the spasmodic high-pitched drone of the mosquito. There were sand flies, wasps and moths all living in the same environment and all starting to make a nuisance of themselves.

Walking as quietly as he could, after only a few minutes Trent thought he may have been gaining ground on Nathan. Suddenly, he caught sight of him up ahead, so he darted behind a tree. Nathan had stopped and was looking around. Trent observed this and wondered whether Nathan was conscious of being followed. Or was he looking for something on the way? Maybe he just wasn't fit and needed to keep stopping to catch his breath.

Trent looked down at his own T-shirt. It was saturated. The humidity level today was extremely high. Maybe it was intensified because he was in the forest. He didn't know, but it was very draining and energy-sapping. It was still only mid-morning and was probably going to be a lot warmer and more humid this afternoon.

Nathan was on the move again. Trent came out from behind the tree trunk and very slowly approached the area where he had last seen Nathan. Looking ahead for any movement and watching where he was stepping wasn't easy and was made more complicated as he approached a rocky stream. The mosquitos came alive and stuck to his sweat-soaked T-shirt, feasting on the back of his neck. He moved through as quickly as possible but maintained a safe distance. The smell of pine and rotting matter was very prominent now as he moved from tree to tree, ready to take cover at any second.

Nathan came across more marked trees, the latest of which seemed to be pointing towards two o'clock, so he diverted accordingly. The incline now started to increase and the soft spongy ground made it difficult to manoeuvre through. He noticed a slight drop in temperature but no drop in the level of humidity. It was stifling and the sweat was running down his face and stinging his eyes.

He walked for another hour then looked for a suitable clearing or fallen log so he could sit down and take on some water. He found just the place; a large tree stump that didn't look too old or rotten and there was certainly no evidence of soldier ants on a route march either on or around it. He sat down on the floor with his back to the stump and opened his backpack. He took a gulp of cool water from a plastic bottle and relaxed.

Although humid, the air was so fresh with the familiar hint of pine sap. Nathan closed his eyes and could hear a bird singing in the background. Then his mind took him to a more unpleasant place … *the image of his mother and father pinned up against a wall by a reckless driver under the influence of drugs. Then he was walking across an open field. It wasn't yet dark but would be in another hour. Behind him was a pig farm where the animals were bred for best pork. He was walking away and had blood on his hands …*

Nathan awoke with a start. His head was lolling forward and his chin was on his chest. He straightened his neck then looked to the sky to ease the stiffness. 'Damn nightmare,' he muttered. He looked at his watch and saw that he had been asleep for forty-five minutes. He could have done without it. He had lost a lot of time and felt worse now than when he had sat down. He took a gulp of water, replaced the lid and put the bottle into his backpack. He stood up, stretched his back and arms and threw the backpack over his shoulders, ready to continue on the path to the cabin.

Trent was watching carefully. Now that Nathan had stood up, he could see him clearly. His own legs felt stiff, but he was grateful for the break and now ready to go again. The trek was relentless. Nathan continued to stop regularly so the progress was slow. Fortunately, the higher they got, the cooler and less humid it became. The conditions were now more suitable for long-distance walking. But how long? What was the target and how much further would it be?

21

A COUPLE of detectives had been despatched to Margaret's house first. When they arrived, they found no one home but they did find evidence of a burglary. One of the detectives called Broadwell to inform him and he flew into a rage, threw his mobile phone at the office wall and demanded from all of his team present, 'Get your act together or find yourself amongst the unemployed!'

The team at the churchwarden's house had been told to find her in no uncertain terms and not to return to the police station until they had news. Broadwell and Lima headed for Fern Heights but when they arrived there was no car on the drive and no one was answering the door. The details of Nathan's car were circulated and Broadwell called his mobile but there was no answer.

Broadwell called Rico to see whether he had heard from his friend. He hadn't but offered to call Nathan's girlfriend Loretta to see whether she had heard from him. Loretta told Rico that she hadn't heard anything from Nathan since yesterday and had no idea where he could be. Rico reported back to Broadwell.

After some painstaking work dialling through the numbers in Margaret's address book, the police eventually located her at her sister's in Wellington. A detective from Wellington was on his way to interview her. Meanwhile, all and sundry were out looking for Trent Allen's Commodore and Nathan's black RAV 4.

In the incident room at Wellsford, Broadwell stood in front of a whiteboard, discussing with his investigation team the possible connection between Trent Allen, Nathan Mason and Margaret Mills. One of the landlines rang and a detective answered, before passing the call to Broadwell. It was the detective from Wellington. He had ascertained from Margaret Mills that Nathan Mason was on his way to the Wall family home in Kaipara Flats Road the previous afternoon. Broadwell updated the team then told Lima to drive him to the location. He also asked for an armed officer to accompany them in the event that they came across Trent Allen.

The three officers made their way at speed to the Wall's residence but not before having to knock on a couple of doors to ascertain which was the correct house. Eventually, they found it, sat way back from the road. They approached in the car then Broadwell jumped out and banged on the front door.

Inside, Marlene didn't want to answer and wouldn't have if she hadn't heard the word 'police' shouted out by Broadwell in such an angry manner. Eventually, she opened the door and invited her visitors in, showing them into the lounge.

Broadwell began by informing Marlene of the urgency and the need to locate Nathan Mason because it appeared that he may be in some danger. As soon as she heard this, she told the whole story. Now Broadwell knew why Trent Allen was so desperate to find out information from the people he had killed. It was all about gold. And Allen was inevitably going to go head to head with Nathan Mason.

Marlene was helpful and was able to roughly draw a map showing the beach and approximately where the cabin was. However, she was unable to tell them how to get there.

On arrival back at Wellsford, Broadwell called a gathering of his troops and organised for all the armed personnel to prepare for a substantial search party in the Dome Forest hills.

In the meantime, a couple of patrol officers drove down to Tauhoa and were able to find the Holden Commodore, then the RAV4. That would be the starting point for the search. Both cars were now isolated and would be dealt with by forensics. Broadwell also posted a car and officers to stay at Marlene Wall's house. Everything was now in place. The difficult bit would be to apprehend both men.

22

NATHAN WAS having doubts about his decision to come on this quest. He knew that he was in a predicament and that he should consider turning back. The chances were that if he carried on and didn't find the cabin in the next twenty minutes then darkness would fall during the second part of his downward and return journey. This was one of the things warned about in the biscuit tin writings: 'Don't be in the forest after dark.'

Suddenly, underfoot Nathan felt something firm and flat. He cleared away the forest debris with his boot to reveal a small flat piece of wood. He picked it up and turned it over. It read 'URUPA' in capital white letters on what was once a black painted board. The rest of the writing had been weathered off. It was strange to see some human trace in the middle of the forest, miles from anywhere. The sign looked incredibly old.

Nathan had a flashback to one of the books that he had recently read. He could see this image of a man in a field, standing next to a post, and on the post was a sign that read 'URUPA. THIS IS A MAORI BURIAL GROUND'. Why would there be a urupa all the way up here in such a remote location? Nathan thought that perhaps many years ago there had been a settlement here that had eventually died off for whatever reason, probably due to its location and the more attractive draw of the coast.

He noted that a directional eye on the tree in front of him was directing him to the right and presumably around the burial ground. He followed the route as instructed, which took him around a square plot about fifty metres before he returned to his normal line to the cabin.

Trent was watching. He couldn't understand why Nathan had gone on this roundabout route just to get back to his original direct line. He decided that unless there was an obstruction he was going straight ahead. He wanted to save as much energy in his legs as possible.

He could see through the trees about 150 metres ahead of him, where Nathan seemed to be moving with more intent now, then suddenly stopped and turned around. Trent's only option was to dive for cover and lie flat on the ground. He waited before he dared to look up, and when he did, Nathan was nowhere to be seen.

Not panicking but with more haste, Trent upped his pace and within no time was roughly at the point where Nathan had deviated from his route. There were no obstructions or water, so he continued straight ahead to try to catch up. He could no longer hear anything up ahead. There were no twigs or branches breaking under Nathan's feet, nor birds singing; no mosquitos or bees buzzing.

It felt surprisingly cold now and Trent suddenly felt a bit lightheaded and started to wonder whether he was becoming dehydrated. He decided to stand still for a moment but the lightheaded feeling wouldn't go away. He started to feel dizzy, his head reeling. The atmosphere began to shimmer and change around him. The pine straw beneath his feet seemed to shape-shift into a mass of earthworms. He didn't know or understand what was happening.

Trent turned to look at the trunk of a tree immediately to his right. It appeared as if its bark was being stripped to reveal a brightly coloured sap-ridden core beneath it. Then the trunk of the tree was being carved by invisible hands and tools. Working the trunk at high speed, pieces of the wood were meticulously chiselled and removed to display a huge Maori sacred spirit guardian, then the completed carving suddenly changed to a weathered nut-brown colour. There were fearsome eyes and facial tattoos carved deep and dark. The wood cuttings, which were piling up around the base of the tree, were in the process of change to what looked like thousands of black cockroaches.

Trent looked into the eyes of the carving and was filled with immense fear. He felt as if it was looking deep into his soul as the fingers of a chilled hand wrapped themselves around his heart. He could take no more. He ran with fear etched across his face. He didn't know which direction. It didn't seem to matter. He was running up a steep incline, looking for higher ground, when suddenly he felt a sharp pain to the side of his head and everything went black.

~~~

Nathan came across a small stream just to the east of the burial ground. He stooped over and washed his hands then splashed water all over his face. He was sure that he was near the cabin now. As he walked over the next rise only a few metres in front of him was his goal – the cabin in all its splendid glory, looking more like a shotgun shack or a large shed.

Nathan approached. It was only a small building with no windows and just a single door. The only thing that wasn't made of wood were the hinges on the door, which was securely closed by a wooden hasp and staple, with a wooden peg through the hoop. That was it. There was no locking device. He removed the peg and opened the door.

It was dark inside the cabin and Nathan was overcome with a smell of musty dampness. There was a rock on the floor nearby so he moved it and used it as a door stop to keep the door open as wide as it could go. Giving himself a few seconds for his eyes to adjust, he noticed that there were quite a few posters pinned to the timber walls. A couple of them were just hanging on by some rusty old drawing pins. In the centre of the cabin was a stone fireplace with a chimney breast that rose up through the middle of the roof. There was also some basic homemade furniture – a table and a chair. On the table was a box but Nathan couldn't see what it contained.

There were several old candles lying about, so Nathan delved into his backpack and extracted his lighter, pleased that he had brought it with him. He flicked the wheel of the lighter with his thumb and it lit first time. He then found six candles strategically positioned on the table, fireplace and in each corner of the cabin. As he went around and lit each one, more of the cabin was revealed.

The cabin walls, apex and floor were all logs. The floor logs had been shaved and were more in the form of planks. The place was strewn with cobwebs, particularly in the apex, and a good layer of dust covered everything. There were a few patterns on the floor where the roof had leaked and droplets of water had fallen and left little hollows in the dust. But all in all, for its age it looked in rather good condition.

Nathan looked in the box on the table. Through the dust he could see that there was a collection of colourful stones, several of which matched up with one of the posters on the wall – pounamu or greenstone. Fred was obviously some sort of collector, but where could he have hidden the gold? If it was here, it had to be found, even if it meant taking the cabin to pieces.

Out of the blue, Nathan's thoughts turned elsewhere. He sat down for a moment in the wooden chair. He decided that he was going to try to make up with Loretta and Rico. He was going to call Millie and Margaret and Marlene Wall. The long walk seemed to have cleared his head; given him some kind of therapy to not give up on people as he had in the past. He had to forge friendships. They weren't just going to fall into his lap. It was the fear of loneliness that subconsciously bothered him. They were the feelings that he was experiencing right now.

He pulled his mobile phone out of his backpack. He should have known there wasn't much chance of a signal bouncing through these wooded valleys. He had wondered why in the last few hours his mobile hadn't chirped, beeped or made any other kind of electronic notification noise that he was familiar with. There was no signal. He was totally isolated and for now he had to live with it.

Trying to shrug off the feelings of loneliness and feeling sorry for himself, Nathan was now concerned about the lateness of the afternoon and whether he would be able to make it back before dark. It would be madness to just turn around now and head back, then have to make the gruelling journey again. But likewise, he didn't fancy sleeping in the cabin in that old chair, waiting for daybreak. But what choice did he have? Maybe it was just a wild goose chase anyway.

Dismissing the negative thoughts, he carried the chair, table and box outside. There was an old handmade broom in the corner made of a branch, with a bunch of small twigs tied to one end. He picked it up and swept the old cobwebs away from above his head and in the corners. Then he brushed everything on the floor to the door, although most of the dust and dirt just fell through the small gaps in the floor timbers.

Seeing this, Nathan was intrigued and went outside to investigate. He noticed that the cabin had actually been built about half a metre off the forest floor, with the corner posts acting as stilts that were driven into the ground. These corner posts went up to roof level, where they formed the start of the apex. This was a strong, well-constructed little building.

But he had to see what was underneath. He walked around the cabin, looking for the best point with the widest gap for him to crawl underneath. The best location was below the entrance door as the ground had been well compacted in the past and the gap was at its widest.

On his knees and then lying flat, Nathan pushed himself under. There was natural light coming in on each side, which enabled him to scan the area. There were a couple of boxes and what looked like an old hessian-type sack on a dusty, mainly earthen section of forest floor. He crawled over to the boxes. *Surely the gold wouldn't be just sitting here in a box*, he thought. But as soon as he grabbed them, he knew there was little inside, as they were too light.

Nathan pulled the boxes over to take a look inside. A cloud of dust appeared as one box fell over on its side and a couple of old books fell out. The other box was pretty much the same size. He put his right arm around the box and pulled it towards him. The box came away from its bottom and he ended up with just a collapsed piece of cardboard in the crook of his arm. There had been something heavy in this box. He crawled over to where the box remnants lay but clouds of dust hampered his view.

Nathan waited for a few seconds and lay there completely still. He could feel the dusty grit in his eyes and on his tongue. Then he could see some sort of bag sitting on a damp piece of cardboard. He crawled a bit closer and grabbed the bag, which felt like it could have been made of leather. He decided to drag it out from its damp dungeon. It was heavy. *Could this bag contain the missing gold?*

As he pushed himself backwards towards his entrance point, Nathan came across the hessian sack and pulled it towards him. He sensed there was movement inside and it looked like a small nest of vermin, then to his horror a large stoat-like creature jumped at him from the shadows and sunk its teeth directly into his left cheek.

'Fuck,' Nathan shouted, brushing the animal away, but it stayed where it had landed and watched him. Nathan backed away slowly, dragging the bag. His heart was nearly pumping through his chest. He kept his eyes on the creature and slowly made his way out under the doorway and into the daylight. He rubbed his left cheek, which was pouring with blood.

He could feel his heart beating in his chest. He didn't know whether it was because he had been bitten or because he could have found the gold. He opened the bag as the blood dripped from his face. Turning the bag upside down, the contents fell to the ground. Two lump hammers, three steel chisels and a selection of other old and well-worn tools.

Nathan was disappointed but not disheartened. He reached for his backpack as in a plastic bag he had a few sticking plasters and cotton wool balls. He pressed one of the cotton balls to his cheek and then secured it with a sticking plaster. He mumbled to himself, 'Damn stoat … or weasel … whatever it was. I'm going to try to avoid going under there again.'

He rummaged through the tools but there was nothing of any great significance. He picked up one of the lump hammers then went inside the cabin, where he proceeded to tap every timber within the building with the head of the hammer. He was listening out for any potential hollows or hiding places. There was nothing. So, he turned his attention to the stone fireplace and chimney, tapping every piece of stone to see whether any were loose. Nothing. The whole area was so well built it would be there for centuries, even after the building had rotted away.

Nathan decided to check the exterior of the cabin. Again using the lump hammer, he checked every timber of the construction for any hollows or anomalies but there was absolutely nothing that looked or sounded anything like a hiding place.

Next, he started to look at the forest floor around him and that's when he realised that darkness was starting to fall. There was a beautiful sky, or what he could see of it, which was blue with a reddish tinge. That usually meant that another nice day was in the offing for tomorrow. For now, he had to accept the fact that he was going to be staying in the cabin for the night, as unappealing as that was. He would search the immediate area in the morning, and if he had no joy, he had to accept that he would be leaving empty-handed.

As the temperature dropped, he decided he was going to make a campfire. There were plenty of logs. In fact, there was a pile of them in the form of a pyramid at the rear of the cabin. He collected a good number of them, while keeping an eye open for his furry attacker. Having found a suitable spot to make the fire, he shaved some of the logs with his Swiss Army knife, added a pile of pine straw, then used his lighter to ignite it. He added some small twigs then gradually increased the volume to branches and eventually logs. Within half an hour the fire was burning a treat and Nathan, having finally brushed down the old chair, sat down with what was left of his water, biscuits and a badly bruised apple.

The smoke was going straight up through the canopy and out into the dark sky above. There wasn't even the slightest breeze but the air temperature was much cooler compared to earlier in the day. The only noise he could hear was the crackling of burning wood and the odd sizzle as a flame lapped across a run of bubbling pine sap. The day's exertions washed over Nathan and he fell asleep.

23

BROADWELL HAD gathered a substantial number of officers, some armed, some with dogs. They were spread out in a line approximately two hundred metres wide near the area where Nathan's car had been found. They advanced into the forest.

The officers had previously been instructed to stay in line as they marched forward but already the line had taken on the form of a dog's hind leg as some slowed to look at something or go over an obstacle. One searcher was trying to follow a trail left in the forest floor by Nathan and Trent, but he was seeing mixed signs as it looked as though several wild animals had recently gone through the area.

The police dogs were having the same problem. It had been about eight hours since the two men had made their way through the forest, so quite a time had elapsed. Now the scent was mixed with boar, possum, turkey and a mix of police searchers' body sprays. The trackers, both humans and dogs, were unsuccessful at this stage but may prove their worth later on.

Broadwell's team had been going for a couple of hours and he was conscious that in a couple more hours it would be dark. He couldn't afford to have any members of his team up in the forest in the dark. It wasn't safe. He didn't want to call the search off for the day but he had to. There were hidden dangers, but worst of all, there were two men up there and one was extremely violent. Everyone was told to return to the muster point. An even larger team was going to resume the search the following morning at 6am.

Later that day, Broadwell spoke to Rico Manu and updated him on the search for Trent Allen and Nathan Mason. Rico was upset when he heard that Nathan was missing, that the murderer Trent Allen was on his tail and that it was all about gold. Regardless of their past disagreements, Rico wasn't going to give up on his old friend. He asked Broadwell for the details of the search and he reluctantly emailed Rico a copy of the drawings of the West Dome Valley and the location of the cabin provided by Marlene Wall.

Rico knew the area but no one as far as he knew was aware of or familiar with the forest, especially the upper reaches. It could be a bit creepy and quite often in early morning was shrouded in cloud until the sun strengthened and evaporated them away.

Looking at the drawing provided and comparing it to an official scale map, Rico saw that the cabin was such a long way from the beach. The best route would be from Kaipara Flats Road and north up into the forest. It was a steeper route but it was half the distance. It meant he could get there quicker and there was also a good possibility that he would bump into Nathan on his way down. There was also the added danger of Trent Allen in the mix. However, Rico didn't believe Nathan would head back the way he went up. He would take the shorter route and drop down to Kaipara Flats Road and probably Marlene Wall's house, especially if he thought he was being followed or was in trouble.

Rico was well aware of the danger involved, particularly as far as Trent Allen was concerned. He would be prepared to leave early in the morning. He informed Broadwell that he would be joining the search but he had no intention of joining Broadwell's team.

24

WHEN NATHAN awoke, the fire was nearly out. He looked at his watch. He had been asleep for a good couple of hours and it wasn't yet midnight. Unless he could fall asleep again it was going to be an awfully long night.

Feeling a bit out in the elements and vulnerable, he wanted to be indoors, so he picked up the backpack and the chair and took them inside the cabin. Having relit the candles, he decided he needed a fire inside. Using two small branches, he picked up the remnants of the last burning log from the campfire and took them inside, nestling them in the stone fireplace surrounded by dry logs.

The fire soon took hold and the smoke was drawn up the chimney and out through the roof. The smell of the burning pine reminded him of his childhood and in particular Guy Fawkes night when he and his friends would stand around the burning bonfire that he had helped to build on the local playing field.

Nathan sat down in the chair in front of the fire and wondered whether he was doing the right thing being up here in this cabin in the forest in a foreign country. And next to an old Maori burial ground. He suddenly felt as if he was invading someone's privacy. Was he being watched? He doubted it. He had to find this gold, which must be here somewhere.

The only place in the cabin that Nathan hadn't checked was the inside the stone fireplace and chimney. He had visually checked the stonework but now it was getting quite hot so he would give it a quick look over in the morning. He also planned to do a thorough search of the area immediately around the cabin to see whether there were any obvious hiding places.

Sat in front of the fire with the candles glowing in each corner, Nathan could think of worse places to spend the night. His mind wandered and he began to think about London, the police and the friendships he had made and lost. The death of his parents was no doubt the darkest time of his life and he never expected to get over it, but he hoped that one day it might not hurt quite as much. He was enjoying watching the flames flicker and their reflection on the cabin walls.

Suddenly, he sat up in his chair and looked at the door. He thought he had heard a noise outside. He quietly got up from the chair, walked to the door and gently opened it enough to see outside. It was pitch black and he was unsure whether to go for his torch or wait for his eyes to adjust. He grabbed the thermal-imaging binoculars from the backpack and stepped outside. The fresh coolness swept across him like a mist and temporarily misted over the lenses of the binoculars.

Switching to night vision, Nathan was looking down the hill in the direction of the burial ground. For a second, he thought he saw a bright spot indicating a heat source, or was his mind playing tricks on him? He stood there waiting, his eyes scanning the area for any telltale movement or light.

He began to see a little clearer. The moonlight was shining through the canopy at irregular intervals in the forest and he could see the tree trunks, any one of which could have been a man, but with a dull glow it was difficult to tell from such a distance.

There it was again – just a flicker of light. Nathan was now unsure what to do next. Standing up on edge by the door there were some small branches about the size of a baseball bat. He had collected them earlier as firewood. He grabbed one of the branches, feeling slightly more confident but was still unsure what to do next, so he waited and watched.

Whatever it was must have been at least two hundred metres away. Could there be someone down there watching him? Maybe it was time to find out. Nathan went back into the cabin and grabbed his torch. Then in near total darkness, thanks to the moonlight, and with the binoculars around his neck, a torch in one hand and a weapon of wood in the other, he made his way back down the hill very slowly and very quietly.

For a second, Nathan thought he could hear several voices chanting, but very quietly. As he got nearer, a flickering flame shot across his eyeline from left to right about a hundred metres ahead of him. Then it shot back from right to left, occasionally disappearing behind a tree trunk. He thought he could smell some sort of wood burning or maybe incense.

Nathan was frozen in his tracks but he needed to see more. He advanced slowly, conscious that he was now approaching the urupa, the Maori burial ground. He could see movement up ahead. Perhaps what he thought were tree trunks were actually people or some kind of shape shifters. They seemed to shiver in the strange light around them and Nathan's brain couldn't comprehend what was occurring. He was scared. He couldn't explain or understand what he was seeing but it didn't seem right. He automatically started to step backwards, feeling threatened.

Suddenly, a breeze swept through the trees from nowhere and everything stopped. There were no more moving lights or shimmering trees. Nathan turned on his torch and shone it directly at the area in front of him that had him transfixed only a few moments ago. His torch lit up the tree trunks and the forest floor. There was no sign of anything unusual. All the same, he turned around and almost ran back to the cabin. He would be glad to see the back of this creepy forest. He couldn't understand what he had just seen happen. It was unexplainable.

Back in the cabin, Nathan angled a log against the inside of the door. He felt he needed the extra security but he didn't know why. Perhaps he was seeing things, maybe he had a temperature after the stoat bite and was running a fever. Either way he had no intention of going out again until daybreak. He placed a couple of extra logs on the fire, flopped down into the chair and pulled his mobile from his backpack. As expected, no signal so no messages or email.

Nathan took a sip of water and ate a biscuit. He needed to go easy on the water as he was running low. He was also hungry. He promised himself a full, all-day English breakfast when he was back in civilisation. He then thought about Loretta and whether he would ever be able to win her back.

The time spent in the cabin dragged and Nathan knew he wasn't going to sleep. Regardless of all the thoughts going through his head, he was still on high alert for any sound outside. And there were sounds. On one occasion he heard a branch snap quite nearby, probably only within a few metres, and it was a branch not a twig, so it must have been something of size and weight out there. However, he wasn't going to do what commonly occurs in the movies and walk out there to confront whatever it was. He was going to stay put, stay safe and protect his space.

It was quiet again. The flames from the log fire gave a warm flickering glow, which was just as well as the candles had long since expired and the thought of sitting there in the total darkness wasn't appealing. Nathan touched the sticking plaster attached to his cheek and pressed it ever so slightly. It was quite sore and he hoped he wasn't the recipient of some sort of animal infection. He placed the palm of his hand on his forehead but there was no sign of a temperature.

So how could he explain what he had seen in the burial ground? A shiver went down his spine. He threw another log on the fire. It was now 2am but at some point Nathan drifted off to sleep, only to be awoken by another nightmare, which felt so real … *He was in the forest. This forest. He was walking away from the burial ground. He had blood on his hands. He stopped at a small stream to wash them clean ...*

~~~

Four hours later, the fire had long gone out. Nathan had run out of logs and he wasn't prepared to go outside to retrieve more. Eventually he saw a gap of daylight around the door, so he removed his security log and opened the door. He stepped outside and shivered in the cool morning air. He was surprised to see it was foggy. He could feel the moisture on his face and everything was dripping wet. Then he realised that it was probably low cloud.

Everywhere was fresh, the trees were greener, the pine straw and soil were darker. And the smell of pine sap was stronger than ever, reminding Nathan once again of his holiday in Corfu. There were some huge cobwebs hanging from branches and the eaves of the cabin. They were heavily laden with water droplets and just about holding together under the immense strain on their tiny fibres.

It was barely light, but Nathan knew it was time to finish his search. He would be pleased to see the back of this forest once and for all. He would be doubly pleased if he could find the gold and deliver it to Marlene Wall. He looked down the hill towards the burial ground, which was dark and grey as the moisture-filled cloud drifted between the trees. He didn't believe in the supernatural but that place gave him the creeps. His intention was to stay as far away as possible.

He went back into the cabin and after a quick sip of water decided to have a look at the stone fireplace and chimney for any possible hiding places. Standing on the chair, he stretched as far as he could, grabbing each piece of stone on the outside of the chimney breast and working downwards. He noticed that they all seemed to have been pointed with mortar and he contemplated the journey up here with the sand and cement to do the job. It really must have been a labour of love.

Just above the fire opening Nathan finally came across a piece of stone that didn't seem to be secured with mortar. He wiggled it from side to side and was able to gradually withdraw it from its recess. He was excited, thinking this could be it. He hoped it was. As the brick-sized stone was eventually removed, he put his hand inside the cavity but could tell that the hole wasn't much bigger than the stone that had just come out of it. However, there was something at the back of the hole.

Nathan pulled the items towards the front of the opening, and he could see from what little light was coming through the open door that it was a Castella cigar box and Zippo lighter. He opened the box and it contained four cigars. The lighter did spark when he rubbed the wheel but its fuel had probably dried up, so there was no way it was going to ignite. What a strange thing to find. Maybe the cigars were to celebrate a good find. There was one missing out of the box and Nathan wondered whether Fred Wall had smoked one after he found the gold.

Disappointed but with no time to waste, Nathan continued his search. He found no more loose stones in the external stonework, so he decided to take a quick look inside the fireplace and chimney breast. It was pretty dark in there, so he used his torch to illuminate the internal stonework. It was jet black with soot as he expected and the stones were still warm from the recent fire. He gingerly put his left arm up the chimney breast while trying to illuminate the way with the torch in his other hand.

Grabbing the warm stones, they seemed to be secure, then suddenly his hand came across something that felt considerably hotter than the stones. He touched it again but this time it moved ever so slightly. He tried to get his hand around it but it was just too hot. He let go and it fell into the ashes of the fire. A cloud of dust ashes and a few sparks flew into the air as the object hit the remnants of the seat of the fire. Nathan's face and upper body were engulfed with sooty dust. He removed himself quickly and ran outside to cough and to rub his eyes.

Looking like a chimney sweep, he returned immediately to the fireplace. Rummaging through the hearth ashes with a twig, he saw the brick-sized object right in the middle. He scraped the top of it and he could see straight away that it was metallic. It was hard to tell in the light but it looked gold.

Nathan was now breathing heavily in his excitement. He grabbed the object and quickly pulled it out of the fireplace and dropped it on to the log floor. He inhaled sharply as the pain from the hot metal penetrated the end of his fingers. He ran outside, grabbed a handful of pine straw and ran back in, before wiping away the soot from the top of the object with the straw.

Nathan's eyes opened wide with amazement. It was a beautiful bright gold ingot. It looked as if it had been cast yesterday. He punched the air in excitement, shouting, 'Yes, yes.'

Knowing that there could be two more bars to find, Nathan got back into his previous position, and sure enough, he could feel another two hot metallic objects. They must have all been next to each other. He pulled them both down at once and they crashed into the hearth. A plume of ash and soot covered him yet again but he didn't care. He grabbed them in turn and threw them out on to the cabin floor. Using the pine straw he wiped the top of each bar to confirm they were gold. He then reached inside the chimney just to make sure there were no more sitting conveniently on the shelf. He didn't expect there to be and there wasn't.

Nathan sat there for a moment, just contemplating and looking at what he had found. He picked up one of the bars. It was extremely heavy for its size. A good comparison would be the size of a house brick. He cleaned the bar as best he could and could tell it was roughly cast as he could see the mould marks and slight imperfections. All the same, it was a beautiful sight.

With some urgency, Nathan jumped and loaded the three gold bars into his backpack. He just managed to fit them in then realised that their combined weight was considerable. He lifted the backpack on to the table then put his arms through the straps, positioned it on his back and took the weight. He had done a quick calculation and concluded that these three bars must be about eighty or ninety kilos. It was like carrying a medium-sized child on your back. And he had a long way to travel.

He took the bag off and put it back on the table then pulled the maps out of one of the pockets. He studied both maps and knew that if he headed south he would eventually come to the Kaipara Flats Road. He knew that this route was shorter than the westerly one but the decline was much more severe and he was unsure of the landscape. One consolation was that it would all be downhill. The thought of carrying a bag with that weight uphill for hours was one of nightmares. He wondered how on earth Fred Wall did it in the first place and considered what difficulties he must have endured.

Nathan picked up his mobile but there was still no signal. The implications were that none of the apps were working so he was unable to use the compass. He made sure everything was packed in his backpack, then went outside and put the peg through the hasp and staple securing the cabin door. He looked down the hill in front of him towards the burial ground.

Last night's nightmare came back to him. Why would he be in there, and why would he have blood on his hands? Like most nightmares it didn't make any sense but it unnerved him and he was going to leave right now. He knew the direction of the burial ground was west, so the southerly direction was to his left. He turned to start his long walk back to civilisation with the cache of gold on his back.

25

B ROADWELL HAD amassed a substantial search team. There were more dogs, there were more armed officers and there were teams of men and women following on behind, dealing with anything evidential connected to either Trent Allen or Nathan Mason. There was even talk of a possible helicopter search.

Today everyone seemed to be more prepared, with the correct clothing, footwear and headgear. There was even a team following on behind carrying supplies such as drinks and food to take up to the searchers as and when required. It was being run like a military operation.

~~~

Meanwhile, Rico parked his car in a small layby on the Kaipara Flats Road. He too was prepared to spend the day looking for the two men. He had water, food and his service-issue sidearm just in case. He stepped out of the car and grabbed his backpack.

The day was still quite cool as the sun had yet to rise so this was a great opportunity to cover some good distance before the heat of the day slowed him down. He was in the forest more or less straight from the road. At these lower levels, the forest was thick with cordyline and huge fern trees, which grew in between the pine and other trees. It was a mass of colour and insect life – butterflies, moths and bees – and the birds were singing. It was going to be another beautiful day weather-wise.

Rico was acutely aware of the dangerous situation he was putting himself in and he had to be aware of what was going on around him. Trent Allen was a dangerous killer and by the sound of it would stop at nothing to get his hands on the gold. If he or Nathan got in Allen's way, they would be added to the murder statistics.

Rico was also aware that mobile phone coverage in the area was poor, so he had come equipped with some old-school technology. He had a compass around his neck and a folded map in his back pocket. He had the cabin marked on the map and knew roughly the direction to travel in.

In between his current location and the cabin was a very steep incline and miles and miles of dense forest. There were fence boundaries and signs informing that the land was private forestry commission land. There were gullies, streams and many other hazards. Like Nathan, Rico had no path to follow, so he made his own path and hoped that he was heading in the right direction and that his limited orienteering skills were adequate.

~~~

Broadwell's team was making good progress. The gradual incline had enabled the front runners to make good advances deep into the forest; however, now that the sun was up, the temperature was on the increase and their only relief would be when they reached the upper limits of the forest.

They had found no evidence that they were on the right track but this search party was spread along a line that must have been four hundred metres long. They were in touch with each other by radio and Broadwell was in the middle directing operations. The mood amongst the search party had been tense. They were all under pressure. There was a madman on the loose and no one knew what he was going to do next.

~~~

Nathan stopped for a sit down and to take some deep breaths without the pressure of the weight on his back. The straps of the backpack had been digging into his shoulders and he could feel that they were sore when he touched them through his T-shirt. He had made good progress but the constant weight, along with the odd jerk on the shoulder straps as he cleared an obstacle, was playing havoc with his shoulders and back.

He took his last sip of water. That was it but he put the empty bottle in his backpack so that he could fill it if he came across a clean water supply. He touched his cheek and realised that the sticking plaster was no longer there. He had been sweating so much, particularly since he got out of the low cloud, that it must have lost its adhesiveness and just fallen off. He looked around him on the forest floor but there was no sign of the plaster, which could be a giveaway, indicating that he had passed this way. The incident in the urupa the previous night had unnerved him but he wasn't unduly concerned and neither did he sense that he was being followed.

Nathan picked up the backpack and sucked air through his teeth as the straps dug into the sore spots on each shoulder. He continued slowly down the hill again, then stopped suddenly. He could hear a helicopter quite a distance away. He wished it would fly over and drop a line right down to his feet and rescue him. But he knew it wasn't for him. No one was looking for him because no one was missing him as far as he was aware.

He had been on the move for a good couple of hours now and knew he must already have covered more than half of the distance to Kaipara Flats Road. It was now much warmer as the dappled sunshine crept through the canopy to the east. All of a sudden, he walked into a cloud of small midge flies, some of which stuck to the sweat on his skin. He brushed them off his face and the back of his neck. Then as he looked to his right, lying on the forest floor was a wild boar. It was huge, at least six feet in length with a large roughly haired body. It was just lying on its side surrounded by thousands of small flies, which gathered around its eyes, nose, mouth and backside. It had menacing-looking tusks, probably about two to three inches long, which protruded from its bottom jaw.

Nathan was glued to the spot. He hoped that the beast was dead but the cloud of flies around it prevented him from seeing any telltale signs of life. Even worse, he noticed some smaller boars half hidden in the brush nearby. He had to move; this was an extremely dangerous place to be, so he stepped to his left until he had made a good space between himself and the beast, then continued downhill.

There was a crack as he stepped on an old rotten branch. Nathan heard a squealing screech from behind him and he turned to look round. To his horror, he saw that the huge boar was charging at him. He pulled his backpack off and held it in front of him as some sort of protection. The beast came to a halt about two metres in front of him and just stared. Nathan slowly made his way backwards until he could feel a tree trunk behind him. Suddenly, the beast charged at great speed, heading straight for him. At the last second, Nathan shuffled himself out of the way and around the rear of the tree. The beast hit the tree hard but within a flash it had followed him round to the other side.

All Nathan could do was to stick his leg out to try to keep the thing away but it wrapped its jaws around his boot and the horrible stinking green tusks latched on. It was a fearsome creature. Its head was huge and its small pig-like eyes were running and mortified by small black midges. The boar looked as if it wanted to kill and eat him for getting too close to its young.

With this thought in mind, Nathan grabbed the backpack straps in both hands, swung the bag as far as he could and with a blood-curdling scream made sure that it impacted on the side of the boar's head. As it made contact, the boar grunted, released, then turned around and staggered away. Nathan quickly put the backpack on and continued down the hill.

He was now dripping with sweat and the straps were digging into his shoulders so hard, but this was no time to stop. He approached a bank of fern trees and moved through as quickly as he dared. There was a small stream in front of him. He was too heavily laden to jump over so he walked through and immediately felt mosquitos biting his legs, arms, face and the back of his neck.

He carried on a little further in extreme discomfort before stopping, putting the bag down and breaking a branch off a small fern tree to give himself a good brush down. Already his legs looked a mass of red blotches and he noticed a tear in his left boot, no doubt caused by the boar. He touched one of his shoulders and saw that his fingers had turned red with a mix of blood and sweat.

He was extremely tired but more determined than ever to get to Marlene Wall's house with his consignment of gold. He noticed that up ahead there was a hill to climb. Maybe this was the last hill before the descent to Kaipara Flats Road. He hoped so, as the weight on his shoulders was becoming unbearable and he would be needing a long rest by the time he reached the top.

Nathan started the ascent but became aware of noises both to his right and from behind him. He turned back for a quick look and could see some movement in the ferns. He tried to scramble up the hill, not knowing what was coming up behind and from the side. He felt as if he was in an ambush situation. Then he lost his footing and fell to his face. He turned over to see the same huge wild boar on the charge and heading straight for him, snorting as it ran. It was only about five metres away from him and he was thinking the worst when there were two loud bangs in succession. The beast fell to the floor in a bloody mess with one hole through its head and one through its side. A large man appeared out of the fern holding a handgun. It was Rico Manu.

~~~

Broadwell heard the shots, which didn't sound close by. He instructed his team to continue but to pick up the pace. The dogs were already becoming more active and pulling on their long leads. Broadwell's radio crackled into life. It was Rico Manu informing him that he had found Nathan and his consignment and that he was safe. They would be going to Marlene Wall's house on the Kaipara Flats Road via the southern route from the cabin.

'Damn you, Manu. You were supposed to be with me on my team,' Broadwell cursed.

'Just as well I'm not,' replied Rico. 'I've just had to keep Nathan from being gouged by a huge pig. The two shots you probably heard were me. I had to put it down. Any news on Trent Allen?'

'Nothing. His car has been here since yesterday. As far as we're concerned he'll be on your tail and I bet he isn't far behind you. He's letting Mason do all the carrying then he'll strike at the end. You had better be prepared. I take it Mason hasn't heard sight nor sound?'

'I haven't asked him yet. We'll be prepared if Allen appears. It sounds as if you and your team are hours away from us.'

'How were we to know that Mason was going to go south? Anyone in their right state of mind would head back to their car. But then I think we know that your friend isn't in the right state of mind is he?' Broadwell said with a sneer.

'You're fucking useless Broadwell. It will all come out how incompetent you are and what a bad decision it was to put you in charge,' said Rico.

'Today is a classic example of why I'm in charge and not you Manu. You're a loose fucking cannon.'

'You're in charge because you went sucking up to the chief and told tales about me behind my back. You're a disgrace and I wouldn't trust you as far as I could spit.'

''Well let's hope that you don't have to rely on my trust then,' said Broadwell in a threatening tone.

They ended the conversation then Broadwell ordered half of his dog and firearms team to move on up to the cabin at speed while he stayed with the follow-up team. One of the dogs in his team had become particularly excited. It was a cadaver dog and was able to smell dead bodies or remnants of bodies, in some cases up to a hundred years old. One of the searches to Broadwell's left shouted, 'Stop.' Broadwell went over to speak to a young police officer who had been drafted in from Auckland North Shore.

'What's the problem?' Broadwell asked. She pointed to the floor at a sign that said 'URUPA'. 'What does this mean?' he added.

'It's an old Maori burial ground. We should walk around it,' the officer said.

Broadwell turned to his team and announced over the radio, 'This is a Maori burial ground. Anyone who doesn't want to come through, follow this young lady and she'll lead you around the outside.'

'I didn't mean ... I was just pointing out what it was,' the young officer said.

'Well now you have a job to do to take your conscientious objectors around the burial ground,' Broadwell said with sarcasm. But he was then surprised when the majority of his team followed the officer on an alternative route, out of objection at the way she had been spoken to and the fact that several of them were Maori.

Knowing that the cadaver dog was overrun with scents from the burial ground, Broadwell and his small team moved through quickly. Then the same dog insisted on going up on to a large, raised area, which consisted of an overgrown rock formation surrounded by brush, fern and other types of small trees and shrubs. It looked totally out of place, a bit like an oasis in a desert.

Due to its gradual incline, the dog and his handler were able to walk up the rock face. As they reached the top the dog nearly dragged the handler through the greenery in its enthusiasm and they both disappeared from view. A moment later the handler shouted out, 'Boss, you had better come and see this.'

Broadwell marched up the rock face and pushed through the greenery. The dog was lying on its front with its tail wagging, and its handler was on his knees next to him. They were both staring into a huge crevice in the rock. It looked to be about five metres long and about a metre wide. There was warm air emanating from the depths, and the side walls appeared to be covered in moist-looking lichen.

'What the hell?' exclaimed Broadwell. 'It looks like some sort of earthquake fracture.' He had never seen anything like it in this part of the country. He picked up one of the numerous small boulders that were nearby and dropped it into the fracture, listening carefully for a thud as the rock hit the bottom. He waited and waited. There was nothing, absolutely nothing. 'Jeez, this thing is bottomless.'

'Yes, and we're still in the burial ground, so the fracture is going right through the earth beneath us. No wonder the cadaver dog is going crazy,' said the dog handler.

Broadwell thought about the situation for a few seconds, then said, 'Okay, let's get out of here. Let's move on.'

~~~

Nathan couldn't believe it. He had thought his time was up. And it would have been, were it not for Rico appearing from his position of camouflage. Once Rico had finished his radio call to Broadwell, he walked over to Nathan. 'Nice to see you two are still getting on,' said Nathan.

Rico ignored Nathan's remark. 'Are you trying to get yourself killed?' he asked.

'Just trying to get this property back to where it belongs.'

'Look Nathan, I know all about the gold but so does somebody else and he's on your tail and wants it. He's killed three times already. There's a huge search party out in the hills looking for him and he's probably just heard my gunshots. He'll be coming Nathan.'

'Who is he, and how do you know he's following me?'

'His name is Trent Allen. Recently released from prison. He obviously got a sniff of the gold story and has been trying to extract information from people ever since. He must have been following you because his car is parked not that far from yours near the beach.'

'I guess we should crack on then,' Nathan said as he looked over Rico's shoulder at the huge boar lying there surrounded by flies. 'Thanks Rico. You saved my life.'

'Yes, I did, didn't I.' Rico smiled and they high-fived.

'Before we carry on,' Nathan said, 'have a quick look in the bag.'

Rico stooped over and looked inside the backpack. 'Wow! That's some haul. How many ingots?' he asked.

'Three large ones.'

'That's two for me and one for you,' said Rico.

'That's exceedingly kind of you to offer to carry two ingots. That will be a great relief off my shoulders,' said Nathan with a smile.

'Ha, ha, very funny but I'm afraid that I have the gun and I have to protect you, so no carrying for me.'

'Typical Kiwi,' Nathan muttered with a grin.

'I'll share the load with you mate. Let's just move on a bit further,' suggested Rico.

Rico helped Nathan with his backpack. He could see that Nathan was in a mess and that the straps had been rubbing his shoulders, causing them to bleed. 'What happened to your face mate?' he asked.

'Oh, I got bitten by a … sorry, can't remember, it was a bit like a long rat.'

'You'll need a tetanus when we get back. Okay, let's go quietly now but be aware of what's going on around us. Keep focused.' Nathan gave Rico a thumbs up.

Broadwell's advanced team had reached the cabin first, about ten minutes ahead of the rest. They surrounded the cabin and after receiving no acknowledgement of their stated intention to enter, the firearms team made a tactical entry. They found that the cabin had been occupied very recently and had been vacated only a short while earlier.

When Broadwell reached the cabin he tried to contact Rico by mobile and his police radio but without success. Nothing was getting through; the area was a real black spot. He decided to split his team up again. The armed officers were to head south down the hill towards Kaipara Flats Road. He and the rest of the team would return to their vehicles and then set up a new base at Kaipara Flats Road, leaving one car to watch Trent Allen's vehicle.

~~~

Rico was trying to lead Nathan on his return path but was having trouble identifying exactly where he was. He resorted back to his compass to make sure they were still heading due south. Nathan had checked his mobile for a signal but now the battery was dead. Rico had gesticulated several times for Nathan to stand still while he had a listen to the forest. There was still no evidence that they were being followed. There was nobody nearby anyway.

The temperature was rising as they approached late morning. The sweat was stinging Nathan's shoulders where the skin had been broken by the straps. One of his eyes was black and swollen, no doubt due to the stoat bite to his cheek. His T-shirt and shorts were filthy and he was starting to smell.

'Do you want me to carry a bit for you mate?' asked Rico.

'Thanks, but I'll just go another ten minutes.'

When they did eventually stop, Rico gave Nathan a long drink of cold water from his flask.

'Water has never tasted so good,' said Nathan. 'Thanks for this. By the way, I think my future with Loretta is over.'

'How come?'

'Since I was hauled in and questioned for the murder of ... erm ... the treasurer. I presumed that you told her. Can't say I blame her really. The last thing that she wants is to be going out with another guy who's constantly in trouble with the police.'

'I didn't tell her,' insisted Rico. 'What makes you think I had?'

'I've tried to contact her and she hasn't been in touch with me since the other night.'

'That's because her mum and dad had a road traffic accident and they both ended up in hospital.'

'I had no idea. How are they?'

'Marika told me they're both due out today.'

'And you didn't tell Marika about me being taken in for questioning again?'

'No,' said Rico. 'We had a bit of a fight about another matter so we're not really on speaking terms at the moment. Just pleasantries if you can call them that.'

'Well one man's misfortune is another man's gain. I'll tell Loretta all about this when it's all over. I need the chance to clear my name and create a better impression on her.'

'Good luck with that. I'm a bit off women at the moment.'

'You'll be on the phone later apologising to her,' said Nathan.

'You might be right actually,' said Rico smiling. They high-fived again.

Rico swapped backpacks with Nathan and they continued their descent. Rico was leading and Nathan got the impression that he knew where he was. They came across another small stream then a really dense section of fern and cordyline. They pushed their way through, and when they appeared on the other side, they were covered in spiders, their webs and little ticks.

They were brushing each other down when Rico suddenly put his finger to his lips 'Shh,' he whispered. Nathan could hear something but it was still a fair distance away. He could hear noises that appeared to be moving through the ferns in their direction. Rico gave the backpack full of gold to Nathan, then started to walk towards the fern. He now had his gun in his hand and he was prepared to use it again if need be.

Using hand signals, Rico directed Nathan back towards a particularly large tree that could afford some cover. Suddenly, chaos ensued. A large turkey scrambled through the fern with panic and bluster. There were feathers flying and midges scattered into the air as a second turkey ran through, making strained gobbling noises. The birds were being chased by what looked like a possum, which disappeared again back into the ferns when it saw Rico. The turkeys just ran on ahead without stopping.

Rico gave a big sigh of relief. His finger had been poised on the trigger. He turned around and looked at Nathan, who was still standing by the tree. Rico puffed out his cheeks and exhaled, symbolising a release of the pressure he had felt. 'Let's carry on down. There isn't far to go,' he said.

'Okay. I'll take the bag from here,' said Nathan.

'Are you sure? Your shoulders are in a mess mate.'

'This is nothing compared to what Fred Wall must have put up with all those years ago. The least I can do is to get this bag and its contents to his house and to his sister where it belongs and not let it fall into the hands of some criminal who will squander it on drugs and alcohol.'

'Well said,' replied Rico. 'I wholly agree, but do you think she'll want to share some of it out with the finders?' he added, smiling.

'I very much doubt it, but if she does, *I'll* be well sorted,' said Nathan, emphasising the 'I'.

'Typical Englishman,' muttered Rico.

They had only walked for another fifteen minutes or so when the trees started to thin out, allowing more of the bright sunshine to penetrate the forest. Up ahead there was a line of what looked like brush and fern.

'Once we get through that crap up ahead, we drop down on to the Kaipara Flats Road, so we're nearly there,' said Rico reassuringly.

They moved forwards, then suddenly ahead of them came a loud crack – a definite gunshot. Both men hit the ground quickly in a movement of self-preservation. Another crack and Nathan noticed that a small section of bark had been removed from a tree nearby with considerable force. Rico signalled for them to stay low. Although they were in an open area, they were partly hidden by several rotting old tree trunks.

Rico had his gun drawn and was looking towards the line of ferns. Someone was approaching. There was a sound of twigs and branches being crumpled underfoot. *Perhaps the murderer Trent Allen has finally caught up with us*, Rico thought, although the two men, rightly or wrongly, were expecting an approach from the rear not the front.

A huge man in a red, checked lumberjack shirt, blue denims, huge boots and a long grey beard appeared. He looked like a hillbilly from the Deep South of the United States. He was carrying a double-barrelled shotgun. Rico and Nathan both realised that this was a dangerous situation. Rico indicated to Nathan to stay down then jumped to his feet, handgun drawn, shouting, 'Police. Drop your weapon.'

The tension in the air was palpable as Rico waited for the man to comply. He reissued his warning and this time the man threw down his shotgun. Rico approached the man. 'Who are you? he asked.

'Daryl Elliot. I have a smallholding about half a mile down the hill near Kaipara Flats Road.'

'You could have killed us man. That was really reckless,' said Rico.

'Yes, sorry about that. I just bagged a brace of turkeys. I reckon some of the shot deflected off a large rock. It's just on the other side of the brush. I can show you if you wish.'

'No, that won't be necessary. Where are the turkeys anyway?' asked Rico.

'I strung them up to a tree. I thought there were more around but it was obviously you I was hearing. If you don't mind me asking, what are you doing up here anyway?'

Nathan stood up from his hide, much to Daryl's surprise. 'I was lost in the hills,' he said 'and he just found me. He's taking me back home. There's a huge search party going on up there with dogs and guns, so it might be a good idea to make your way back home, but not before you've shown us the quickest route to the road.'

'Yes, not a problem. You look like you've been in a battle.'

'Yes, I suppose I have. I got lost up there and ended up staying the night and had a few run-ins with the local wildlife.'

'That'll be the wild pigs then.'

'Yes,' Nathan replied.

'Vicious bastards they are, and breeding like rabbits. The trouble is, if you kill one, it's getting the bloody thing down the hill, they're that big. Otherwise you have to take all your knives with you and butcher it on the spot, and I can't stand all the flies and shit. That's why I prefer wild turkeys.'

'And nearly humans,' interrupted Rico. 'Anyway, you go ahead and lead the way. But before you do, can you please take any shells out of the gun and leave it open for me across your arm?' Daryl immediately picked up the gun, opened it and put the cartridge shells in his pocket, leaving the gun open.

Nathan picked up his heavy bag and put it on his back. He didn't want to draw any attention to it so he stayed at the back. As they walked through the last line of brush, they could see the road through the trees. They could also see a pair of turkeys strung together hanging over a low branch.

'What do those things taste like?' asked Rico.

'They taste like normal turkey; they're just a bit tougher. But my wife makes lovely curry from them. She leaves them in the slow cooker all day.'

Nathan realised how hungry and thirsty he really was and couldn't wait to sit down at a table to gorge himself and wash it down with a bottle of chilled Chardonnay. Then fall asleep in a comfortable warm bed.

'Would that be your car parked by the Whangaroa creek bridge?' said Daryl looking at Rico.

'Yes it is,' Rico replied.

'Okay, well it's about three hundred metres, something like that up the road to your left.'

'Okay. Thanks for helping us man, but do me a favour, please be more careful when you're out hunting and using that shotgun. I take it you have a licence for the gun,' said Rico.

'Yes, I do, and I keep the gun in a lockable box.'

'Do me a favour,' said Rico. 'You and your wife stay indoors for the rest of the day. We believe there's someone else in these hills, who's responsible for several serious crimes and there are a lot of police officers up there looking for him.'

'Oh right,' replied Daryl.

'Okay, we best be on our way,' said Rico.

'I'll be going this way; quickest way back for me.' Daryl walked off to the left in the direction of his farm.

Nathan shouted after him, 'I hope the turkey is good.'

Daryl didn't turn around. He just continued walking and simply raised his right arm in a leisurely wave as the two turkeys lay over the front and back of his left shoulder.

'Stupid bastard could have killed us,' said Rico, turning to Nathan. 'Anyway, let's keep alert. There's still a real nutcase floating around this area and we don't want to be caught by surprise again.'

The last few metres seemed like agony to Nathan as they walked out of the forest on to Kaipara Flats Road. His legs, his back, his shoulders, his face – everything ached with a severe intensity and the bag on his back got heavier and heavier.

'Give me the bag,' said Rico.

'No,' replied Nathan. 'Let's just get to the car.'

Both men were sweating heavily in the now bright sunshine. There was no breeze and it was sultry, humid and sticky.

'There's the car,' said Rico, pointing up ahead. The feeling of relief welled up in Nathan and a tear ran down his cheek, stinging the skin around the stoat bite as it went.

There was huge relief as they reached the car. Nathan threw the bag into the boot and they both climbed in. The engine was soon on and the air conditioning on full fan. Rico made a quick call to Broadwell on his mobile. The signal wasn't good but he was able to let him know that Nathan was safe and on his way home. He told him that there was no sign of Trent Allen, to which Broadwell replied with a few expletives before the line went dead.

'Rico, do you mind taking me to get my car?' said Nathan.

'Of course not, just direct me.'

They travelled through Kaipara and were stopped by police at Tauhoa. It was part of Broadwell's team doing vehicle checks and looking for the fugitive. They were waved through and crossed SH16. As they approached the mangroves they knew they were by the sea. They came across the dark Holden Commodore, which had been parked in a manner that rendered it partly hidden.

'I recognise that car,' said Nathan.

'Yes, that will be Trent Allen's,' Rico replied.

Suddenly, two armed police officers appeared and waved them down. Once again, when the officers realised who was driving, Rico and Nathan were ushered through. They moved through the narrow track with mangrove on either side before it opened out to the lovely sandy beach. Rico headed straight over to Nathan's car. The armed officers must have radioed through because the officers at the beach were obviously expecting them.

'Let's not get the bag out of the boot here. We'll stop on the way back to do it,' said Rico.

'Okay, as long as you don't do a runner and leave the country.'

Rico looked at Nathan with a smile on his face, which indicated he liked the idea.

Nathan noticed that the police officers treated Rico with great respect. They were clearly pleased to see him and ready to ask him about family members and so on. Rico reciprocated with, 'How's your dad doing?' or 'What's your sister doing these days?' and such like. That was the side of Rico that Nathan was familiar with. It had only been on this visit to New Zealand that he had seen the other side to him –

combative, short-tempered and, in Nathan's opinion, suffering from stress. Having said that, Rico had been there when he needed him and had saved his life when the boar attacked.

Nathan jumped in his car and left the beach, with Rico not far behind. They stopped nearby in a secluded spot and Rico handed over the bag.

'Rico, I just wanted to say a big thank you for what you've done for me. You saved my life up there.'

Rico looked at Nathan with intensity and said, 'You would have done the same for me, right?'

'You know I would,' replied Nathan.

'What are you going to do with the gold?'

'I'm going to Marlene Wall's house right now to give it to her. It's her gold.'

'I'm not sure about the law on treasure finds. I would have to look it up, but it will probably have to be declared to the authorities,' said Rico.

'Then she'll have to declare it. It's her gold and not my problem,' replied Nathan.

'Nice problem to have though, eh?'

'Just a bit.'

Rico was going to make his way back to Auckland as he had pressing matters to deal with on his own patch. The two men shook hands and agreed to stay in touch.

A few minutes later, Nathan pulled into the drive of Marlene's house and drove up to the front door. He got out of the SUV, opened the boot and lifted out the heavy bag, then knocked on the front door. Surprisingly, Marlene opened the door very quickly. She must have seen him arriving, Nathan assumed.

'Oh my god,' Marlene said with a look of horror on her face. 'What on earth happened to you?'

'It's a long story Marlene, which if you don't mind, I would like to come back tomorrow to tell you all about, but first of all I have a special delivery for you.'

'Come through,' Marlene said.

Nathan quickly took off his boots and carried the bag through into the lounge. He sat down on the sofa while Marlene remained standing in front of him. He could see she was full of anticipation and the tears were welling in her eyes as he handed her the first gold bar. She buckled a little under the weight and Nathan got up and took her over to her seat.

'I can't believe it after all these years. The remaining gold is here at last,' Marlene said, then she kissed the gold bar. Her tears fell upon the cold shiny metal.

'I have another two in my bag Marlene. I hope you have a secure place to keep them.'

'I do,' she said, still sobbing.

'Here are the other two,' Nathan said and opened the bag so she could see the contents.

Marlene was regaining her composure now. 'We had a safe built into the floor underneath the coat and boot cupboard,' she said. 'My mum organised it after Fred's find.'

She walked out of the room and Nathan followed her into the hall. There was a small cupboard off to the right. She opened the door and said, 'If you can pull that shoe rack out and move those old gum boots, then lift the carpet, you'll see what's underneath.'

Marlene walked away and came back a few seconds later with a large key. Nathan had removed the contents of the cupboard into the hall and pulled out the old piece of carpet, which lifted a cloud of dust into the air, causing him to cough.

'Sorry about that,' Marlene said. 'I never clean that cupboard out.' She handed him the key and he inserted it into the lock and turned it. He pulled the door open by the key. It was very heavy and squeaked on its hinges as he opened it. He took the keys out, which enabled him to lay the door almost flat on its back.

Nathan couldn't help noticing that there was a quantity of notes with rubber bands around them already in the safe. 'Do you know there's cash in here Marlene?' he said.

'Yes, I usually go in there every six months or so to get some money out. It's what I live off. We never had any pensions or savings, you see.'

Nathan pushed the cash to the side so that it was easily accessible then he took the three gold bars, placed them in the safe, locked it, put the carpet back in place and moved everything back into the cupboard. Meanwhile, Marlene had been into the kitchen and returned with a large tumbler of ice-cold water.

'Sorry, I should have offered you a drink when you arrived,' Marlene said.

Nathan made short work of the water and handed the glass back to Marlene. She clamped his hand against the glass with her two hands. 'I can never thank you enough,' she said, and her eyes started to fill again.

'You already have Marlene. You already have,' Nathan said, smiling at her.

'I'll see that you get recompense.'

'No Marlene, please, there's no need. You may have to declare it anyway; I'm afraid I don't know the law on treasure finds.'

'I have a friend, similar age to me. She used to work in the library in Warkworth, then in the museum. She helped us last time when Fred brought the gold back. She'll know what to do.'

'I'm just so pleased I was able to get this gold back to you. I couldn't stand the thought of it falling into the hands of a criminal who would squander it on his own pleasures and improve the profits of the local drug dealers in the process.'

'You're a good man Nathan, but tell me, what about this evil guy that's out there. Should I be worried? Should we all be worried?'

'I think we should always be on our guard but we have to get on with our lives and not allow it to be run by a sadistic maniac.'

'I have a shotgun you know,' said Marlene, as if she was letting Nathan know about a national secret.

'On that note, I'm leaving,' said Nathan with a snigger. 'One encounter with a shotgun is more than enough for me today.'

'What do you mean?' replied Marlene.

'I'll come by and tell you the whole story tomorrow, but for now, if you don't mind, I need to get back, get showered, get some food and some rest.'

'Thank you again Nathan.'

Nathan leaned forward and gave Marlene a peck on the cheek. He left the house, jumped into his RAV and made his way back to Fern Heights. He very nearly fell asleep at the wheel while he was on SH1 and was relieved beyond belief when he eventually approached his turn-off and made his way up to the house. He opened the gates but didn't bother to close them behind him.

He parked up, made his way into the house, up the stairs, stripped off and jumped straight into the shower. The warm water and shower gel washed over him like silk. It felt so good until the stinging started. His face, his arms, his legs. He jumped out of the shower and dried off then stood in front of the bedroom mirror. What a sorry state. Legs and arms reddened and covered in mosquito bites, his face swollen and sore thanks to the stoat. Funnily enough, the largest of his creature assailants and the deadliest, the wild boar, had created the least damage. Thanks to Rico.

Nathan lay on the bed in his clean boxer shorts and instantaneously the inevitable happened.

~~~

The following day around lunchtime Nathan was woken by a loud banging on the front door then a consistent ringing of the bell. He jumped up and, with a sore head, he trudged down the stairs to the front door. Still half asleep, he opened the door to find his sister standing there with her suitcase.

'Nathan, what the hell!' Millie shouted. She stormed past him as the taxi drove away down the drive. Nathan closed the door and turned to see her standing there and she was clearly not impressed.

'I've been ringing your mobile and the house phone. You said that you would pick me up at the airport,' Millie said.

'But you said on Monday,' Nathan replied.

'It is Monday, you silly sod. I was so worried. I thought something had happened to you and by the looks of your face I was right to be concerned.'

'I'm so sorry, I really am. It's a really long story. Come through and I'll make you some tea.'

They walked through into the kitchen and it dawned on Nathan that the whole house was a mess as he hadn't had chance to clean it. Preparing for the onslaught, he gritted his teeth.

26

BROADWELL AND his team had concluded their search of the West Dome Forest hills. Although they had only searched about five per cent of the area, the DI concluded that Trent Allen had somehow fallen down the crevice and would probably never be recovered. This conclusion was based around the behaviour of the cadaver dog, regardless of the fact that they were in a burial ground. A thorough search of the cabin and two others that they came across en route all proved inconclusive for anything relating to Trent Allen.

Broadwell visited Marlene Wall, who confirmed that Nathan had been to her house and was in a poor condition. Marlene thought Broadwell asked her some strange questions: 'Did Nathan appear to be frightened?' 'Did he look like someone on the run from someone or something?' 'Did he come across anyone else while he was in the forest' 'Did he appear to have any blood on him?' 'Did he have any injuries?' 'Was he carrying any weapons?'

The questions had been relentless. Some Marlene could answer and some she couldn't. All Broadwell seemed to be interested in was Nathan and his behaviour. Then right at the end just before he left, he asked, 'I assume he gave you the gold?'

'Yes,' replied Marlene, 'and it's been safely deposited.'

'Well, I'll get back to you about that. I'm not sure what your legal requirements are with regards to ownership.'

Marlene was pleased to see the back of Broadwell. He wasn't a pleasant man and she even considered relocating the gold so he would be unable to get his hands on it. In the end she decided that if she did that it would appear dishonest. If she had to hand it in, then hand it in she would.

A couple of hours later, Broadwell was on the telephone to Marlene. 'Hi Mrs Wall, Detective Inspector Broadwell here.'

Marlene's heart sank. 'Hello again.'

'I just wanted to let you know about the find of gold that you're now in possession of and what you need to do.'

'Okay,' she replied.

'According to the treasury you have to take reasonable steps to determine who the owner might be before you can say that it's yours.'

'Okay. I have someone who will act on my behalf to ensure that the procedure is followed.'

'In that case I would like to say congratulations.'

'Thank you.'

'I must go, I have things to do.'

'Have you caught the fugitive yet?' Marlene asked.

'No, I'm afraid not, and at this point we have no reason to believe he's still alive.'

'Oh, have you found a body?'

'No. I'm sorry, I must go now, so take care.' Broadwell hung up.

Marlene was confused, although delighted at the thought that she may never have to have dealings with Broadwell again.

~~~

Nathan had spent a good couple of hours explaining to Millie what had been going on while she had been away. Millie had cried. She was devastated at the loss of three members of the church and the fact that it had all been about gold. 'I would rather that he had got the gold than gone on his murderous rampage,' she said.

'But there lies the problem. Nobody knew about the gold, so he had started to make his way down a list of prominent church members, hoping to strike lucky,' said Nathan.

'Then what happened?' Millie asked, glaring at Nathan.

Nathan hesitated. 'Somehow he found out about me and my connection to the church. He must have realised that I was privy to police information and was working closely with them. I believe he's been following me.'

'What here, to my home!' Millie shouted in anger and with tears running down her face.

'Yes, I'm sorry.'

'Sorry? There's a lunatic out there probably watching this house, desperate to get his hands on a cache of gold that you're responsible for and all you can say is sorry!'

'I don't believe we're under any imminent threat.'

'How do you know?' Millie snapped back. 'What is it, just a feeling you have in your gut that we'll be okay?'

'Basically, yes.'

'Well stop being so fucking naïve!' Millie screamed at her brother and stormed out of the room. Nathan heard her walking up the stairs and into the master bedroom. He assumed she had gone to unpack her suitcase, so he decided to begin clearing up the house, starting with the kitchen.

When Millie had completed her unpacking, she came downstairs, loaded up the washing machine and then went and sat outside on the patio. As she sat down, a car came up the drive. She flew inside into the study, where she looked at Chris's gun cabinet. For a second, she was so scared that she thought about reaching for one of his guns. She could see through the window as the car pulled up and two men in suits got out. She waited and watched as they banged on the door. They looked like police.

Nathan opened the door pretty quickly and he wasn't best pleased when he saw Broadwell and his sidekick standing there. 'This is an awfully bad time; my sister has just got home from Australia and she isn't in the best of moods,' Nathan said.

'That's okay,' said Broadwell. 'It's not her we want to speak to.'

Millie suddenly appeared at the door behind Nathan. 'If you want to speak to him, I want to be present. I want to know more of what the hell has been going on around here,' she demanded.

'Okay then,' Broadwell said nonchalantly.

'Come in. We'll go and sit on the patio,' said Millie.

They marched through the hall and kitchen and out on to the patio. The four of them sat around the table. Broadwell was the first to speak. 'Just to get things rolling, I wanted to put you in the picture about where we're up to with the investigation, but I'll keep it brief. We believe the three murders were committed by a man called Trent Allen. He has a long prison record and hasn't been out for that long.

'Somehow, he found out about a donation that was given to the Wellsford church in 1969 in the form of a substantial gold ingot. For whatever reason, he convinced himself that if he could locate somebody with knowledge of the mystery benefactor there could be more gold at the end of the rainbow. As we know, Trent Allen was actually right, but he was never actually able to identify the benefactor. In the end, after being responsible for three horrific murders, he decided that you were the man in the know and the man on the inside helping the police. I'm interested to know, Mr Mason, how you came to find out who the beneficiary was.'

Nathan was slightly unsettled by this question, mainly because Broadwell had called him mister for the first time and was generally being respectful. Nathan suspected that it was Millie's presence that was keeping Broadwell's language in check.

'It wasn't easy,' Nathan started to explain, 'but neither was it rocket science. Firstly, it was obvious from the break-in at the church that he was after information, the way he had been searching through the minute books. I decided to do some research and found out that there was a mystery benefactor who had given a considerable amount of money to get the new church building completed in 1969. But you see, the Church Council minute book for the year in question, 1969, was missing and that was the one that he wanted.

'Anyway, he was able to find names and addresses of the people who have given money to the church because there was a box of donation envelopes in the vestry. Each box had the name and address of the recipient on the cover and these were all due to be hand-delivered. These were the names and addresses of people that he was interested in who may even have been the mystery benefactor. However, after killing Brenda Massey, who obviously provided him with no information, he decided to corner the vicar at the church. He obviously got no information from the vicar either, so decided to refocus back on the church elders who may have known in person who the beneficiary was.

'But it was poor John Selwood who was the next victim. He couldn't give any information because he couldn't remember it. But that afternoon, John informed Margaret and me that he had passed all the earliest minute books to Margaret in a large plastic packing box. It was only when I eventually managed to get a look at the records from 1969 that the vicar, or secretary maybe, had written on them the initials C. W. in pencil. The fact that it was written adjacent to the section in the minutes that thanked all beneficiaries indicated that the initials could be those of the mystery benefactor. I then did a search of the church electoral roll in 1969 and identified Catherine Wall as the potential benefactor.

'Fortunately, the Walls still have a family home on Kaipara Flats Road, which is where I met Marlene, the daughter of Catherine. She was able to confirm that they were the mystery benefactors of the day and there was indeed more gold hidden away. Unfortunately, that night John Selwood was murdered in his home. Marlene provided me with rough directions in the form of a handwritten map showing how to find the cabin where the remainder of the gold was hidden.'

'Can you tell me about your journey up into the forest and what you saw?' Broadwell asked.

'Yes, I drove to a beach in the mangrove, which was sort of shown on the map, then I headed east up into the forest hills. It wasn't easy with the temperature and the mosquitos but the higher it got the cooler it became. I came across a urupa Maori burial ground and my map fortunately diverted me around it. Strange place to have a burial ground though, so high up in the mountains. There must have been a settlement up there years ago. Anyway, I got to the cabin eventually, but it was too late to head back so I lit a fire with the intention of sleeping over.'

'Did anything else happen while you were up there?'

'Oh yes,' said Nathan with meaning.

'Well, just carry on,' said Broadwell.

'While I was searching for the gold, I checked under the floor of the cabin. I found some old tools and stuff but I also found a stoat that was protecting its young. As you can see from my face it was very vicious. Anyway, later that night I heard something out in the forest down in the direction of the burial ground. I used the thermal-imaging binoculars that I had taken with me and I saw things that I couldn't explain.'

'Such as?' Broadwell probed.

'Moving light and heat sources. Shifting shapes that didn't make sense, so I moved in for a closer look. I didn't know what was going on down there but it frightened the life out of me. I was starting to doubt my sanity. I thought I might be hallucinating with a fever after being bitten by the stoat. Then a gust blew through the trees and it was as if it just blew everything away – the images and hallucinations – they just disappeared.

'Anyway, early next morning I did a search of the chimney breast and I found three large gold ingots sitting on a shelf inside the breast itself. I was delighted. This was what I had come for. I decided to leave more or less straight away and decided on the quickest route, which was to head south towards the Kaipara Flats Road. On the way down I was attacked by a wild boar, which wanted to eat me. Fortunately, a bag full of gold is quite a heavy weapon and I was fortunate enough to bring it down on the side of its head. The pig was stunned and I made my exit.

'It caught up with me again and was in the process of charging me when Rico shot it twice from the bushes. He saved my life. He was out searching for me and Trent Allen. Rico decided to lead me down and we took turns in carrying the gold. It was painfully heavy. At one point we were nearly shot by a local farmer who was out turkey hunting. But we made it eventually.'

'That's quite an adventure you've been on,' said Broadwell in a manner that Nathan couldn't read. 'What about Trent Allen?'

'What about him?' said Nathan.

'When did you come across him?'

'I didn't. I had no idea he was following me.'

'Did you not see him in the burial ground?'

'If he said he didn't see him, then he didn't see him,' interrupted Millie impatiently.

'I wouldn't go into that burial ground; it's a sacred place and I was warned to stick to my route,' said Nathan.

'By whom?' asked Broadwell.

'It was a note left by Fred Wall, the original finder. It sort of gave directions to the cabin and said to stick to the route.'

'So, you didn't enter that area at all?'

'No. Why do you keep asking me?'

'Because the cadaver dog led us into the burial ground and to a large crevice on a mound that seemed like a fracture in the forest floor. Probably some old volcanic fault.'

'So, you think he fell in?' said Nathan.

'Or was pushed,' replied Broadwell.

'Right, I've had enough of this,' insisted Millie.

'No, it's okay Millie, I have nothing to hide. I had no idea I was being followed, if indeed I was,' said Nathan.

'Well his car was parked not far from yours and he still hasn't returned for it,' Broadwell said.

'Like I said, if he was following me, maybe he tried to shortcut me and ended up falling to his death. Can you rely upon a cadaver dog in a burial ground anyway?' asked Nathan.

'It's just that you never seemed too concerned that there was a killer after you and that's either because you genuinely didn't know or you've done away with him, and I'm struggling to make my mind up which one it is.'

'This must be quite a dilemma for you,' said Nathan. 'Not knowing whether there's a killer still out there on the loose and knowing that if there isn't, how you're going to pin this on me.'

'It just seems a coincidence,' said Broadwell, 'how people tend to go missing when you're around.' The two men locked eyes. Nathan was fuming and Broadwell was waiting for a response.

Then Millie shouted, 'Right, I want you two out of here right now. You're no longer welcome in this house.' The two detectives stood up and without saying a word followed Millie, who was leading them to the front door.

Nathan stayed at the table. He was wringing his hands when Millie returned. She sat at the table opposite him, still breathing quite heavily. She was upset at the way she had to speak to Broadwell but her baby brother came first and she would defend him always. She composed herself. 'I'm sorry Nathan,' she said.

'You don't need to say that to me. It's me who's trashed your house, forgotten to pick you up from the airport and generally disrespected you. It's me who's sorry.'

'If I hadn't got you involved with the church, you wouldn't have had to go through all this.'

'And I wouldn't have found the gold.'

'What was it like Nathan, finding such a large amount like that?'

'I was absolutely ecstatic and so happy for Marlene, but conscious that I had an unbelievably valuable consignment and I needed to get to safety.'

'How did it get there in the first place?' Millie asked.

'Well, in the late 60s Marlene's brother was doing some beachcombing when he came across the gold buried in the beach. Apparently the cabin was the safest and nearest place to hide it but he managed to get two ingots home before dying of a heart attack that very night.'

'That's a really sad story. I wonder where the gold came from originally?'

'There have been many shipwrecks along the west coast and quite a few near Kaipara harbour. There was one in particular that I've recently read about. It was a ship called the *Tory*. It was owned by the New Zealand land company and was one of the early expedition ships. She set sail from London in 1839. Anyway, to cut a long story short, in December of the same year the ship put into Kaipara harbour but was wrecked on entering. It nearly lost its passengers and had to jettison all its cargo to remain afloat before it was run ashore near Tauhoa.'

'So how come that particular ship would be carrying all that gold anyway?'

'It wasn't actually a colonist ship, although it did play a conspicuous part in the development of New Zealand as a colony. They were basically going around buying land off the Maori. Whether they were paying them in gold, I very much doubt, but perhaps they were using gold to buy the things that were of interest to the Maori. I know at the time some of the main bargaining tools were items such as muskets, tobacco, iron, lead, soap, fishhooks, clothing, material, gunpowder, shoes and many other items. Maybe these were purchased with gold in Australia and they still had some gold left over. That part is supposition, but the story of the *Tory* is fact.'

'You've certainly done your research,' said Millie.

'Yes, it's what I love doing. My love of history and research has taken over from policing. I just don't seem to be able to shake off my feelings for fighting crime. It follows me around but when you're not a police officer you tend to be considered a villain. Just like Broadwell does of me.'

'You just need more time to adapt,' suggested Millie. 'Perhaps Rico isn't the right person to be around at present. It must be a constant reminder for you of your past. Your only friends seem to be police officers in the UK and here. That reminds me of someone who isn't a police officer – how is Loretta?'

'I must call her. Her parents were involved in a road traffic accident, so I haven't heard from her for a few days, plus there was no signal in Dome Forest.'

'So, why don't you call her now?'

'I will shortly but first tell me about Melbourne and the funeral, and how's Chris doing?'

'Chris is fine; it will take time for him to get over the death of his mum. Don't forget we went to put her into a care home. The move for her must have been too much. She just sat down and died; her heart just gave up. It was so upsetting. Chris was traumatised, then there was all the organising for the funeral. It's a good job I went over there to help him.

'But once the funeral was over, we had to deal with emptying the house. Several of the local charities have done very well out of it. All Chris will be bringing back here are memorabilia from when he was a child, which was all boxed up in the loft. His mum has a solicitor in Melbourne who's going to deal with the will and hire an estate agency to look after the sale of the house. I suspect he'll be back in a few days. He'll tell you all about it when he gets back. Now go and call Loretta.'

Nathan wisely did what he was told and he went up to his bedroom to do so. He felt surprisingly nervous. It reminded him of the time when he had met his first girlfriend at school and she had given him her number. He had been so worried what he would say if her mother answered the call or, god forbid, her father or brother.

This is ridiculous, Nathan thought. *I'm calling her personal phone, so only she will answer.* He called Loretta's number and she picked up immediately. 'Hi Nathan, how are you?'

It sounded as if she was pleased to hear from him. 'I'm good thanks,' he replied. 'I heard about your mum and dad. Are they okay?'

'Yes, they're okay. Nothing too major but I spent a lot of time at the hospital, then my phone died. I meant to call you but—'

'It's okay,' Nathan interrupted her. 'I meant to call you but I got involved in a bit of an adventure and my phone wasn't working, then it died on me too.'

'An adventure. That sounds interesting. We should get together so you can tell me all about it.'

311

Nathan could tell that Loretta was smiling when she said that. 'I can come to pick you up this evening,' he suggested. 'Let's go out for dinner in Auckland.'

'Yes, I fancy that, but can I call you back later to confirm the time. I just have to sort Mum and Dad out first.'

'Of course, no problem. Hear from you later then.'

'Okay, bye.'

Nathan was happy and relieved that he and Loretta were still on track. He told Millie, who was delighted. 'You must invite her over,' she insisted.

'All in good time,' Nathan replied coolly, but inside he was ultra-happy.

27

A FEW months down the line and things had finally settled down for Nathan and he was enjoying his time in New Zealand. His relationship with Loretta was blossoming and they appeared to be very much in love. Chris had taken Nathan under his wing and he was now making baby steps on the stock markets and earning his own income.

From the doom and gloom of months earlier, the church and its community were getting their act back together. A new vicar had been employed, Margaret had returned to continue her churchwarden duties and Millie was now enjoying her role as the new church treasurer.

Marlene's gold had been rubber-stamped as no additional claims or ownership rights came to the fore. As a result, the financial rewards were significant, not only for Marlene but also the Wellsford Ecumenical Church and several local Maori groups associated with the church. Due to this, several Maori folk now attended the church every Sunday.

Trent Allen was never found and had been presumed dead at the bottom of the crevice. It was too dangerous and too deep to attempt to recover the body – if that's indeed where it lay.

DI Broadwell was as unpopular as ever. During an enquiry at police headquarters in Auckland, the hierarchy had accepted that he was no longer suitable to be carrying out murder investigations as a team leader as he was too abrasive, too aggressive and too insensitive when it came to dealing with indigenous people and their land and property. It was agreed that Rico Manu would be far better suited to that role.

Rico was no longer with Marika. He still frequented the rugby club at Wellsford and regularly visited his parents. He remained mates with Nathan but it was now more of an occasional friendship.

The East Dome Valley forest, of course, remained as beautiful and in parts as creepy as it had been for millennia. Workmen had erected a gated fence around the urupa and multiple signage indicating it as a Maori burial ground. The small hill within it was securely fenced off to prevent anyone from falling down the crevice. Occasionally, small groups of scientists, volcanologists and geologists appeared to test the air and collect fragments of earth, but they never stayed long.

Because of its proximity to the rear of the burial grounds, the cabin in the clouds was left abandoned and remains today. Local Maori folk say that anyone who enters the urupa or the cabin does so at their own risk. No one goes there, not even the Maori.

28

NATHAN LAY on his bed. He was happy. His world had come back together again and the stars were aligned. He had just come back from an exceedingly long walk and was looking forward to seeing Loretta later. The weather was changing; it was late autumn but the temperature was like a summer's day in England, although it was much cooler by night.

As Nathan's window was open, a light breeze lightly rattled the blind. A small bee had become trapped between the blind and the glass and was unable to find its way out. It was as if it was trying to force its way out by flying at the glass, hitting it with a thud and nearly knocking itself out. The bee soon tired and fell silent and Nathan drifted off to sleep ...

He was in England, in the Cotswolds. It was dark as he pulled the body into the pig pen. When the pigs realised someone had entered their domain, the adult males appeared from their little sties. Nathan closed the gate quickly but quietly, and as he walked away, he could hear the pigs grunting and gorging on the large luxurious slab of meat. Nothing would be wasted, down to the last bone or tooth. Nathan walked away into the trees. He had blood on his hands.

Suddenly, he was in New Zealand and on the small hill in the urupa. The warm air vented from the fissure in the earth's crust. He looked into the blackness and then pushed the body in. He walked away. He stepped over the sign and washed his hands in a stream nearby …

Nathan's eyes opened suddenly and with a gasp he couldn't help himself saying, 'This is a figment of my imagination … I think … I hope. Please God …' He screwed up his face in pain and rolled into the foetal position.

About the Author

The author was born in 1960 and is based in the north-west of England. His hometown is Warrington, Cheshire. He has a passion for archaeology, an enthusiasm for history as well as an enjoyment of watching cricket and rugby.

He began writing articles and newsletters in 2015 and progressed to be a novelist. *Cabin in the Clouds* is his second novel.

www.jacksonbeck.com

Afterword

Thank you for reading *Cabin in the Clouds*. I hope you enjoyed this book.

If you want to know when I release my next book, please join my mailing list at www.jacksonbeck.com

You can also like me on Facebook, Jackson Beck

Or on Instagram @jacksonbeck66

And if you have a moment, please review *Cabin in the Clouds* on Amazon, Google, BookBub, Goodreads or any other social networks and inform other readers why you enjoyed this book.

Many thanks
Jackson Beck
www.jacksonbeck.com

Printed in Great Britain
by Amazon